# The
# MORGANS

# The MORGANS

## WILLIAM W. JOHNSTONE

### AND J.A. JOHNSTONE

## PINNACLE BOOKS
### Kensington Publishing Corp.
www.kensingtonbooks.com

# Chapter 1

*Arizona Territory*

The sudden hush that fell inside the cantina told Frank Morgan that something was about to happen. Long years of experience told him it wouldn't be anything good.

He lifted the cup of coffee in his left hand and took a sip. Most people who came into a cantina ordered tequila, mescal, or pulque. Whiskey, maybe. Beer, at the very least. Frank wasn't much of a drinking man, though, and never had been. He preferred a phosphate or a good cup of coffee.

This brew wasn't particularly *good*, but it was recognizably coffee, and Frank had smiled and nodded to the fat, moon-faced bartender who'd poured it for him. The man had smiled, pleased by the acknowledgment.

Now, wide-eyed with anxiety, he peered past Frank toward the arched entrance door that had a curtain of beads hanging over it to diffuse the hot sunlight and keep out at least a few of the flies.

Unlike bigger saloons, a cantina like this didn't have a mirror behind the bar, only shelves where bottles and jugs of liquor sat. So Frank couldn't check out the reflection to see what had happened. The beads had clicked together for a moment, though, like a miniature set of castanets, so he knew someone had come into the cantina. The sudden quiet in the place told him it was someone who frightened the other customers.

He set the coffee cup on the bar and half turned to his left so he could look over that shoulder. The move put his right hand and the holstered Colt on his right hip out of the view of whoever had just come in.

Actually, two men had just strolled into the cantina, Frank saw, and as he watched, that pair split apart and a third man came in between them, almost as lean as an ax blade against the sun.

Frank recognized what had just happened here. The first two had stepped into the cantina to check the place and make sure no imminent threat waited for the third man, who hadn't come in until one of the others gave him the word. That made him the boss. Maybe the most dangerous of the trio. Hard to say at this point.

All three wore gray, steeple-crowned sombreros, charro jackets, and tight pants. They might have been vaqueros, but vaqueros didn't dress quite that well.

"You know those hombres, amigo?" Frank asked the bartender, quietly enough that his voice didn't travel far.

*"Sí, señor."* The moon-faced man swallowed hard. "The man in the middle is El Serpiente. The famous gunman."

"El Serpiente," Frank repeated softly. *The Snake.* Probably because he was both quick and deadly, or at least fancied himself so. El Serpiente might be famous in the vicinity of this small settlement in the border country, but Frank had never heard of him.

The lean gunman sauntered forward, flanked by the two burlier hombres. He asked in English, "Who owns that ugly dog outside?"—then repeated the question in Spanish.

Frank stiffened at the mention of a dog. One of his trail partners was a big, wolflike cur who answered only to the name of Dog. Frank had left him outside the cantina along with his two saddle mounts, Goldy and Stormy, and the packhorse that carried his supplies.

"That sounds like my dog," he raised his voice in answer to El Serpiente's question. From the corner of his eye, he saw the beads of sweat that suddenly popped out on the bartender's round face.

El Serpiente turned slightly so he faced Frank head-on as he said, "Eh, so, señor. I would like to buy the beast from you."

That surprised Frank a little. He said, "He's not for sale, but why would you want to do that?"

"The creature growled at me."

"You must have gotten too close to the horses," Frank said. "They're old friends, and he's a mite protective of them."

El Serpiente's chin lifted in defiance and anger.

"I was merely examining the golden sorrel. He is a fine-looking animal, and I gave thought to buying him. Then the cur threatened me."

"Goldy's not for sale, either," Frank said, "but I apologize for Dog growling at you." He made it a habit not to look for trouble. A mild word sometimes turned away hard feelings and prevented a killing. Frank had seen enough killing in his life.

El Serpiente made a curt gesture with his left hand.

His right hovered near the butt of the low-slung revolver he wore.

"It is not enough! I must buy the animal. You see, señor, I respect other people's property. I intend to shoot the beast, but first I would pay you a fair price for him."

Frank drew in a slow, deep breath, then said, "You'd shoot a dog for growling at you?"

"No one is allowed to disrespect El Serpiente. Not even a dog. Now, name your price, señor, so we may proceed. But I warn you, I will make this offer only once. Refuse it, and the dog will die anyway, and you will have nothing."

Frank didn't have any more mild words in him. His voice was hard as flint now as he said, "Dog's not for sale."

El Serpiente took a deep, angry breath, too, at being defied this way. In Spanish, he snapped at his companions, "Watch this old fool. I will deal with the dog. If he tries anything, do not kill him. Save him for me."

Frank's Spanish was fluent enough for him to understand what the gunman said. In English, he said, "Move and I'll kill you, snake."

El Serpiente's minions had been smiling and chuckling at the idea of the stranger at the bar trying anything. True, Frank Morgan was a big man, tall and broad shouldered, but his face was weathered and considerable gray streaked the dark hair under his brown Stetson. He had the look of an old saddle tramp who had been riding the grub lines for more than thirty years.

Actually, it had been more than thirty-five years since Frank Morgan had come home to Texas following the Civil War, and he had spent nearly all of that time drifting. He had seen all there was to see of the West, from below the Rio Grande all the way up to the snowy wastes of Alaska, from the vast, slow-moving waters of the Mississippi to the pounding waves of the Pacific under rocky, tree-topped cliffs.

His restless nature had led some to call him the Drifter. He had another name, though, given to him because of his blinding speed and deadly accuracy with the Colt Peacemaker he wore, and because so few of his breed still lived, here in the early days of the twentieth century.

*The Last Gunfighter.*

El Serpiente and his men knew none of that. All they knew was that some foolish *viejo* had challenged them, and therefore he must be killed swiftly and mercilessly, so none of the other sheep around here would get the idea that they might stand up to El Serpiente, too.

The three men clawed for the guns on their hips.

Since El Serpiente was the one with the reputation, Frank figured he was probably the fastest member of the trio. So as he palmed out the Colt and finished his turn, he brought the gun up and triggered it just as it came to bear on El Serpiente's slender form. To Frank's keenly honed senses, he didn't seem to move all that fast, but the gun in his hand bucked and roared just as El Serpiente's weapon cleared leather.

The bullet punched into the Mexican gunman's chest and knocked him backward with such force that he flew through the entrance and caused the strings of beads that formed the curtain to swing wildly. The frantic clicking provided a counterpoint to Frank's next two shots, one for each of El Serpiente's companions. They had managed to get their guns out, but, like their leader, they had no chance to raise and fire the weapons before Frank's lead ripped through their bodies.

One man folded up and collapsed immediately. The other did a jittery little dance on tiptoes that lasted for a couple of seconds before his knees buckled and he pitched forward to land facedown on the cantina's hard-packed dirt floor.

Frank stalked forward, Colt poised and ready if he needed to fire again, but it took him only a moment to see that that wasn't going to be necessary. He used a boot toe to roll the two men inside onto their backs and saw their sightlessly staring eyes.

El Serpiente's thin, bloody chest rose and fell spasmodically as he lay on his back, mostly in the sun. His arms were flung out limply at his sides. Labored breath rasped in his throat. He wasn't long for this world, Frank knew.

He was coherent enough to stare up at Frank and gasp, "This . . . this is not right! You are . . . an old man . . ."

"How do you reckon I got to *be* this old?" Frank said.

El Serpiente didn't answer. He sighed, the gush of air turning into a grotesque rattle as it came out, and he was gone.

Frank replaced the three rounds he had fired from the Colt and then pouched the iron. As he turned and stepped toward the bar, he saw the bartender and the other half-dozen patrons in the cantina staring at him with a mixture of awe and horror on their faces. Frank had seen that expression too many times in his life. His skill with a gun couldn't help but impress people, but the thought of human lives being snuffed out so swiftly and easily made their stomachs go cold and queasy.

"This El Serpiente . . . he was a bad man? I'm not

talking about his gun-handling, but rather the way he conducted himself."

The bartender's head bobbed up and down as he said, "*Sí, señor*, a very bad man. *Un hombre mucho malo.* And the other two, they were no better. El Serpiente, he would goad men into fights they had no chance of winning. He and his men took what they wanted . . . food, drink, supplies . . . women . . . and girls. They never cared who they might hurt."

Frank smiled faintly.

"Reckon I won't lose any sleep over killing them, then."

"Oh no, no, señor," the bartender bubbled. "No one will mourn them. In more than one house tonight, prayers of thanksgiving that they are gone will ascend to the Lord."

Frank said, "I'm obliged to you for the coffee," and started to reach into his pocket for a coin to pay for it.

The bartender held up his pudgy-fingered hands and waved them back and forth.

"No, señor, no. Your money, she is no good here. Not today, and not ever again, as long as you remain here among us."

"Afraid that won't be very long. I'm just passing through on my way to Tucson." Frank lifted a finger to the brim of his hat. "Adios."

When he stepped back outside, the big, wolflike cur was sniffing around the body of El Serpiente.

"Always know I can trust you to be a good judge of human nature, Dog," Frank told the shaggy animal. "I'm glad you didn't bite that fella, though. If you had, you might've come down with hydrophobia."

He untied the reins of the three horses and swung up into the saddle, which at the moment was on the back of the big golden sorrel. With Dog bounding out ahead, Frank rode northwest toward Tucson to answer the summons that was taking him there.

# Chapter 2

*San Francisco*

Not for the first time, Conrad Browning thought what a shame it was that beating the hell out of somebody wasn't considered a proper tactic for business negotiations.

Some people sure had it coming, whether he was allowed to give it to them or not.

"We'll shut down the docks, by God," Raymond Moffatt said as he clenched his right hand into a fist and slammed it down on Conrad's desk. "Then your ships can't unload at all, you fancy-pants young scalawag! What do you think of that?"

Coolly, Conrad said, "I think if you do that, the families of a lot of the men you claim to represent will go hungry."

"*Claim* to represent?" Moffatt repeated. "What in blazes do you mean by that?"

"There is no . . . what do they call it? No federation or union of dockworkers. You walk in here, start issuing demands, and claim that the men have gotten together and elected you to speak for them, but what means do I have of knowing whether or not that's true?"

"Are you callin' me a liar?" Moffatt said with a murderous scowl on his face. Both hands were clenched into fists now as he loomed over Conrad's desk. Over on one side of the room, at a smaller desk, Conrad's secretary watched with a frightened expression on his face. He looked like he wanted to bolt out of the office.

Conrad put his hands flat on the desk and pushed himself to his feet. Standing, he was several inches taller than Moffatt, and although it was difficult to tell in the elegantly tailored brown tweed suit he wore, he was powerfully built as well, although the burly older man probably outweighed him by twenty or thirty pounds.

"I'm not saying you're a liar, Mr. Moffatt, but I'm saying I'd like confirmation of your bona fides." The sandy-haired young man smiled. "That's why I'm going down to the docks to talk to the men myself." He nodded to the secretary. "Phillip, apologize to anyone who has an appointment with me this afternoon and tell them that I'll return as soon as possible."

Moffatt stared at Conrad in apparent disbelief and said, "You're goin' down to the docks?"

"Why shouldn't I? The company owns several warehouses in the district, and our cargo ships tie up there frequently, as you just pointed out yourself."

Moffatt sneered and shook his head.

"A fella like you in a place like that . . . well, that's just askin' for trouble, Browning. Real workin' men don't like it when soft-handed pencil pushers come around botherin' 'em with a lot of foolish questions."

"I'll take my chances," Conrad said as he snagged a dark brown homburg hat from the hat tree just inside the office door. The recently crowned English king, Edward VII, had made that particular style of headgear popular when he was still a prince. Conrad didn't like it as well as a Stetson, but it was more suitable as business attire.

And he had made himself a promise that he would try to be "suitable." There had been a time in his life when nothing had been more important than being stylish and proper.

That was a long time ago. A lot of dusty trails, burned powder, and spilled blood ago. Conrad was trying to put all that behind him, but sometimes he felt like it was a losing battle.

He settled the hat on his head and turned toward the door. Moffatt stopped him by gripping his upper arm.

"Hold on. I say you're not goin' down there, and the docks are my territory, not yours, Browning."

"The streets are public, and I'll go where I want. Anyway, if you're telling me the truth, your friends on the docks will back you up, won't they?"

A muscle lying along Moffatt's jaw twitched and jumped, but he let go and didn't say anything else as he followed Conrad out of the office.

A simple, unostentatious sign on the outside of the building read THE BROWNING COMPANIES. Similar offices were located in Denver, Chicago, Philadelphia, New York, and Boston, showing the vast reach of the various holdings owned primarily by Conrad Browning. Shipping, railroads, real estate, banking . . . all those enterprises and more funneled wealth into Conrad's pockets. His mother,

Vivian, and her husband—Conrad's stepfather—Charles Browning had done a superb job of establishing this financial empire, and it had only grown larger under the astute leadership of the men Conrad had put in charge.

Over the years since he and his real father, Frank Morgan, had assumed ownership of the holdings, Conrad had had very little to do with running things. At first he couldn't be bothered, because he'd been busy living the life of a rich, arrogant wastrel. Then he had fallen in love with and married a Western girl, and for a while it seemed as if her influence would be enough to make him grow up.

Then brutal violence had stolen her away from him, and that tragedy had plunged him into a new life . . . a life where he roamed the West as the gunfighter known as Kid Morgan, surviving by his wits and the gun-handling skill he had inherited from Frank Morgan.

From the first moment Conrad Browning had discovered who his real father was, he had hated Frank Morgan. Over time, as fate made them allies in numerous battles, that feeling had softened into an uneasy truce, and finally that grudging acceptance had turned into affection on Conrad's part.

As for Frank, he had always loved the son he had never known he had until the boy was almost grown, although he was practical enough to admit that Conrad was pretty much of a horse's ass at first. Conrad had realized that about himself and tried to make up for it.

After several years of salving his grief with the adventurous life he led as Kid Morgan, Conrad's mourning had faded to a more bearable level. It was time to go back to his previous life, his real life, as a young businessman. He'd been trying hard in that effort.

Like putting up with Moffatt's bluster, for example. The man continued trying to persuade Conrad to turn back as they headed toward the docks, but Conrad ignored him.

Quite a few tall-masted sailing ships were tied up along the waterfront, but this was the age of steam, and vessels made of iron and steel instead of wood, with smokestacks instead of masts, were numerous, too. Noise filled the air, the shouts of men and the rattle of machinery blending to form a racket that was almost musical in its own distinctive way. The sharp tang of coal jabbed Conrad's nose. He didn't find any of the sensations particularly appealing, but he supposed men could get used to them, maybe even revel in them.

A Browning ship was being unloaded. A crane swung a big cargo net full of crates from the deck to the dock. A burly older man with a bristling white mustache was supervising the operation. The sleeves of his work shirt were rolled up over brawny forearms.

He spotted Conrad and Moffatt approaching and bushy white eyebrows rose at the sight of the two men together. He motioned for the crane operator to stop the machine.

"Hello, Ward," Conrad greeted the man.

"Mr. Browning," the man replied with a curt nod. Then he glared at Moffatt and went on, "What are you doin' with this scoundrel?"

"By God, Ward, you can't talk about me like that!" Moffatt burst out. "You may be the boss of this crew while they're working, but they've chosen me to represent them when it comes to their wages, and you know it."

Ward shook his head and said, "I know nothin' of the sort. You came around here with your bully boys and tried to scare the lads into doin' what you want, but it didn't work, did it? Most of 'em told you to take a flyin' leap!"

"That's a damned lie," Moffatt said, clenching his fists again as he moved closer to Ward. The stevedore boss squared his shoulders and looked like he was ready to throw a punch, too.

Conrad said, "Both of you take it easy," as he moved smoothly between them. "So Moffatt hasn't formed a union down here after all?"

"Some of the crews have gone along with him," Ward said. "The ones he buffaloed into it."

"I never forced anybody to turn to me for help," Moffatt said with a sneer.

Three men had moved up behind Moffatt, Conrad noted, men who hadn't been there a moment earlier. They were all big and looked like they might have been dockworkers at one time, but now instead of rough canvas trousers and shirts, they wore suits. But like Moffatt, they seemed out of place in them. Clearly, they were roughnecks, and Conrad assumed they were the muscle that had convinced some of the workers to throw in with Moffatt.

Conrad looked the men over and then coolly dismissed them, turning to Ward to say, "Spread the word for me, Jonas, that if any man wants to come and see me to talk about a better wage, my door is open. There's no need to go through Moffatt, who'd probably just take the lion's share of any increase for himself."

"That's a damned lie, too!" Moffatt yelled. "You're gonna be sorry about this, Browning."

"I'm already sorry I gave you the time of day," Conrad snapped. "Now, step aside. I have work to do."

One of the men who had joined Moffatt spat an obscenity. He shouldered up to confront Conrad and suddenly swung a hamlike fist at the young man's head.

Conrad's reactions might have slowed slightly from months of sitting in an office, but he was still faster than the man attacking him. He leaned away from the punch, which merely clipped the homburg's brim and sent the hat flying off his head.

The missed blow threw the man off-balance, so he couldn't defend himself as Conrad hooked a hard left into his ribs and followed it with a straight right to the face. Cartilage crunched under Conrad's knuckles as blood spurted hotly from the man's flattened nose. He reeled back, howling in pain, and sat down hard.

Their companion's misfortune didn't cause the other two to hold back. They rushed Conrad, swinging wild punches. For a moment, he blocked the flailing fists, but then one of them got through and caught him on the jaw. The impact spun him halfway around. That gave one of the men a chance to grab him from behind and pin his arms to his sides.

"I got him, boss!" the man yelled to Moffatt. "Teach him a lesson!"

Grinning, Moffatt cocked his fists and moved in. The evil gleam in his eyes testified that he meant to hurt Conrad, perhaps badly.

Moffatt had forgotten about Jonas Ward, though. The burly stevedore grabbed his shoulder, hauled him around, and slammed a punch to his jaw. Moffatt staggered but didn't go down. He caught himself and bored in on Ward like a badger, peppering him with short but powerful blows.

Meanwhile, the third bruiser was standing close enough for Conrad to lift both feet from the ground, draw his knees up, and then straighten his legs in a powerful double kick that landed on the man's chest. The man flew backward—right off the edge of the dock. He yelled as he tried futilely to find something to grab in midair. A second later, water flew high in the sky as he landed in the bay with a huge splash.

Despite his wastrel ways in his youth, enough of Conrad's education had stuck for him to be familiar with Newton's third law. So he wasn't surprised when the kick he launched made the man holding him stumble backward. He stuck a foot between the man's ankles and got their legs tangled up so that the man toppled over. He hit the cobblestones hard enough that it knocked his grip on Conrad loose.

Conrad rammed an elbow into the man's midsection, rolled over, and grabbed him by the throat. He pulled the man up, then banged his head against the pavement. The man went limp. He was knocked cold.

Shouting filled Conrad's ears as he scrambled to his feet. He saw that a lot of the dockworkers had gathered around to watch the fight. Nothing drew attention like a battle—unless it was a beautiful woman, and none of those were in sight at the moment.

Instead, Moffatt and Ward were slugging away at each other, and as Conrad watched, Moffatt landed a blow to the other man's stomach that doubled him over. That put Ward in perfect position for Moffatt to lift an uppercut from ground level. It exploded on Ward's chin like a bomb and knocked him a couple of inches into the air before he crashed down on his back, senseless.

Breathing hard, Moffatt glared in triumph at Ward's motionless form for a second, then swung around. His expression of savage satisfaction disappeared when he saw that Conrad was on his feet and the three bruisers were down and out of the fight. One man was unconscious, one was floundering in the bay trying to find a place to climb out, and the third sat cross-legged on the ground cupping his hand under his broken nose to catch the blood that welled from it. What he intended to do with a handful of gore was anybody's guess.

Moffatt said, "How . . . how did you . . . ?"

He didn't finish the question, but Conrad answered it anyway, saying, "Maybe I'm not the soft-handed pencil pusher you thought I was, Moffatt."

Hate and rage twisted Moffatt's face. He reached under his coat as he started toward Conrad. Sunlight glinted on the knife he pulled from a hidden sheath.

Faster than the eye could follow, Conrad drew a gun from a holster under his coat at the small of his back and pointed it at Moffatt, who stopped in his tracks when he found himself staring down the weapon's barrel. His face was dark with angry blood, but now it began to pale as Conrad thumbed back the little revolver's hammer.

"You made a fundamental negotiating mistake, Moffatt," he said. "It takes a man who's highly skilled with a knife to go up against a man with a gun." Conrad smiled. "How about it? Are you that good?"

Moffatt cursed and opened his hand. The knife clattered to the street.

"You can't shoot me," he said. "I'm unarmed."

"I don't know. I might find some men around here who would swear that you never dropped that knife. If they told the law you attacked me with it, and I was just defending myself . . ."

That drew some jeers of agreement from the onlookers. Conrad didn't believe that Moffatt had many friends here, only men he had paid off or intimidated, and neither of those things created much loyalty.

"What do you want, Browning?"

"For myself? Nothing. I just want you and your hooligans to leave these honest, hardworking men alone. Try living on the sweat of your own labors, instead of leeching off the work other men do."

The gun in Conrad's hand might have scared Moffatt, but that didn't stop him from sneering.

"You're a fine one to talk! Fancy rich boy who inherited all his money! What have you ever done to earn your own way?"

The man had a point, even though Conrad didn't like to admit it. Sure, the Browning holdings had grown larger and even more lucrative while he was running them, but in truth, "running" the business meant putting good people in charge and staying out of their way, for the most part. Conrad couldn't take personal credit for much of that success.

Then why was he here, sitting in an office instead of out on the trail somewhere? He couldn't answer that.

He pointed the gun in the air and lowered the hammer off cock. As he slipped the weapon back in its holster, he said, "Just remember what I told you, Moffatt. Everyone here today saw that you're not invincible after all. It won't take long for word to get around to the rest of the docks. People will stand up to you now."

Jonas Ward had regained his senses and climbed back onto his feet. He called, "Damn right, we will!"—and more shouts of agreement and support came from the crowd. The hangdog look on Moffatt's face said that he knew he was beaten.

The man Conrad had kicked into the bay had finally gotten out. With water streaming from him, he came up to Moffatt and asked, "What do you want to do, boss?"

"Get those other two on their feet," Moffatt snapped. "Let's get out of here."

Within minutes, all four men had slunk out of sight.

Ward clapped a hand on Conrad's back and wrung his other hand.

"That was a mighty fine fight!" he said. "Did you mean that, Mr. Browning, about giving the men higher wages?"

"I think we can work something out," Conrad said. "I'll leave instructions for my manager to talk to you and all the other men who unload my ships and see what can be done."

Ward frowned and asked, "You're not gonna handle it yourself?"

"I may not be here."

"May not be . . . Where are you goin', Mr. Browning?"

Conrad shook his head and said, "I don't really know."

# Chapter 3

*Tucson*

Frank had to spend one more night on the trail, then arrived in Tucson the day after the shootout with El Serpiente and his men. It had been a number of years since he'd been in the city, so he didn't know if the livery stable owned by his old friend Pete McRoberts was still in business. He was happy to see that it was.

"Frank Morgan!" the toothless, bandy-legged liveryman exclaimed as he gazed up at the head-and-a-half-taller visitor. "I figured for sure you was dead by now!"

"Why, did you read about me dying?" Frank asked.

"No, just figured the kind of life you led, somebody would've plugged you before now!" McRoberts slapped the leg of his overalls, raising some dust, and laughed. "Reckon I should've knowed better, as slick on the draw as you always been. You still as fast as ever, Frank?"

"Fast enough that I'm still here."

"Reckon that's fast enough, all right!" McRoberts cackled. He looked at Goldy and Stormy and let out a whistle of admiration. "Lord have mercy, them's two fine pieces o' horseflesh. Bring 'em on in here. You're lookin' for a place to stable 'em, I reckon?"

"Yeah, and I've got that pack animal, and my dog, too."

"Dog? I figured a wolf done followed you in off the desert. I can tell by lookin', he ain't no ways tame, is he?"

"Tame enough," Frank said. "He won't chew your arm off or rip your throat out if you don't bother him. He's particularly partial to old Stormy there, so if you let the two of them stay in the same stall, Dog will behave himself."

"He'd better," McRoberts said as he cast a leery eye toward the big cur. "I charge extra for gettin' chawed on."

He quoted a price for feeding and looking after all four animals, and Frank paid for three nights in advance. Money was no problem. Since he had inherited an equal percentage in the Browning business holdings from his former wife, he had been one of the wealthiest men west of the Mississippi, although he never dressed or acted like that. Having money hadn't changed him. As long as he had enough for supplies and ammunition, that was plenty, just as it always had been.

"I'm looking for a hotel called the Plaza del Sol, Pete," he said once the arrangements had been concluded. "I don't recall it, so it must not have been in business the last time I was through these parts. Reckon you can tell me how to find it?"

"Shoot, you can't hardly miss it. Just go on down Congress Street and keep an eye out for a fancy, hacienda-lookin' sort of place." The old-timer cocked his mostly bald head to the side. "You supposed to meet somebody there, Frank? Is it work that brung you to Tucson? Gun work?"

Frank frowned. He knew the reputation that had followed him around for all the long years. People always believed that because he was a fast gun, that talent was for hire to the highest bidder.

As a matter of fact, that wasn't the case. Frank had never earned his living as a gunfighter. He had worked as a bounty hunter from time to time, and he had pinned on a badge as a town-taming lawman. He had fought in range wars and railroad wars, but only because he believed one side was in the right and people needed his help. He had hired on as a guide for wagon trains and ridden as a shotgun guard on stagecoaches. But as far as taking money just to shoot somebody's enemies . . . that he had never done. And never would.

But it was indeed a summons for help that had brought him to Tucson. A letter had caught up to him in El Paso, and he had started in this direction to find out what it was about.

*Dear Señor Morgan,* the letter had read.

*I write to you in the hope that you can assist me in a dire situation. We are not acquainted, but Don Felipe Almanzar, an old and dear friend of my father, gave me your name and suggested that you might help us. My father, Eduardo Escobar, has a ranch near Tucson that is under a veritable siege by outlaws and rustlers whose lawless activities threaten to ruin it. The authorities have been unable to run them to ground but Don Felipe believes that you are equal to the task. I cannot promise you a great deal of money if you were to assist us, but you would have my eternal gratitude. If you can see your way clear to do this, please write to me in care of the Plaza del Sol Hotel in*

*Tucson and I will meet you there anytime you*
*would like to discuss the situation. I very much*
*hope you can help us. I fear you are the only one*
*who can.*

The letter was signed *Antonia Escobar.*

Over the years, Frank had been contacted many times by people with similar problems. Sometimes he took a hand, sometimes he rode away, depending on what his judgment of the situation turned out to be. The fact that this Escobar woman had gotten his name from Don Felipe Almanzar spoke well of her. Frank both liked and respected the Mexican rancher, having gotten to know him several years earlier when a perilous adventure had led him south of the border.

Of course, without looking into things, he had no way of knowing if what Antonia Escobar said in her letter was true. But Frank had figured that drifting toward Tucson was as good a direction as any, so he had bought some supplies and headed out.

Now he told Pete McRoberts, "I'm supposed to meet somebody at the hotel, but I don't know if anything will come of it."

"Well, I hope you don't wind up shootin' up the town. That'd be bad for business. Tucson's civilized these days, don't you know. O' course, you get outta town and things is just about as wild as they ever was. You heard about that fella Diego Ramirez who's runnin' high, wide, and handsome down along the border?"

"Can't say as I have," Frank replied with a shake of his head.

"He started out claimin' to be a revolutionary and sayin'

that he wanted to replace ol' Presidente Díaz, but you know as well as I do what that really means. He's just a durned ol' *bandido*. The Rurales done run him outta Mexico, so he's been raisin' hell on this side of the border, just like in the old days."

"I've been over in Texas, and I didn't hear anything about this fella there. I guess every place has its own troubles."

"Truer words were never spoke," the old-timer agreed solemnly.

Frank left the livery stable and followed the directions McRoberts had given him. A few minutes later, he saw a large building on the left side of the street that matched the liveryman's description, three stories tall, made of adobe and thick wooden beams, with a slate roof. The architecture was Mexican, and an ornately painted sign on the side of the building identified it as the Plaza del Sol Hotel, as if Frank had had any doubts.

He crossed a wide, shady veranda to a pair of heavy wooden doors. People were coming and going, but Frank wasn't the sort of man who blended easily into a crowd. He felt eyes on him as he walked into the big lobby. The building's thick adobe walls made it cool in here, and that felt good after the heat of the sun.

Stopping in front of the counter where people checked in and out of the hotel, Frank waited until the clerk looked up at him and then said, "I'm looking for Señorita Antonia Escobar."

"You were supposed to meet the lady here, sir?"

"That's right, but not at any set time because I didn't know for sure when I'd arrive. If you could send a message up to her room . . ."

"That's not necessary. I saw Miss Escobar go into the salon a few minutes ago." The clerk pointed across the lobby toward the arched entrance into another room. "I believe she takes tea in there every afternoon about this time."

Tea. Well, that was all right with Frank. He preferred coffee, but a cup of tea now and then was fine. He nodded to the clerk, said, "Obliged," and started to turn away.

"Did you wish to rent a room, sir?" the clerk called after him.

Frank looked back over his shoulder and said, "Don't know yet. Probably won't know until I talk to the lady."

"I just thought you might like to freshen up a bit . . ."

"Wash off some of the trail dust, you mean?" Frank grinned. "I'll try not to get your fancy salon too dirty, sonny."

The clerk looked flustered but didn't say anything else. Frank walked across the lobby and into the salon.

About the time he got there, he realized he should have asked the clerk what Señorita Escobar looked like. He really had no idea. But as he stepped into the room, which was furnished with a number of dainty tables and chairs, he spotted a young woman sitting alone at one of the tables and had a sudden hunch that she was who he was looking for.

She was the only woman in the salon who was by herself. Three middle-aged women were sitting with men who were pretty obviously their husbands. The one Frank pegged as Señorita Escobar was in her twenties, he estimated, and very pretty with golden skin and raven-black hair pulled into a bun at the back of her head. The dress she wore probably wasn't terribly expensive, but she made it look elegant anyway.

Frank was long past the age when the charms of a pretty girl had much influence on him, but he still admired beauty and this gal fell into that category. He took off his hat as he approached her. She glanced up at him, then looked again, sharply, and came to her feet, the cup of tea in front of her momentarily forgotten.

"Señor Morgan?" she said.

"Señorita Escobar?" he replied as he held his hat in front of him in his left hand.

"That is right. I was not sure you would come, but now that you are here . . ." She paused for a moment, as if unsure how to go on, then said, "You are a large, impressive man, just as Don Felipe described you."

Frank smiled and said, "How is the old rapscallion? I haven't heard from him in a long time."

"He is well," she said. She waved a hand at the empty chair on the other side of the table. "Please, Señor Morgan, sit down."

Frank eyed the fragile-looking chair with some wariness. He supposed it would hold him up, as long as he was careful. He said, "You first, *por favor, señorita,*" then when she had sat down again, he lowered himself onto the chair and set his hat on the floor beside him.

"You are a gentleman," she commented.

"That's the way I was raised. Figure being polite doesn't cost anything, so a man might as well. Or at least try to."

"I can already tell that I did the right thing by writing to you. Will you have a cup of tea?"

"Sounds fine," Frank said, nodding.

Antonia smiled and signaled to a white-jacketed waiter who brought over another cup of tea in a fine china saucer. Frank sipped it and nodded appreciatively.

"You are not quite what I expected, Señor Morgan," Antonia said as she toyed with her cup. "Oh, you are big and tough, no doubt about that, but you are well-spoken, like an educated man. I mean no offense."

"None taken," Frank assured her. "As for being educated, most of it is because I like to read and always have a few books in my saddlebags. It's been like that for many years. Plenty of nights on the trail spent reading by firelight. I'm reading a novel by Jules Verne now."

Antonia smiled slightly and shook her head to indicate that she wasn't familiar with the French author. Then she grew solemn and said, "I am so relieved that you have come to help us. My father does not know that I wrote to you. His pride, you know . . . He sees it as somehow shameful to need to ask for help."

"I haven't agreed to take a hand in this yet," Frank reminded her. "I'm going to need to know a lot more about what's going on."

"Of course. Perhaps you could come up to my room, and I can tell you all about it . . . ?"

Frank shook his head and said, "That wouldn't do your reputation any good, señorita."

She opened her mouth to say something, stopped, then laughed softly.

"You are right, Señor Morgan. Then we shall have dinner together tonight in a respectable manner and discuss everything then. There is a good restaurant near here called the Ruby House."

"That sounds fine to me," Frank agreed. He grinned.

"The clerk out yonder in the lobby seemed to think I needed to clean up, and that'll give me a chance." He took another sip of the tea, then stood up and reached into his pocket for a coin.

She stopped him with a shake of her head.

"There is no need, señor."

"Well, then, dinner will be on me. We'll meet in the lobby in about an hour?"

She inclined her head and smiled as she said, "As you wish."

Frank nodded farewell and didn't put his hat on until he was in the lobby again. He went to the desk and told the clerk, "Reckon I'll take that room after all. And do you think you could have a tub and some hot water sent up?"

The clerk looked a little dubious until Frank dropped a double eagle on the counter in front of him. Then the man said quickly, "Certainly, sir. Right away. Welcome to the Plaza del Sol."

Frank grunted and said, "Glad to be here."

At least he would be once he found out what was actually going on, he mused . . . because as much as he wanted to accept what pretty little Antonia Escobar had told him, he wasn't sure yet that he believed a word of it.

# Chapter 4

Frank walked back to the livery stable to get his saddle-bags and Winchester. By the time he returned to his hotel room, a tub was waiting for him, full of water so hot that little wisps of steam curled up from its surface. He stripped off his dusty clothes and sank into the tub with a grateful sigh as the water's warmth enfolded him.

The clerk had given him a wary glance as Frank walked through the lobby carrying the rifle. The fella probably thought it was bad enough that Frank was packing the Colt on his hip. The long gun just made it worse.

Pete McRoberts was right: Tucson was civilized now, like most other big towns. It was more and more uncommon to see a man carrying a gun, let alone two of them and a bowie knife, which Frank normally had sheathed on his left hip. A lot of places had uniformed police now, instead of a town marshal and deputies. Folks relied on them to keep the peace and no longer knew what it was like to depend on themselves to protect their families in times of trouble.

Frank stomped his own snakes and always would. If that put him out of step with everybody else, then so be

it. He was too old to care what people thought of him—
not that he had ever really worried much about that.

Once he had soaked the trail dust off him and some of
the aches out of his muscles, he dried and got dressed in
fresh clothes, then buckled on his gun belt. He left the
Winchester there in the hotel room, not expecting to need
it while he was having dinner with Antonia Escobar.

When he reached the lobby, he didn't see Antonia, but
he was a little earlier than the time they had agreed upon.
The same clerk was at the desk. He didn't look down his
nose as much now that he knew Frank had money and
could afford to stay here. He even managed a smile as
Frank approached.

Nodding toward the opposite side of the lobby from the
salon where he and Antonia had talked earlier, Frank said,
"I see you've got a bar here in the hotel. When Señorita
Escobar comes down, send a boy in there to fetch me."

"Of course, Mr. Morgan."

"The Ruby House, is it a good place to eat?"

The clerk's smile was genuine as he said, "Oh yes, it's
very good. Are you and, ah, Señorita Escobar going to
dine there this evening?"

"And talk business," Frank said. He didn't care for the
slight smirk on the clerk's face as the man asked the question. He supposed that being in the hotel business, the
clerk was accustomed to seeing older men with much
younger women, but Frank wasn't that sort.

He turned and walked into the bar, which had a lot of
dark wood and polished brass to go with the adobe walls.
Two men were drinking at the far end of the hardwood bar,

while the tables were empty except for one where a quiet poker game was going on.

A bartender wearing a red vest over a white shirt with sleeve garters came over and nodded to Frank as he asked, "What can I get you, mister?"

"Wouldn't happen to have a phosphate, would you?"

"Lemon flavored?"

Frank smiled and said, "That sounds mighty good."

"Comin' right up."

The bartender began preparing the drink, which involved putting lemon juice in a glass and then pouring in phosphate from a bottle and watching it foam up. The men at the other end of the bar noticed what he was doing, and one of them said, "That's a kid's drink you're making. I don't see any youngsters in here."

The bartender nodded toward Frank and said, "This gentleman right here ordered it."

"He did, did he?" The man hooked his thumbs behind the gun belt he wore and sauntered along the bar toward Frank. His friend followed him. The one who had done the talking so far wore a brown tweed suit and vest and had a string tie knotted around his skinny neck. A derby hat sat atop his angular face. He came to a stop a few feet from Frank and grinned as he asked, "Something wrong with your belly, friend?"

"Not that I know of," Frank said.

"I just wondered 'cause, you know, you're fixing to drink what a little kid would, instead of a real man's drink. Maybe you can't afford a whiskey. Tell you what, I'll buy one for you."

"No need. I can afford what I want. And I'd rather have

this," Frank said as the bartender set the foaming glass of lemon phosphate on the bar in front of him.

"Why, that just don't make a lick of sense, a grown man acting like that. When somebody offers to buy you a drink, you damn well ought to accept it."

"You can pay for this phosphate if you want to, I suppose," Frank said. He reached for the glass . . . with his left hand.

"Pay for one of those blasted fizzy things? Hell, I got more self-respect than that. More self-respect than you, if you plan on actually drinking that concoction."

Frank lifted the glass to his lips, took a sip, and nodded in satisfaction.

"Good," he said to the bartender.

The man in the derby sneered as he said, "I guess a man with a yellow belly needs a yellow drink."

Frank had sized this hombre up the minute the man started talking to him. He was looking for trouble, looking for somebody he could bully and harass just for the fun of it. He must not have been a very good judge of character, because clearly he believed Frank would stand for that.

The man with him wasn't quite so oblivious. He put a hand on his friend's arm and said, "Listen, Bracken, maybe you'd better just—"

Bracken shook him off and said, "Don't interrupt me, Kern. I'm talking to this fella and his yellow belly."

Frank swallowed some more of the phosphate and then set the glass on the bar.

"That's twice you've said that," he told Bracken. "Probably be a good idea not to say it again."

Bracken snarled at the bartender, "Pour a damn drink. Pour two of 'em."

The bartender said, "This is a nice quiet place, no trouble—"

"I'm not starting trouble," Bracken insisted. "If this gent will have a drink with me, we'll just call it square and move on. Now pour the damn drinks."

The bartender swallowed and shifted his feet nervously, but he took two glasses off the back bar, set them on the hardwood, and splashed whiskey from a bottle into them.

Bracken nudged one of the glasses closer to Frank and said, "How about it? Have a man's drink."

"I'm fine with this," Frank said as he picked up the phosphate in his left hand again.

"Well, I'm not, you yellow-bellied son of a—"

Bracken's hand dived toward the gun on his hip even as he called out angrily. His fingers hadn't closed around the revolver's grips when Frank, with a flick of his left wrist, threw what was left of the phosphate into Bracken's face.

Bracken jerked back, let out a startled yell, and pawed at his stinging eyes with his left hand. He was determined enough to complete his draw with the right hand, but as the gun came out of its holster, Frank closed his left hand around Bracken's wrist and prevented him from raising the gun. An instant later, Frank's right fist crashed into the man's jaw and slewed his head to the side. The derby hat went flying. Bracken's knees buckled.

Frank plucked the gun from his hand and stepped back to give Bracken some room as the man fell to his knees.

He toppled forward and landed with his face on the floor, out cold from the sledgehammer punch Frank had landed.

Frank flipped the gun up and caught it deftly so that its barrel pointed at the other man. His thumb rested easily on the hammer.

"You taking cards in this game, mister?" Frank asked quietly.

The other man held up both hands and backed away hastily as he said, "Not hardly, mister. Bracken dealt the hand and it was his to play."

"That's the way I'd look at it, too. I don't go hunting for trouble." Frank placed Bracken's revolver on the bar and went on, "Why don't you get him out of here? He can come back for his gun later."

"That's a good idea." Bracken was starting to move around a little and make incoherent noises. His friend bent, got hold of him under the arms, and hauled him to his feet. His legs were pretty rubbery, but his friend managed to steer him in staggering fashion toward the lobby. Frank was surprised to see Antonia Escobar standing in the bar entrance watching. She smiled as she stepped back out of the way to let Bracken and his friend past. They stumbled on through the lobby and out of the hotel.

"Bravo," Antonia said as she came on into the bar and walked up to Frank.

He grunted and said, "I told the clerk to send a boy in here to fetch me when you were ready to go."

"I know, but I told him I could fetch you myself. I'm not such a delicate flower that merely stepping into a bar will cause me to wilt, you know."

"I never figured it would."

The bartender spoke up, saying, "I'm obliged to you

for not killing that loudmouth, mister. I purely do hate mopping up blood."

Frank looked over at the man and asked, "Is he a regular in here?"

"Never saw the man before today. He and his friend must have drifted into town. With any luck they'll keep on drifting."

Frank nodded. He hoped that would be the case, too. But he would keep his eyes open for the two men while he was still here in Tucson. More than once, some fellow had braced him and he'd allowed the person to live, only to have to deal with him again later in fatal fashion. Some men just had too much foolish pride to let such a thing go.

"Let's go on and have supper, if that's all right with you," he said to Antonia.

"It's very much all right." She offered him her arm, and he took it. As they walked into the lobby, she went on, "Don't worry about what I saw back there. I know you're capable of violence, Señor Morgan. I would not have written to you if that were not the case. And yet clearly, you are a man capable of restraint as well."

"I never believed in letting a man live who needed killing, you can count on that. It's not always necessary, though."

Dusk was settling down softly on Tucson as they walked a couple of blocks to the Ruby House, an impressive false-fronted building. The tables in the restaurant had white linen cloths, the lamps burned with a warm, subdued yellow light, and the air was full of delicious smells. Most of the women in the place were dressed fancier than Antonia, but Frank thought she still outshone them all for looks. Most of the men were in dark, sober suits, in contrast to his clean but well-worn trail clothes, but that didn't matter. He was the sort of man who never felt out of place.

The food was as good as Frank had been told. They dined on excellent steaks with all the trimmings, washed down with strong coffee. After a lot of time on the trail eating his own cooking, Frank really enjoyed the meal, so much so that he was reluctant to bring up the reason they were there.

Eventually he did, though, as they lingered over coffee.

"Tell me about the trouble you and your father are having on your ranch."

"It started about six months ago," she said. "We began losing cattle to rustlers, and some of our vaqueros were shot at while they were out on the range. It has only gotten worse since then. At first only a few head of stock were taken, but now they are being run off as many as a hundred at a time. And our men . . . one was killed, and two more were badly wounded. Many of them have quit and left. They are afraid to work there anymore." She shook her head sadly. "I cannot really blame them for feeling that way."

"You've notified the law, I reckon?"

Antonia made a face and blew out a disgusted breath.

"The sheriff sent out a deputy. He claimed that he tried to follow the rustlers' tracks but lost them. I do not believe he tried very hard."

Frank took a sip of his coffee and then asked, "Do you have any idea how many men are in this gang?"

"I have heard our riders talking about it. They believe there may be as many as a dozen. Those are not good odds, I know."

"Could be worse," Frank said. "When you're taking on a big bunch like that, sometimes the trick is to whittle them down a little at a time."

Antonia leaned forward and asked, "Is this something you believe you can do, Señor Morgan?"

Frank still had his doubts that she was telling him the whole story, but he had to admit that she seemed genuine enough and truly worried about her father and their ranch. And there was only one way to find out what the situation actually was.

"I believe I ought to ride out there with you and take a look around," he said. "I'm not making any promises, but there might be something I can do to help you."

She closed her eyes and breathed a sigh of relief.

"I am so happy to hear you say that." Her tone became more brisk as she went on, "Now, we should discuss your payment—"

Frank held up a hand to stop her and said, "Hold on. I haven't agreed to do anything yet except ride out there with you. Where is this spread of your father's?"

"About twenty miles north of here."

"Then, if we make an early start in the morning, we'll get there by the middle of the day."

"*Sí.* That is best. It will give you time to meet my father and look around. I warn you . . . he may not be happy that I have summoned you."

"I expect you can win him over."

She laughed and said, "Yes, I have . . . how do you say it? I have him wrapped around my little finger. No?"

Frank smiled and said, "I don't doubt it. How did you get from the ranch here to Tucson?"

"I have a buggy. I drove in."

Frank raised an eyebrow and asked, "By yourself?"

A bit of a haughty tone crept into her voice as she replied, "I am accustomed to taking care of myself, Señor Morgan."

"I don't doubt that, either. Where's the buggy?"

"A shed and corral are in back of the hotel, and a man who cares for the animals that are left there. I will have him hitch up my two horses in the morning. Shall we leave at first light?"

"That's fine. My horses are at a livery stable down the street. I'll get them saddled and meet you around back at sunup."

"We have a deal, then." She held out her hand, extending it over the table like a man to seal the arrangement.

Frank took it and was a little surprised by the strength of her grip. Definitely not a delicate flower, he thought, even though she was as pretty as one.

# Chapter 5

Frank slept well and was up early the next morning, well before dawn. He was naturally an early riser.

The hotel didn't have a dining room, and he didn't figure a fancy place like the Ruby House would be open for breakfast, but the previous evening while he and Antonia Escobar were walking to the restaurant, he had noticed a café in the next block that looked like a place where a man could get a good cup of coffee and a hearty breakfast.

When he went down there, that proved to be the case. A Swedish couple with several buxom blond daughters ran the place. One of them brought Frank a plate piled high with thick slices of ham, fried eggs, biscuits, and hash brown potatoes. The coffee was strong enough to get up and walk around by itself, just the way Frank liked it.

The proprietor came over as Frank was finishing up his breakfast and said, "You don't remember me, Mr. Morgan, but I remember you, *ja*, I do. From Dodge City, ten years ago. I ran a café there, and my daughters, they were just little girls."

Frank thought for a second and a name came back to him. He said, "I do remember you, Mr. Sorensen."

The man beamed because Frank recalled his name. Then his expression grew solemn as he said, "Some men came into my place one evening when you were there. Trail hands. They were drunk and began to cause trouble. But you stood up to them and made them leave."

Frank had remembered Sorensen's name but truly didn't recall the incident the man described. Over the years, he had run into too many obnoxious varmints who needed to be taken down a notch to be able to remember most of them. But he nodded because what Sorensen was saying sounded exactly like something he would do.

"We have always been grateful to you for your help," Sorensen went on. He gestured toward one of the empty chairs at the table. "Do you mind if I sit?"

"Not at all," Frank said.

Sorensen sat down and leaned forward, frowning now. He said, "Last night, two men came in here. I could tell that one of them was very angry, and his friend was trying to calm him down. I did not intend to eavesdrop, but I heard them mention your name."

Frank's eyebrows rose slightly in surprise.

"What did these two hombres look like?"

"One was stocky, dressed like a cowboy, and had a small beard. The other was tall and skinny and wore a fancy suit and one of those derby hats. He was the angry one."

Frank nodded slowly and said, "I had a run-in with them in the barroom over at the Plaza del Sol. You say they knew my name?" He didn't recall ever mentioning it during the brief conversation.

"*Ja*, the one in the derby said he did not care if you are

the notorious Frank Morgan, he was going to settle some score with you. When I heard the name, I could not help but take notice. As I said, we have never forgotten you and the help you gave us, Mr. Morgan. Now good fortune has brought you into our humble café this morning, so I can warn you."

"I appreciate that, Mr. Sorensen," Frank said. "I was already keeping an eye out for those fellas, but now that I know they're actually planning something, I'll be even more careful." He smiled. "I wouldn't worry too much, though. They're probably still asleep this morning, and I plan on riding out soon."

"You are leaving Tucson?"

"Yep." Frank didn't explain where he was going or why. He trusted Sorensen, but he was in the habit of playing his cards pretty close to his vest. He drank the last of his coffee and reached in his pocket for a coin.

Sorensen tried to wave that off, saying, "The breakfast is on the house—"

"I appreciate that," Frank said, "but you've got a business to run and a family to support." He slid the gold piece across the table and grinned. "Are any of those daughters of yours married off yet?"

"Not yet, but they all have beaus!"

"My best to them and your wife," Frank said as he stood up and put his hat on. He nodded his farewell and left the café.

The sun wasn't up yet, but an arch of orange-gold light was visible in the eastern sky. Frank knew that by the time he walked down to Pete McRoberts's stable and got his horses ready to travel, Antonia's buggy team ought to be hitched up to depart Tucson as well.

One of the livery barn's big double doors was open, but only a couple of feet. Frank didn't see McRoberts around the front of the place, and no lamp burned in the office, behind which the old-timer had his living quarters. But that didn't matter. Frank had already paid more than what he owed, and he was perfectly capable of saddling his own horse. If McRoberts was still asleep, that was fine. Frank didn't see any reason to disturb him.

The barn's cavernous main area was dark at this early hour, with only a little gray light leaking in through the partially open door. Frank pushed the door back a little more to give himself enough room to step inside. He knew a lantern hung on a post to his left, so he stepped over and found it. Lifting it from its hook by the bail, he used his other hand to dig an old-fashioned lucifer from his pocket and snap it to life with his thumbnail.

The glare from the match spilled out around him, and from the corner of his eye he saw something that shouldn't have been there. A booted foot stuck out from an empty stall about halfway down the aisle that ran through the center of the barn. Frank hung the lantern back up without lighting it and hurried along the stalls as the lucifer burned down. He noticed now that some of the horses stabled here seemed restless, as if something had disturbed them. Goldy and Stormy both tossed their heads and nickered as if to warn him.

*Where was Dog?*

That question suddenly blazed through Frank's mind. If anyone had tried to cause trouble in here, Dog likely would have taken action. Worry over the big cur put a frown on Frank's face.

He had just reached the stall where he had seen the foot sticking out when the match burned down and went out.

The glimpse into the stall he got before darkness closed in around him was enough to make alarm course through him. He had seen Pete McRoberts lying there unmoving, with blood on his head, and sprawled beside the old-timer was the big, shaggy form of Dog.

Frank twisted to put his back against the thick beam at the front corner of the stall. His right hand went to his gun while his left delved in his pocket for another lucifer. The sound of something whipping through the air toward him warned him that he was under attack. He crouched but couldn't avoid the lasso that dropped neatly over his head and shoulders and jerked tight, pinning his upper arms to his sides.

He was still able to draw his gun, but as he brought it up, something cracked sharply across his wrist and made his hand go numb. The Colt slipped from his fingers and thudded to the hard-packed dirt at his feet.

The bludgeon that had knocked the gun out of his hand slammed across his face. Pain exploded through Frank's head. He didn't pass out, though. Anger fueled his efforts to fight back against this treacherous attack. He didn't know if McRoberts and Dog were even still alive, but at the very least they were badly hurt, and he wanted to settle the score with those responsible.

As he charged forward, despite the rope around his arms, the thought of settling the score reminded him of what Sorensen had said. The man called Bracken who had fancied himself a gunman, along with his burly friend, knew who Frank was and had been plotting revenge on him. He suddenly had no doubt they were the ones who had lain in wait for him here in the stable.

His shoulder rammed into someone. The unseen figure let out a startled yell. Frank heard him crash to the ground. That was enough of a respite for Frank to get hold of the rope and try to push it up over his shoulders.

That was a mistake. The rope snapped taut again, but this time around his neck. The rough strands chafed his skin as whoever had hold of the lasso hauled hard on it. Frank tried to get his fingers under the rope before it crushed his windpipe.

Somebody—probably the man he had knocked down—tackled him around the knees. Frank fell as his legs were driven out from under him. The choking pressure was still on his neck. He hadn't had much air in his lungs when the rope tightened, and now he was short enough of breath that a red haze was beginning to descend over his eyes. He knew he was going to black out soon if he didn't get the rope off. He bulled up onto his knees and tried again to wrestle the loop off his neck.

Something crashed into his head again and laid him out on the stable floor. The toe of a boot thudded into his ribs in a savage kick, then landed again in his side, equally brutally. Still, he would have summoned up the energy to keep fighting if one of his assailants hadn't kicked him in the head.

That was more than Frank's battered brain could withstand. He slumped back down, out cold.

# Chapter 6

He hadn't had time to think about it during the fight in the stable, but if he had, Frank would have said it was likely his attackers would stomp and beat him to death if they were able to knock him out.

Instead, he gradually became aware that consciousness was seeping back into his brain. The pain that thundered in his head with every beat of his heart told him that he was alive. Nobody dead could hurt like that.

Bit by bit, other sensations wormed their way into his body. He was moving, rocking back and forth a little, sort of like he was at sea. Frank had been on a ship more than once and was familiar with what it felt like. After a few minutes, though, he decided that wasn't the case here. What he was experiencing was different somehow.

The soft, regular thuds he heard gave him a better idea of what was going on. Those were the hoofbeats of a team of horses or mules, he realized. He was in a wagon moving along at a slow but steady clip, and the irregularities of the road it followed were what caused him to rock back and forth.

He was lying on something hard, almost certainly the

wagon bed. Musty-smelling darkness enveloped him. He moved his head just slightly. The scrape of coarse fibers against his cheek told him somebody had thrown a woolen blanket over him.

Had they done that to conceal him, or because they believed he was dead? Was he being taken out into the desert to be dumped in a shallow, unmarked grave?

The heat under the blanket was stifling. Frank had trouble getting his breath. That reminded him of the rope that had been around his neck. At least it was gone now, although the skin of his neck stung in places where it had been rubbed raw.

The pain in his head that had throbbed at first, keeping time with his pulse, had subsided to a dull ache by now. He was able to ignore it as he lay there without moving and took stock of his situation.

At least two men had attacked him in the livery barn, and he wouldn't be surprised if both of them were his captors now. They might both be riding on the wagon, or one could be handling the reins while the other rode horseback next to the vehicle. Frank was confident, though, that if he tried to escape he would have to deal with both of them. And there could easily be more enemies he didn't know about.

He tensed the muscles of his arms and legs to see if they worked. It seemed to him that they did, but he couldn't move much because he was tied hand and foot, with his arms pulled behind his back. They had done a good job of trussing him up before they tossed him into this wagon. They had to know that he was alive, or else they wouldn't have gone to that much trouble.

No gag in his mouth, so he could yell if he wanted to, but that wasn't going to do him any good. He didn't know how long he had been unconscious, but it had probably been a while. More than likely, by now they were well out of Tucson, on their way to wherever they were going.

Frank lay there gathering his strength. He wondered about Dog and Pete McRoberts. Were they alive? Or had the two men killed them? If they had, that was two more scores Frank had to settle with them. Not that he needed any more reasons to kill those two. He figured they already had it coming.

He thought then about Antonia Escobar. Had she waited at the hotel corral for him until she finally gave up and decided he wasn't coming? He hoped she hadn't come looking for him and wandered into the stable just in time to get herself caught by the same two varmints. She might be a prisoner in this very same wagon and he just didn't know it.

A voice asked suddenly, "Think we'll be there by dark?" It sounded vaguely familiar to Frank.

"Damned well ought to be," another man replied. He was farther away, probably on horseback, as Frank had speculated a few minutes earlier. Frank knew who the voice belonged to, as well: the derby-hatted bully called Bracken. That meant his stocky friend was driving the wagon.

But that didn't answer the question of where they were going. From what they had just said, they had a definite destination in mind.

"How about we haul Morgan out of there and kick him around some more?" That was Bracken again, obviously holding a grudge.

"You know better than that. We need him alive."

"Alive, sure, but as long as he's breathing, it don't matter what kind of shape he's in, does it?"

"The money we stand to make from this is more important than you getting even with Morgan. You know that."

Bracken heaved a sigh and said, "Yeah, yeah, I suppose so. Before this is all over, though, I'm gonna square accounts with him."

Frank was more puzzled than he had been before they started talking, but right now it didn't matter if he knew all the details of the trouble he had landed in. He wanted to know why he was valuable to these two hardcases, but finding out would have to wait.

He knew he would be running a risk by moving around enough to reveal that he was conscious, but he believed the chance was worth taking. He moved his head and pushed the blanket down a little. He continued working at it, and after a few minutes he had uncovered enough of his face for him to be able to see as he looked around the back of the wagon.

He was alone. By twisting his neck, Frank could look toward the front of the vehicle enough to see through the opening in the canvas cover over the bed. The back of the driver's head was visible as he sat on the seat and handled the reins.

Frank's wrists were tied behind his back. Despite that, he was able to use his hands enough to catch hold of the blanket and pull it down even more. Without making any noise, he wiggled around and got himself clear of its cumbersome folds. Then he turned, slowly and quietly, and wedged his knees underneath him. Heaving himself upright from that position took a lot of strength, but Frank was a powerful man. Fortunately, the steady *clip-clop* of the team's hooves and the creaking of the wagon wheels covered up any small sounds he made.

He inched forward on his knees until he was only a couple of feet behind the man on the driver's box. He could see better now. Bracken was riding ahead of the wagon by about fifty feet and was off to the left a short distance.

Frank drew in a deep breath and then flopped over on his back. That made enough noise to alert the driver. He yelled, "Hey!" and started to stand up and turn around.

Frank pulled up his knees and kicked out with his bound feet. His legs shot over the top of the seat. His bootheels caught the man on the shoulder and knocked him forward. He yelled as his feet struck the angled lip of the floorboard and he toppled onto the backs of the team.

That startled the horses, as Frank had hoped it would, and they bolted forward. Frank heard the driver screaming, so he must not have fallen underneath the flashing hooves. He had to be hanging on for dear life to the harness or to the wagon's singletree.

Frank clambered back up and awkwardly lunged forward through the opening so he hung over the back of the driver's seat. He could see now. He caught a glimpse of Bracken's startled face as the runaway four-horse team stampeded past him.

The driver clung to the side of the right-hand wheel horse with a precarious grip on the animal's harness. His feet dragged. He kept trying to throw a leg up over the horse's back, but he couldn't make it.

Frank rolled over the top of the seat and barely caught himself before he slid on down to the floorboards. His coiled gun belt lay on the seat where his captors had put it after taking it off his unconscious form. He wasn't that interested in the Colt at the moment, but the sheathed bowie knife was also attached to the gun belt. That was what he had to get his hands on.

He turned his back to the coiled belt and scooted

toward it. He had to be careful. If he knocked it off the wagon seat, all his efforts would go for naught. By now Bracken must have realized what was going on and would be galloping after the runaway wagon. It wouldn't take him long to catch up. Frank had to get his hands free before that happened.

*Then* the well-used Colt would come into play.

Frank's fingers brushed the bowie's handle. He closed one hand around it and worked it out of the sheath. The blade was razor sharp, so he had to be cautious as he turned it around until it rested on the length of rope wound around his wrists. If he cut himself very deeply, he might bleed to death before he could get free.

With maddening slowness, he sawed at the rope and felt the strands parting one by one. Every bounce of the wagon made him grimace as that just increased the chances of him slashing his own wrists.

Because of the rolling thunder from the hooves of the stampeding team, he didn't hear Bracken galloping up beside the wagon until it was almost too late. He spotted something from the corner of his eye, looked over, and saw Bracken brandishing a revolver at him. The gun roared and spat flame, but Frank could tell that Bracken had aimed high, trying to scare him. He remembered that they wanted to keep him alive.

The knife nicked his wrist, but not deeply enough to do any real damage. That told him the bonds had almost parted. He heaved with his arms and shoulders and broke them the rest of the way. Turning the bowie, he drove its point into the seat beside him so it stood up there, quivering slightly. Then he plucked the Colt from its holster and snapped a shot at Bracken, who jerked his horse away and caused Frank's bullet to go wide.

Frank glanced at the man who had been driving the wagon. He still hung on to the horse, although he had gotten his arms around the animal's neck by now and had a leg over the horse's back. He was trying to pull himself up but not having much luck.

Frank grabbed the knife with his left hand and bent down to slash the rope around his ankles. He was free now, but still in a bad spot. The reins had fallen down among the horses' legs, so he couldn't control the wagon. Bracken had fallen back a little so Frank couldn't shoot him out of the saddle, but he was still nearby and a threat. Frank wondered if he should risk a leap from the wagon, since it was careening along so wildly it might crash at any moment.

When he was younger, he would have done it without hesitating. Now the odds were that he would break an arm or a leg with a leap like that. But if the wagon overturned going this fast, the wreck definitely would bust him to pieces.

He hadn't really had a chance until now to study the terrain through which the wagon was passing. It was flat and sandy, dotted with scrub brush and an occasional clump of grass or cactus. But an arroyo meandered across the terrain up ahead to the right, and Frank decided that if he could reach it, he could use it for cover while he tried to hold off Bracken. Quickly, he buckled on the gun belt, sheathed the knife and holstered the Colt, and slid to that end of the seat.

A bullet ripped through the wagon's canvas cover, then another. Bracken's shots were coming closer now as he got frustrated. Frank waited a few seconds longer, gauging where and how he wanted to jump, then launched himself off the seat.

He flew through the air, hanging there for a breath-taking instant, and then came down to earth with a bone-jarring, teeth-rattling crash. He landed cleanly, though, and was able to roll over and over to steal some of the momentum from the impact. The ground dropped out from under him, just as he had planned, and he rolled down a steep bank into the arroyo.

He came to a stop at the bottom and scrambled back up eight feet so he could look out over the edge. The wagon was still racing along at high speed as Bracken pursued it. Had the hardcase not noticed when Frank jumped off? For a second Frank thought he might be able to give his erstwhile captors the slip.

Then hoofbeats pounded up the arroyo behind him and as he whirled to face the new threat a rifle cracked twice. Bullets slammed into the slope on either side of him and threw dirt and rock into the air. A magnificent black horse slid to a halt about twenty feet away, and the rider, also in black, leveled a Winchester at Frank.

"Don't reach for your gun, Señor Morgan! I won't kill you, but I will put a bullet in your knee so you never walk again. Please don't test my aim."

As a matter of fact, Frank was too flabbergasted to attempt a draw. The rider who had galloped up the arroyo and gotten the drop on him was none other than Antonia Escobar.

# Chapter 7

The tight, black leather trousers she wore allowed her to ride astride, like a man. Above them was a black jacket decorated with ornate beadwork. Her long dark hair was pulled back and tied behind her neck so it hung down her back, and a flat-crowned black hat was on her head. She didn't appear to be armed except for the Winchester, but the way she held the rifle told Frank she was accustomed to using it—and good at it, too.

Even so, for a second he considered reaching for his Colt. A couple of things stopped him.

One was the cold determination in her eyes as she gazed at him over the Winchester's sights. She *would* pull the trigger, he knew, and if her aim was as good as it seemed to be, a bullet through his knee would cripple him for the rest of his life.

The other thing that held him back was the fact that she was a woman. He knew now that he'd been right not to trust her, and a bullet from a woman's gun could be just as deadly as one fired by a man. But even so, Frank couldn't disregard the way he had been raised and how he had lived his life. He just didn't want to kill Antonia Escobar.

Now, taking her over his knee and blistering her butt might be a different story . . .

She had to be working with Bracken and the other man, and they wanted him alive, Frank reminded himself. It might be better to let this hand play out until he discovered what was going on.

"Take it easy, señorita," he said. "I'm not going to try anything. You want me to get my gun out with my left hand and toss it away?"

"I think not," Antonia said coolly. "I know a great deal about you, Señor Morgan. You may not be *quite* as dangerous with a gun in your left hand, rather than your right, but I'd rather not take the chance. Please keep both hands well away from that gun until my men get here."

"Your men, eh? So those two work for you?"

"I am in charge right now, yes."

That answer was sort of intriguing, he thought. Who else was in charge at other times?

"You know, there's no telling how long it's going to take for those two hombres to get back. Most women aren't strong enough to hold a Winchester steady for very long."

"I am not most women," she said, still with that cool, arrogant tone in her voice. She appeared to be telling the truth, too. So far, the rifle was steady as a rock in her hands.

"Well, then, why not tell me what this is all about?" he suggested. "You claimed that you and your father needed my help."

"And so we do," Antonia said. "If everything goes as

planned, you will be a great help to us, indeed, Señor Morgan."

Frank was getting annoyed. He didn't like mysteries. He snapped, "Have those two varmints been working for you all along, even when they braced me in the hotel bar?"

"I wished to see what kind of man you truly are, so that we could make our plans accordingly. You obliged with that little demonstration in the bar. Bracken carried things a bit further than he was supposed to, but it all worked out. We knew that we could not take you head-on. Some subterfuge would be required."

"Ambushing me in the livery stable, you mean." Frank's voice was harsh with anger as he went on, "Did you kill Dog and the old man?"

"You worry about an animal and a worthless old man?"

"Either of them is worth a lot more than you and your pet snakes."

Anger flared in her dark eyes. Her finger tightened a little on the trigger. Frank saw that and wondered if he had goaded her into shooting him. Maybe he ought to make a try for his Colt after all.

Then she controlled her reaction and said with a sneer, "Both were alive when we left, merely knocked out, as far as I know. My orders were no shooting, because I did not want to draw attention. Bracken suggested cutting their throats once they were unconscious, but I saw no need of that. The old man never got a good look at us, and the dog cannot talk."

Frank sighed in relief, knowing there was a good chance Dog and the old-timer were alive. Right now, he would take whatever good news he could get. The barrel of that rifle pointing at him still hadn't wavered.

Hoofbeats sounded not far off, followed by the creak and rattle of the wagon as it approached. Bracken must have been able to catch up to the vehicle, grab the harness on one of the leaders, and bring the runaway team to a halt.

A minute later, Bracken appeared at the top of the bank and slid down into the arroyo. He had a gun in his hand, and he glared at Frank as he said to Antonia, "What the hell's the matter with you? Shoot him—or I will!"

"Have you forgotten that our plan was to capture Señor Morgan alive?" she asked, sounding as cool and haughty when she talked to Bracken as she had when she was addressing Frank. This was one señorita who had a pretty high opinion of herself and was used to giving orders—and being obeyed.

"You ain't even disarmed him," Bracken said.

Instead of responding to that, Antonia said, "Where's Kern? Is he all right?"

"Yeah, I'm fine," the answer came from the top of the bank. The stocky, bearded man appeared there, also holding a gun. "A little shaken up, but nothing to worry about. Nearly getting trampled by that runaway team probably scared five years off my life, though. I don't want to ever do *that* again."

"Come down here and help me cover Morgan," she told him. "Now, señor, unbuckle that gun belt and let it drop."

Surrounded by enemies who had the drop on him, Frank had no choice but to do as she said. When the gun belt, along with the holstered Colt and sheathed bowie, had fallen to the ground, Antonia went on, "Now step back away from it. Bracken, get the belt."

Still muttering unhappily, Bracken jammed his iron back in its holster and stalked forward to pick up Frank's gun belt. He was careful not to get in the line of fire of either Antonia or Kern as he did so.

Once Bracken had backed off with Frank's weapons, Antonia lowered the rifle a little but kept it pointed in Frank's general direction.

"Now, Señor Morgan, you will climb out of this arroyo. Please do not try any tricks."

"I'd have to be kind of foolish to do that, wouldn't I?" Frank said.

"I told you, I know a great deal about you. I know you are the sort of man who believes he can overcome any odds, given the chance. You have decided to, what is the expression, play along with us for now. But I promise you, if you cause too much trouble, you will regret it. You may not die, but you will wish you had."

"Pretty girls don't normally make such threats."

"And have you not noticed, I am not just any pretty girl?"

That was the truth, Frank thought. He wasn't sure he had ever run into a gal like this one before.

Kern climbed out of the arroyo first so he could keep Frank covered while he clambered up the bank. Then Bracken followed. Antonia wheeled her horse around and rode off in the direction she had come from, disappearing around a bend. More than likely the bank was caved in somewhere up there, so she could ride out of the arroyo. That had to be how she had gotten down into the dry wash.

She'd probably been following the wagon all along, Frank mused. He just hadn't noticed her in the excitement of his attempted escape. He hadn't had any reason to think she was anywhere around. To the best of his knowledge at that point, she was still back in Tucson, wondering why he hadn't shown up at the place and time they had arranged.

He wasn't surprised when she rode up again a few minutes later. Her Winchester was back in its saddle boot now. That saddle was impressive, just like the horse. Gleaming black leather with silver trappings and trim. A saddle like that cost a lot of money. She was a young woman with expensive tastes to go along with her superior attitude.

"Tie him up again," she told Bracken and Kern.

"It may not be as easy this time," Bracken warned her. "He's not out cold like he was in the stable."

"We can knock him out again," Kern suggested pragmatically.

"He has already been unconscious once," Antonia said. "A man who continually gets hit in the head risks great damage. Do you want to take a chance on that, Señor Morgan, or would you rather cooperate?"

"I'd just as soon not get walloped again," Frank said honestly. "I've been banged around enough in my life."

"I can imagine. And truthfully . . . you are curious, are you not? You desire to find out why all this is happening."

Frank shrugged and said, "Got to admit, I wouldn't mind."

"Then put your hands behind your back and do not struggle." She slid her rifle from its sheath and pointed it at Frank again. "Bracken, you cover him as well. Kern, tie his wrists."

It galled Frank to cooperate with his captors like this, but he swallowed the bitter-sour taste in his mouth and allowed Kern to bind his wrists again. Then he climbed into the wagon, and the man tied his ankles together, as well. At least this time he was sitting up with his back against the wagon's sideboards rather than lying down with some dirty, smelly old blanket flung over him.

Antonia looked in at him through the opening at the back of the wagon and warned again, "Do not try anything. Bracken will be riding behind the wagon, and I will be up front."

"And I'll be driving," Kern said from the seat. "I've got a grudge against you, too, now, so I won't mind shooting your legs out from under you if I have to, Morgan."

Frank ignored him and looked at Antonia. He said, "Tell me one thing, Señorita Escobar . . . was there any truth in that yarn you spun for me?"

"Not really," she replied with a smile, "and my name is not Escobar. I am Antonia Ramirez."

With that she wheeled her horse and rode out of sight, and Frank was left wondering where he had heard the name Ramirez recently.

It didn't take him long to come up with the answer. Pete McRoberts had mentioned a Mexican outlaw named Diego Ramirez who had been raising hell along the border. Ramirez claimed he was leading a revolution against the dictatorial Mexican president, Porfirio Díaz, but as with almost every other self-styled revolutionary in that strife-torn country, Ramirez's real goal was to get his hands on as much loot as he possibly could.

At least, according to the old liveryman that was the case. Frank supposed there could be some rebels in Mexico whose actions were motivated by a genuine desire to do what was best for the country . . . but he had never run across any or even heard tell of them. Most politicians, even would-be ones, were bandits at heart.

Was Antonia connected somehow with Diego Ramirez? She had mentioned that Frank was worth something to her and her father. Could she really be Ramirez's daughter? The more Frank thought about it, the more possible that seemed.

If that was true, then what in blazes did some *bandido*/revolutionary want with him? Ramirez couldn't be trying to recruit him to his cause, could he? Knocking him out and kidnapping him would be a mighty poor way of doing that.

Unable to come up with any real answers to the puzzles facing him, Frank cleared his mind and let himself rock along in the wagon. They stopped in the middle of the day to let the horses rest. With obvious reluctance, Kern held a canteen and gave Frank a drink of lukewarm water, then put a strip of jerky in his mouth.

"That'll have to hold you until we get where we're going," the man said. "We won't be stopped long enough to build a fire and cook a meal. Besides, smoke draws attention."

"What are you worried about?" Frank asked around the jerky. "A posse?"

Kern snorted and said, "Not hardly. We got out of Tucson right at sunup without anybody having any idea you were in the back of this wagon. I'm sure somebody's found that old man before now, but there's nothing he could tell them about who knocked him out. Bracken may not be all that smart, but he's good at things like that."

Frank made a mental note of the disparaging remark Kern had just made about his fellow hardcase. That might not ever come to anything, but knowing how Kern felt about Bracken could be handy information to have at some point.

"What about Indians?" Frank asked. "Haven't heard about them causing any trouble along the border lately, but there are still some bronco Apaches up in the mountains and you can't ever predict what an Indian might do."

"Not worried about them, either," Kern said. "But being careful never hurt anybody. Now, shut up and gnaw on that jerky. You'll get another drink later."

Judging by the way Frank's stomach felt, it had been a good long time since that breakfast at Sorensen's café, so while the jerky wasn't much of a meal, it was better than nothing. A short time later, the wagon resumed its journey.

In the heat of the afternoon, with the rocking motion lulling his senses, Frank dozed off, waking only when Kern stopped the wagon again to give the team a respite. Kern let him drink again, as promised. He didn't see Antonia or Bracken but assumed they were somewhere close by, maybe resting their mounts, maybe scouting the trail ahead.

Late in the day, Kern slowed the vehicle again. A swift rataplan of hoofbeats dwindled up ahead. Either Antonia or Bracken had ridden on.

It was Bracken, Frank discovered a moment later when Antonia rode up behind the wagon and peered through the opening in the canvas cover at him.

"We have almost reached our destination, Señor Morgan," she said. "Your curiosity is about to be satisfied, to a certain extent, at least. My father will tell you as much as pleases him."

"You mean Diego Ramirez?"

Her finely arched eyebrows rose. She said, "You know of my father?"

"I've heard of him," Frank said. "I've heard that he's a no-good bandit."

Antonia's features tightened. "You would be wise to hold your tongue, señor. My father is firmly committed to the nobility of his cause."

"But you're not?"

She didn't reply. Instead she pulled up on the reins and wheeled the black horse away from the wagon. Frank heard the thudding hoofbeats as she rode on ahead.

Frank leaned forward to peer past Kern on the driver's seat. He could see that they were approaching some open wooden gates in what looked like a fairly tall, thick adobe wall. Beyond the entrance were a large plaza and some adobe buildings, and past them . . .

Rearing up was a huge pile of stone, adobe, and logs, a massive structure topped by towers and battlements that reminded Frank of pictures he had seen in books. What he was looking at was nothing less than a castle in the desert.

# Chapter 8

The wagon rolled through the open gates. Frank caught glimpses of men standing guard there, burly Mexicans with high-crowned sombreros and bandoliers of ammunition crisscrossed on their chests. Inside the compound were more men. Most of them were Mexican, but a good number of gringos stood around, too, as well as a few who appeared to be Indians. All of them looked like they had gathered as if in anticipation of seeing something interesting.

Frank had a hunch that "something" might be him.

He looked out the back of the wagon and saw the gates swinging closed. From here he could also see a parapet along the inside of the wall where men could stand to fire rifles at anyone attacking the place. He didn't see any cannon, but he wouldn't be surprised if some of the big guns were around here someplace. He had just entered a veritable fortress.

Kern slashed the reins against the backs of the team and sent the horses forward at a faster pace. That seemed unnecessary to Frank—they had already arrived at their destination, after all—but as he heard cheers erupting from the assembled men, he realized Kern had done it to make an impression on them. Kern hauled on the lines and swung the wagon in a tight turn that brought it to a halt broadside in front of an adobe building with wooden vigas protruding from the wall just below the roof. Netting hanging from those beams cast some shade over a gallery with a stone floor.

Men climbed into the wagon, grabbed hold of Frank, and lifted him out into the late-afternoon sunlight. Those slanting rays flickered on the blade of a knife as one of the bandits cut the bonds around Frank's ankles so he could stand and walk on his own. His wrists remained lashed together behind his back, though.

A rifle barrel prodded him toward the gallery along the front of the building. Antonia stood there under the netting. Her hat was thrust back off her gleaming raven hair now and hung by its chin strap behind her head. She placed one hand on a neatly curved hip and gestured toward Frank with the other hand.

"Look," she said to a man sitting in a large wicker chair on the gallery. "I told you I would bring him, and I did. This is Frank Morgan, the famous Drifter!"

The man in the wicker chair regarded Frank from under the broad brim of a straw planter's hat. His face was dark and hawklike, testifying to some Indian blood in his heritage, but his eyes were startlingly blue, a legacy from his Spanish ancestors. A thick black mustache drooped over his wide mouth. He wore gray wool trousers and an embroidered vest over a white shirt with an open throat. As far as Frank could tell, he wasn't armed.

"Señor Morgan," the man said, "I apologize for any indignities and inconveniences you may have suffered, but such was necessary, I'm afraid. Welcome to the stronghold of Diego Ramirez. I am, as you may have guessed, Diego Ramirez."

"I've met your daughter," Frank said with a nod toward Antonia.

"Quite an exceptional child, as I gather you have already become aware." Ramirez looked at one of the heavily armed men standing under the shade with him and said, "Cut our visitor's hands loose."

"Are you sure that's a good idea?" Antonia asked sharply.

"I never give an order unless I am sure it is a good idea," Ramirez responded with a trace of steel in his voice.

The man he had spoken to drew a knife from a sheath at his waist and stepped behind Frank, who wasn't completely sure he wasn't about to get that blade buried in his back. The bandit did as he was ordered, though, and cut the ropes around Frank's wrists. It felt good to pull his arms around in front of him again. He flexed his fingers and massaged his wrists where the bonds had chafed them.

Ramirez went on, "Nothing I have ever read or heard about you, Señor Morgan, would lead me to believe that you are an insane man."

"I'd like to think I'm not loco," Frank said.

"Then you understand how foolish it would be to try anything while surrounded by fifty armed men who would not hesitate to shoot you down in my defense."

"I don't intend to. As your daughter and I discussed earlier, I'd like to satisfy my curiosity. I figure that if I'm patient, you'll tell me what it is I'm doing here."

"Of course." Ramirez took a pair of cigars from a pocket in his vest and held one out toward Frank. "Would you care for a smoke?"

Frank shook his head and said, "Thanks, but I don't use 'em."

"He drinks lemon phosphates, too," Bracken said in a jeering tone. He was standing to the side with Kern, who had climbed down from the wagon. Bracken's thumbs were hooked in his belt, but his casual pose was obviously just that—a pose. Frank could tell he was tense and wanted to reach for his gun. Bracken wanted to kill him, and sooner or later, the man would try. That was a good thing to keep in mind.

"A man's tastes are his own, and he has a right to them," Ramirez snapped as he directed a slight frown toward Bracken.

"Sure, boss," the gunman agreed quickly.

Ramirez put away the second cigar and stuck one of the cheroots in his mouth. He didn't light it, however, but said around it, "What you are doing here is very simple, Señor Morgan. You will either make me a very rich man . . . or you will die."


Frank Morgan was marched at gunpoint into the big, castlelike building that was Diego Ramirez's stronghold. The inside of the place was as impressive as the outside, with granite floors, tapestries and paintings hung on the walls, heavy, overstuffed furniture, chandeliers and wall sconces with crystal fixtures.

However, when Frank looked a little closer, he saw the patina of dust that covered many of the furnishings, as well as the wear and tear, the damage from the elements and animals. Some of the walls showed signs of recent repairs.

Ramirez hadn't built this hacienda, Frank decided. He had found it when the Rurales ran him and his men out of Mexico. Someone had settled here in the past and poured a great deal of money into establishing a ranch, only to have it fail for some reason. Indian attacks, maybe, or the harsh, unforgiving climate. Frank estimated the house was around a hundred years old, dating back to when this region had still been part of the Spanish colony in the New World. It might be even older than that. But at some point, it had been abandoned to sink back into obscurity . . . until Diego Ramirez came along and made it his headquarters.

Kern, who was in charge of the men guarding Frank, motioned him up a broad, open staircase that curved along one wall.

"The boss said to put you in one of the rooms on the second floor," Kern explained. "The door's mighty thick and has a good lock on it, and the only window has iron bars over it. So don't go thinking you'll be able to break out." The man shrugged. "Even if you did, where would you go? You'd still be in the middle of all of us."

"If it was up to me, I'd throw you in the damn dungeon," Bracken put in. He was part of the detail charged with locking Frank up. He laughed and went on, "Yeah, that's right. This place has a dungeon in it. I reckon those old Spaniards who built the place threw their Indian slaves in there whenever they gave 'em trouble. Probably tortured 'em some, too."

Bracken sounded like he wouldn't mind trying his

hand at that. Frank didn't rise to the bait and respond to the man's jeering comments.

The room on the second floor, behind a heavy door and with only a single barred window, just as Kern had said, was comfortably furnished with a four-poster bed, an armchair, a wardrobe, and a dresser. Indian rugs lay on the floor. Frank supposed he couldn't complain about the accommodations, but the fact that he was a prisoner still grated on him.

Ramirez hadn't gone into detail about why Frank had been brought here. He had uttered only the cryptic comment about Frank making him a rich man. Easy enough to guess what the bandit leader had in mind, though. He had found out somehow that Frank was Conrad Browning's father and a partner in the vast Browning business empire. Ramirez intended to demand a huge ransom for him. Frank had no doubt of that.

He hoped Conrad wouldn't pay these outlaws a damned cent. He would prefer dying to giving them what they wanted. And if it ever came down to that, he would put up a fight and make sure he took some of them with him.

Kern, Bracken, and the other two gunmen who had brought him up here left then, locking the door behind them. Frank immediately checked around the door to make sure it couldn't be loosened in its frame. Seeing that it couldn't, he went to the window to check the bars. They had wrought iron scrollwork attached to them to make the window look decorative, but in reality they would work just fine to keep anybody inside from getting out. Frank examined the way they were set into the thick stone wall. If he'd had a hammer and chisel, he might have been able to chip away at the mortar and loosen some of the bars . . . in a month or so. Since he didn't have a hammer and chisel and wasn't likely to, thinking about it was a waste of time, anyway. But what else did he have to do right now?

An hour or so later, a key rattled in the door lock. Frank was sitting on the bed with his legs stretched out in front of him. He swung them off the bed and stood up as the door opened into the room. The man who had just unlocked the door stepped back in the corridor and raised the shotgun he held. He pointed the twin barrels at Frank and said, "This scattergun will splatter you all over the walls if you try anything, Morgan. The boss doesn't want that, so just stay right where you are."

"I don't want it, either," Frank said.

The man moved into the room. He gestured with the shotgun and said, "Now, move over there and sit down in that chair."

Frank sat. The shotgunner put his back against the opposite wall and kept the weapon trained on the prisoner. Frank thought he had seen the man outside among the other members of Ramirez's gang when the wagon arrived, but he couldn't be sure about that and knew it didn't really matter.

Bracken and Kern came in. Bracken moved up on Frank's left, drew his revolver, and pressed the barrel to Frank's head. The shotgunner stepped away from the wall enough for Kern to pass behind him, so Kern didn't have to get into the line of fire. He moved into position on Frank's right and put his gun to Frank's head, too.

"Now, don't move and don't try anything," Kern warned.

"I'm not likely to with two guns to my head, am I?"

Bracken said, "Who knows just how loco you really are, old man?"

Frank was tempted to give them a demonstration of how loco he could be, but he held down the urge. His time was coming, he told himself. He was sure of that.

Another man came in carrying something that Frank recognized as a camera on a tripod. He'd had a few pictures made in his life, the earliest ones the sort where he'd had to sit still for minutes at a time while the photographer worked under a big black cloth draped over him and his apparatus. This camera was a more advanced type than that. It was smaller, more boxlike, with a leather carrying handle on the top. The man opened the tripod's legs and set it down so the camera was pointed at Frank.

The photographer was a short, heavyset Mexican with thick, curly hair. He wore a dark suit with a white shirt and black string tie. Drops of sweat beaded his face, but he seemed more nervous than overheated.

"Sit very still, señor," he said. "This will not take long."

"I know how cameras work," Frank said.

"Ah, but this is not just any camera," the man said, pride in his profession and equipment blunting his anxiety for a moment. "This is a Brownie 2. The very latest thing. I saved for months to order it from the Eastman Kodak company. It takes only a second—" He reached out and pushed a button on the side of the box. Frank heard the thing click. "You see? It is done."

"Take a few more, just to be sure," Kern ordered.

*"Sí, señor."* The man turned a knob on the side of the box, pressed the button again, and repeated that process twice more. "One of those should be perfect for what Señor Ramirez wants."

"Damned well better be," Bracken said. "If you can't do the job, he'll find somebody who can."

The man squared his shoulders and drew himself up to his full height, which wasn't any more than four inches over five feet.

"No one in this part of the territory knows more about the photographic arts than do I, Señor Bracken," he said with wounded dignity in his voice. "I worked for Señor C. S. Fly himself in Tombstone and learned a great deal from him."

"Yeah, yeah, Armendariz, we've heard you bragging about how you were there when the Earps and Doc Holliday shot it out with the Clanton bunch. Nobody gives a damn."

The man with the shotgun said, "Take your stuff and get out of here, Armendariz. You know what the boss wants."

"*Sí, sí,*" the little man said. He closed the tripod, picked it up along with the camera, and bustled out.

The shotgunner kept Frank covered while Kern and Bracken stepped away from Frank and holstered their guns. They left the room first, then the shotgunner backed out.

"You fellas plan on feeding me?" Frank asked before they shut the door.

"You'll get fed when we're damn good and ready," Bracken said from the corridor outside. He slammed the door and turned the key in the lock.

What had just happened was even more proof that Frank's hunch was right. Ramirez wanted proof that Frank was his prisoner, and a photograph of him with guns being held to his head would provide that. Ramirez probably planned on sending that picture to somebody.

Frank had a pretty good idea who that somebody would be.

# Chapter 9

*San Francisco*

Conrad Browning closed his eyes and massaged his temples for a moment. Even though he had been working all morning, the pile of paperwork in front of him on the desk didn't seem to have diminished any. What was it, he asked himself again, that had prompted him to give up the wandering life of Kid Morgan to resume being Conrad Browning, business tycoon?

The run-in on the docks with Raymond Moffatt and his bruisers had taken place a week earlier. Conrad still thought about it during idle moments. That brief flurry of action had been the high point of his life in recent months. *Was he that addicted to excitement?* It seemed so.

One of the office boys had come in a short time earlier and spoken to Phillip, Conrad's secretary, in an excited whisper. Phillip had said, "I'll be back shortly, Mr. Browning," and left the office with the boy after Conrad distractedly waved him out. Conrad didn't know what it was about, but he was sure that Phillip would inform him if it was anything important. Unless and until that happened, he simply wouldn't worry about it.

Phillip came in wearing a worried frown on his face and holding an envelope in his hand. Conrad laid aside the pencil he had just picked up and figured that whatever was going on, it would be a welcome distraction from the endless reports he'd been going through.

"What is it, Phillip?" he asked.

"This message for you arrived, Mr. Browning," the secretary replied. "You know that your instructions have been for me to go through all the business correspondence and handle everything that doesn't require your personal attention."

"Yes, of course," Conrad said with a hint of impatience.

Phillip glanced down at the envelope in his hand and said, "This isn't *exactly* business correspondence. I thought it was, or I wouldn't have opened it, but . . ."

Conrad held out his hand and said, "Give it to me."

Phillip extended the envelope across the desk. It bore no marks from the post office and had only the words *Conrad Browning, San Francisco* scrawled on it. Conrad frowned.

"Who delivered this?"

"I'm told it was a rather disreputable-looking man," Phillip replied. "Possibly a Mexican."

Conrad opened the envelope and took out a folded sheet of paper. He spread it out and read the message written on it in pen and ink, in an excellent script.

*Your father, Frank Morgan, is my prisoner, and his life is in my hands. If you would save him, you must bring, in person, $250,000 in cash to the*

*village of Saguaro Springs in Arizona Territory.*
*You will be contacted there and instructed how to*
*deliver the money. This must take place within the*
*next two weeks, or Frank Morgan's life will be*
*forfeit. Any attempt to contact the authorities will*
*also result in Frank Morgan's death. This is very*
*serious and you must do as I have told you if you*
*wish to ever see your father alive again. If you*
*doubt what I have said, you will soon receive proof*
*following the delivery of this letter.*

The message was unsigned.

Conrad didn't know whether to be astounded or angry. He hadn't seen his father in quite some time. He got occasional letters from Frank Morgan, and in the last one, Frank had mentioned that he was in Texas.

That had been at least six weeks earlier, though. Conrad had no idea where Frank had gone or what he had done since then. Even though the resentment Conrad had felt toward his real father had long since faded, they weren't so close that they kept in frequent contact. Each lived his own life.

Conrad also had a hard time accepting the idea that Frank Morgan could be captured and held for ransom. It wasn't impossible, he supposed—Frank wasn't superhuman, and he *was* getting older—but every time trouble had come calling, Frank had come out on top. Conrad had assumed he always would.

"Sir," Phillip said, "I apologize for inadvertently reading such a personal message, but since I *do* know what it says . . . would you like for me to start getting together the two hundred and fifty thousand dollars?"

Conrad tossed the letter and envelope on the desk and said, "The ransom money, you mean?" He shook his head. "I'm not going to cooperate with criminals. Anyway, anybody can write a letter and make some wild claims and demands. That doesn't mean anything in this is true."

"The letter speaks of some sort of proof—"

"We'll wait for that before we decide what to do next," Conrad said.

As if he had been waiting for that cue, the office boy who had spoken to Phillip earlier knocked on the door and stuck his head into the office.

"There's another delivery for you, Mr. Browning," he announced. "A package this time."

Those words made a chill go through Conrad. What proof of his father's captivity could be sent to him in a package? Some body part that had been hacked off, maybe?

Only one way to find out. He told the office boy, "Bring it in."

"You bet, Mr. Browning."

Phillip was wide-eyed and apprehensive as he looked at Conrad and said, "Do you think—"

"I don't know what to think," Conrad interrupted as he got to his feet. "But I suppose we're about to find out."

The office boy reappeared, swinging the door open and striding in with a jauntiness that showed he was unaware of the situation's seriousness. He must have realized that something was going on, though, because he slowed and broke stride.

In his hands he held a flat package about an inch thick and eight-by-twelve inches in dimension, wrapped in brown paper tied with a string. The package wasn't big enough to contain anything too grisly, Conrad thought.

He held out his hand and the office boy gulped at the fires he saw burning in his boss's eyes. The boy handed the package to Conrad, who took a folding knife from his pocket and cut the string holding the wrappings in place. Then he dropped the still-open knife on the desk and tore the paper away to reveal a framed photograph.

It was a starkly exposed picture of Frank Morgan sitting in a chair and wearing a grim expression on his face. A man stood on either side of Frank, but not much of either of them could be seen in the photograph. The guns they held to Frank's head were clearly visible, though.

The office boy gulped again and exclaimed, "Good Lord!"

Phillip said, "I've never met your father, sir, but I assume that's him?"

"It is," Conrad said. "That's Frank Morgan." His fingers tightened on the frame. In the photograph, Frank appeared unhurt, but the menace of the guns was unmistakable.

Hesitantly, Phillip said, "You know, playing the devil's advocate here, we can't be certain when that photograph was made . . ."

"No, but why would anybody go to that much trouble if they weren't telling the truth?" Conrad placed the photograph on the desk next to the letter. "I don't know who's responsible for this, but I believe whoever it is actually has my father and intends to kill him if I don't pay that ransom."

"As I said, I can start gathering that money—"

"No," Conrad broke in. "Not yet." His brain was spinning, but certain thoughts had begun to emerge from the mad whirl and were crystal clear. "Send word to Claudius Turnbuckle that I need to speak to him, here in the office, as soon as possible."

"Mr. Turnbuckle, sir? Your, ah, personal attorney?"

"That's right." In the past, Claudius Turnbuckle had handled both business and personal affairs for Conrad, but most of the increasingly complex legal work involving the Browning holdings had been shuffled over to other attorneys in recent years. These days, Turnbuckle was as much friend and mentor to Conrad as he was legal counselor.

Conrad looked intently at Phillip and the office boy and went on, "Are the two of you the only ones who know anything about this?" He tapped a finger on the letter.

Phillip swallowed, nodded, and said, "That's right, sir." He looked at the office boy. "You didn't say anything to anyone, did you?"

The wide-eyed youngster shook his head and said, "To tell you the truth, I'm still not exactly sure what's goin' on, sir."

"Keep it that way," Conrad snapped. "I don't want word of this getting out."

"Of course, sir," Phillip said quickly. He looked at the office boy again. "You know where Mr. Turnbuckle's office is?"

"Sure."

"Get over there and deliver Mr. Browning's message."

"You got it, boss!"

The boy hurried out. Phillip turned back to Conrad and said, "Is there anything else I can do?"

Conrad slumped back into his chair and shook his head.

"Not right now. Claudius will have some instructions for you later."

Phillip looked puzzled by that, but he didn't say anything.

"I want to be left alone," Conrad added.

"Certainly. I'll be in the outer office if you need me."

"Show Claudius in as soon as he gets here."

The door closed behind the secretary. Conrad sat there, looking at the letter and the photograph on the desk but not really seeing them.

Instead, in his mind's eye, he saw himself, a spoiled, helpless young man in the hands of a brutal outlaw gang. They had been holding *him* for ransom and had cut off part of his left ear to prove that he was their prisoner. He still wore his sandy hair long enough to conceal that mutilation.

Frank Morgan had saved him from those outlaws, and not by paying any damn ransom, either. The only thing Frank had delivered to them had been hot lead.

The images in Conrad's head shifted. He saw his late wife, Rebel, eternally beautiful in his memory. She had been kidnapped, too, and had met death at the hands of her captors, despite everything Conrad had done to try to save her. He had failed, and that failure had haunted him for years before finally fading to a dim ache of sorrow and regret that would never go away completely.

He was still deep in that bleak reverie of the past when the office door opened without a knock and the tall, broad-shouldered, middle-aged Claudius Turnbuckle strode in. His beefy face had a look of annoyance on it.

"Your boy was most insistent that I come to see you right away, Conrad," he said. "I'm not accustomed to being at someone's beck and call like that, you know, not even yours. This had better be important. That blasted boy wouldn't even give me a hint of what it's about."

Conrad gestured toward the letter and photograph and

said, "Take a look at those and then tell me if you think it's important."

Turnbuckle picked the items up briskly, still looking put out, but his expression turned to one of shock and concern as the meaning of what he was looking at sunk in on him.

"Dear God in heaven," he muttered. "Can this possibly be true?"

"It looks real enough to me," Conrad said. "I don't know who wrote that letter—you can see it's unsigned— but if he's able to capture Frank Morgan he has to be taken seriously."

"Of course." Turnbuckle placed the letter and photograph back on the desk. He was all business again as he went on, "There's enough money in your various bank accounts to put together that quarter of a million dollars. It'll take a day to do so, but that should still leave you plenty of time to reach this Saguaro Springs place, wherever it is."

Conrad shook his head and said, "I'm not taking the money to Saguaro Springs. I want you to gather the cash and make arrangements to have it delivered there in ten days' time if you haven't heard from me before then."

Turnbuckle frowned and said, "I don't understand. You're not going to Arizona to ransom your father?"

Conrad opened the large bottom drawer on the right side of the desk and reached into it. He brought out a coiled gun belt with an attached holster in which a walnut-butted Colt .45 rested. He stood up and put the gun belt on top of the letter and photograph.

"Conrad Browning isn't going to Saguaro Springs," he said, "but Kid Morgan damn sure is."

# Chapter 10

The room in Diego Ramirez's stronghold where Frank was kept locked up might be comfortable—but it was still a prison. Frank had been locked up more than once in his life, always unjustly, and he didn't like being behind bars.

That first evening, a middle-aged Mexican woman had brought him supper. It was simple fare: beans, tortillas, stew with chunks of *cabrito*, goat meat, swimming in it. The food was good and Frank appreciated it, but when he expressed that gratitude and tried to get the woman to talk to him, she remained silent and just darted glances at the two guards—both armed with shotguns—who had accompanied her to the room on the second floor. Clearly she was afraid of them, as Armendariz the photographer had been.

Frank wondered where they came from. Was there a village near the bandit stronghold? That was entirely possible, and in that case, Ramirez's men could have taken it over and were ruling it with an iron fist. A place like this needed servants to take care of it, and Ramirez would be able to get them from a nearby village and force them to work.

Frank thought Ramirez might show up after supper to gloat, but no one else came to the room that evening. With nothing else to do, and since the day had been a mighty long one, he turned in early and went to sleep without much trouble. Any man who had spent years on the frontier knew how to sleep when he had the chance, because he never knew when another opportunity might come along.

The same woman, accompanied by different guards, brought his breakfast the next morning, which included a single cup of coffee. Frank could have used more, but his suggestion to that effect was met with a blank stare.

A younger woman who bore a marked resemblance to the first one brought his midday meal. Frank figured she was the daughter or maybe the niece of the older Mexican lady. She proved just as unresponsive when he tried to engage her in conversation.

One of the guards laughed at that and said, "You're wastin' your time, Morgan. These señoritas don't like us, and there don't seem to be nothin' we can do to make 'em feel different."

Frank could understand why that would be the women's reaction to this gangling, snaggle-toothed guard, who appeared to hail from the mountains of Arkansas. He couldn't blame the female servants for not wanting anything to do with the man or the others like him. They were outlaws, after all.

The guard went on, "Since they act so stuck-up and all, we just take whatever we want from 'em. It ain't like they can do anything about it, after all. But I reckon you're too old to be thinkin' about such things, ain't you, Morgan?"

Frank ignored the man and his leering comments. He

saw the split-second glance that the young woman directed toward the guards, though, and recognized the anger and hatred burning in her eyes. Ramirez's men might have the upper hand right now, but they had better be careful, Frank thought. One day they might not be in charge anymore.

Instead of one of the women bringing him supper as he expected, Kern and Bracken showed up again with their guns drawn. Frank was sitting in the armchair with his boots off. Kern motioned toward them with his gun and said, "Get your boots on, Morgan. You're going to have supper with the boss."

"Ramirez?" Frank asked.

"Only one boss around here, isn't there?" Bracken said.

"I don't know," Frank said coolly. "You tell me."

"Let's go," Kern said. "Señor Ramirez is expecting you."

Frank pulled on his boots and stood up. Kern backed into the hall and crooked his free hand to indicate that Frank should follow him. Bracken brought up the rear. Frank didn't like having the derby-hatted gunman behind him. He didn't put it completely past Bracken to gun him down and claim that he'd tried to escape, then take his chances with Ramirez for killing the hostage.

If Bracken had that impulse, he restrained it. Frank went downstairs with the two men covering him. They ushered him into a dining room dominated by a big hardwood table with heavy, ornate chairs around it.

Diego Ramirez sat at the head of the table with a cigar smoldering between the fingers of his left hand. He wore a dark brown, Spanish-cut suit today. Gold rings on several fingers gleamed in the rich yellow light that came from a chandelier hanging above the table.

"Good evening, Señor Morgan," he greeted Frank. "I hope your stay with us has not been too unpleasant so far."

"No, other than being locked up," Frank said.

Ramirez's shoulders rose and fell in an eloquent shrug.

"An unfortunate necessity," he said. "I do not believe you would stay here and cooperate with us of your own accord."

"Not hardly."

"But when our objective has been achieved, then you will be free to go, and I hope there will be no hard feelings between us. I bear you no personal ill will."

"Can't say as I feel the same way," Frank replied.

Ramirez chuckled and said, "If you did, you would be lying, and we both know it." He waved the hand holding the cigar toward the empty chairs to his left. "Please, have a seat."

Frank didn't see any point in arguing with that, so he sat down in one of the chairs halfway along that side of the table. A female servant appeared almost instantly and filled his glass from a bottle of wine. She wasn't the same one who had brought him his lunch, but she was also young and attractive, in a coarse way.

As the servant withdrew, Ramirez picked up his own wineglass and said, "Please join me, señor. The wine may not be as good as that to which you are accustomed, but it is passable."

"I've never been much of a drinker," Frank said. "What makes you think I know anything about wine?"

Ramirez frowned slightly and said, "But you are a wealthy man. Every man I have known who possessed a great deal of money had expensive tastes."

"A man can have his name on a piece of paper saying that there's money in a bank that belongs to him, but pieces of paper blow away in a strong wind. I carry enough gold and silver to buy bullets and supplies, and as far as I'm concerned, that's all the money I really have. And your men seem to have cleaned me out of that while I was unconscious."

"Our philosophies differ," Ramirez said with a quirk of his right eyebrow. "But that does not mean we cannot share a drink."

"I suppose not." Frank picked up his glass and took a sip. The wine tasted all right, but he was no expert.

"Perhaps we should drink a toast," Ramirez started to suggest, but then he stopped short and got to his feet as he looked past Frank. Frank glanced in the same direction and saw that Antonia had come into the room. He stood up, as well. He might not like the way she had tricked him, but he was still a gentleman.

Anyway, most fellas would stand up for a woman as pretty as Antonia Ramirez. She wore a dark blue gown trimmed at neck and wrists with white lace. The gown's neckline was low enough to reveal the upper slopes of her high, full breasts. A choker with a blue gem set in it hugged her neck. Her long dark hair flowed loosely around her shoulders and down her back. She was elegant and stunning, especially when she smiled as she did now.

"Good evening, Señor Morgan," she said. "It is good to see you again. You have been treated well?"

"Fine, señorita," Frank said. She was headed toward the chair at the opposite end of the table from her father, so he moved in that direction, too. Kern and Bracken, who had stood by silently while Frank and Ramirez were talking, both stiffened and put their hands on their guns, but as Frank took hold of the chair and pulled it out for Antonia, Ramirez made a slight gesture to indicate that they should relax.

"*Gracias, señor*," Antonia said as Frank held her chair for her. "I knew as soon as I met you that you were a gentleman."

"I was raised to be polite," Frank said.

Antonia sat down and nodded to her father. "Papa."

"You look lovely as always, my dear," Ramirez told her.

The same female servant filled Antonia's wineglass while Frank and Ramirez resumed their seats. Antonia murmured, "*Gracias, Manuela*," to the girl.

"I was about to propose a toast," Ramirez said as he reached for his glass again. "I will do so now. To the future. May it be bright for us all."

"The future," Antonia repeated as she lifted her glass. She looked at Frank.

"I'll drink to the future," he said. "Who knows what it holds?"

"Success for the revolution!" Ramirez said. "That is what it holds."

They all drank. Ramirez set his glass down, motioned with a finger, and more servants began to arrive at the table, carrying platters of food.

The meal tonight consisted of strips of tenderly cooked beef, along with chilis, wild onions, beans, and tortillas. The beef probably came from rustled cattle, Frank thought, although he supposed Ramirez could have brought some stock with him when he and his followers fled across the border. Even if that was the case, though, more than likely he had stolen them down there in Mexico.

The food was good and plentiful. In the same way that he handled sleep, a frontiersman ate when he had the chance, so Frank put away plenty of the vittles and washed them down with wine from the glass that seemed to stay full. Luckily, alcohol had never muddled his brain, except for the stretch when he had been mourning his late wife, Dixie. He had put that behind him long ago.

Ramirez seemed to have a pleasant glow about him, however, and he grew more expansive as the meal went on, saying, "I deeply regret inconveniencing you this way, Señor Morgan. I would never be so ill-mannered if it were not necessary in order to free my beloved country from the cruel grip of the tyrant Díaz!"

"El Presidente has plenty of enemies," Frank said, "but somehow he's managed to hang around for a long time."

"Because he is a murderous dog!" Ramirez clenched a fist and thumped it on the table. "But mark my words, señor, that butcher's time is coming to an end. He knows it, too. He fears me. That is why he sent his Rurales to force me to flee from my own homeland."

Antonia said with a smile, "The fact that you kept holding up trains and robbing his garrisons had nothing to do with it, did it, Papa?"

"A revolution must be paid for. Not every man fights out of sheer patriotism and love for his country. Not every man who supports our cause is from our beloved Mexico." Ramirez waved his glass toward the two gunmen. "Is that not right, Bracken?"

"You're always right, boss," Bracken drawled.

"You fight because I pay you to fight and because you hunger for your share of the loot that comes our way."

Bracken shrugged.

"If someone offered you a better price," Ramirez went on, "you would betray me in an instant!"

Bracken frowned and said, "I don't know as I'd go so far as to say that, boss. You've treated us good, and we've been loyal to you."

"*Sí*, but if the money went away, your loyalty would go with it."

Bracken looked like he wanted to protest some more, but Ramirez didn't let him go on. Instead Ramirez turned to Frank and went on, "You see, Señor Morgan, that is why you are so vital to our cause. With the money your son will pay to save your life, I will be able to recruit more men, buy more guns, perhaps even form a real army with cannons to blow that *bastardo* Díaz right out of his palace!"

"Papa," Antonia spoke up, "you have said enough . . . and drunk too much."

"Nonsense!" Ramirez said with a snort. "Señor Morgan is an intelligent man. He has long since realized why he is here. But one thing he does not know." He looked at Frank. "Would you like for me to explain what that is, Señor Morgan?"

"This is your place," Frank said. "I reckon you can say whatever you want to say."

"Indeed I can! The real reason I brought you here to dine with us this evening is to offer you a position in our revolution."

"Papa!" Antonia said as she sat up straighter. "You said nothing of this to me."

"You are my daughter, but I am the leader of this rebellion." Ramirez's gaze swung back to Frank. He didn't seem so drunk now as he went on, "You have a reputation as a superb fighting man, señor. Just the sort of man I need in my army. I am the general, but I would make you a colonel. You would share in our successes, and there would be a high place for you in the government after Díaz is dealt with and I rule Mexico in his place!"

"And if I was to throw in with you like that, I reckon I'd be expected to furnish the money to build that army of yours?" Frank asked. "Instead of you taking it from my son?"

"Support freely given for a good cause is always repaid in one fashion or another."

"You're overlooking something, Señor Ramirez. I'm not a military man. I had my fill of being a soldier a long time ago, when I went off to fight the Yankees. I wouldn't be much good as a colonel."

"All battle is the same," Ramirez snapped. "One man trying to kill another and demonstrate his superiority. Only the excuses are different."

"I'll have to refuse your offer," Frank said with a shake of his head. "It's not my revolution . . . and I'm not a bandit."

Ramirez's face darkened with anger. He put his hands on the table and lurched to his feet.

"You have been treated well, Señor Morgan, but you should remember . . . a dungeon lies below our feet, and time spent there would be much less pleasant for you."

"I know. Bracken told me about it. But that doesn't change anything. I don't want any part of your revolution, and I hope my son tells you to go to hell."

"Papa . . ." Antonia said in a warning tone, but Ramirez

ignored her. He jerked a hand toward Frank and barked an order to Kern and Bracken.

"Take him!"

"It'll be a pleasure, boss," Bracken said. He yanked his gun from its holster and lunged at Frank, chopping at his head with the weapon.

# Chapter 11

Frank didn't care where he was or what the situation might be, he still wasn't going to just sit there and let somebody wallop him with a gun.

He twisted toward Bracken as he came up out of the chair. His left forearm blocked the slashing blow aimed at his head. At the same time, his right fist shot out and caught Bracken on the chin. The blow snapped the gunman's head back. His momentum made him stumble into Frank.

Frank caught hold of Bracken's coat and swung him around fast. When he let go, that sent Bracken flying into Kern, who was also trying to get close enough to Frank to clout him. Their legs got tangled up with each other, causing both men to fall.

Frank sprang toward the head of the table, where Ramirez was clawing under his coat, probably for a gun. If he could get his hands on Ramirez and use the man as a shield, he might be able to bluff his way out of here.

Before Frank could reach Ramirez, something smashed into the side of his head. Liquid splashed across his face and got into his eyes, stinging and blinding him momentarily. The smell of wine filled his nose, and he knew a bottle had hit him. He staggered against the table and slapped a hand down on it to catch his balance and keep from falling.

A second later, a wildcat landed on his back. Long fingernails clawed at his eyes and forced him to duck his head. Antonia had jumped on him. Elegant and beautiful though she might be, she was a fighter.

One of the men he had knocked down, Kern or Bracken, grabbed his ankles from behind and jerked his legs out from under him. Frank pitched forward heavily and landed on his belly. Antonia still clung to his back.

He was vaguely aware of Ramirez shouting in Spanish, calling for help from his other guards. Frank knew he didn't have much time. Fighting a girl really went against the grain for him, but he had no choice. He rammed an elbow back into Antonia's midsection with enough force to lift her off him.

She let out a startled sound and fell away from him, gasping for breath. He rolled to put some distance between them, and as he did he caught a glimpse of Bracken looming over him with a foot drawn back, ready to kick him. Remembering the savage kicks that had battered him during the attack in Pete McRoberts's stable, Frank figured Bracken had been responsible for them. When Bracken's foot flashed toward him this time, he caught it and heaved upward as hard as he could. Bracken yelled and went over backward. His head thudded against the floor.

Frank rolled again, got his hands and knees under him, and pushed up to his feet. Kern knelt a few yards away and aimed a gun at him, clearly aiming to shoot his legs out from under him. Frank snatched a platter off the table and flung it at the gunman as he dived aside. Kern's gun boomed, but the shot went wild because the thrown platter struck him in the face at the same moment he pulled the trigger.

Another gun went off, this one with the sharp crack of a smaller-caliber weapon. The bullet burned along Frank's hip and spun him halfway around. As he slapped a hand on the table to keep his balance, he saw Ramirez pointing a pistol at him and knew the bandit leader had just wounded him.

Frank also saw a wine bottle lying on the floor and figured it was the one Antonia had thrown at him. His head was still spinning a little from that impact.

Antonia lay beside the table, curled up in a ball as she still struggled to drag air into her lungs after Frank had elbowed her in the stomach. He darted toward her, moving with surprising speed and agility for a man of his size and age, and bent to slide an arm around her.

"Antonia!" Ramirez said as Frank dragged her to her feet. He didn't dare shoot again, and neither did Kern.

A rush of footsteps behind him told Frank that the guards Ramirez had been yelling for had arrived in the dining room. He backed off at an angle so he could see them from the corner of his eye. They couldn't open fire on him because of the danger that their bullets would go through him and strike Antonia.

Using a woman as a human shield like that galled Frank, but vastly outnumbered and surrounded by enemies as he was, he had to use every weapon he could get his hands on . . . and he had gotten his hands on Antonia Ramirez.

"Call off your men if you don't want your daughter to

get hurt," he told Ramirez. He looped his arm around Antonia's neck. He wouldn't harm her seriously, no matter what the circumstances, but Ramirez and his gun-wolves didn't know that.

"Señor Morgan, you are making a terrible mistake," Ramirez said. "Even if we cannot work together, we need not be enemies."

"I reckon you took care of that when you kidnapped me and your men hurt my dog and an old man who's a friend of mine. Now, I want you to have a couple of horses saddled. The señorita and I are leaving, and nobody's going to try to stop us."

"Please, Señor Morgan," Antonia whimpered. "You . . . you are hurting me."

"Sorry," Frank muttered, but he didn't ease his grip.

"And I . . . I am frightened."

"No need to be, as long as your father does what I tell him—"

A lance of fiery pain bit into his right thigh and made his leg buckle momentarily. His hold on Antonia slipped enough for her to writhe free. He made a grab for her but had to jerk his hand back when she slashed at it with the bloody dagger she had just used to stab him in the leg. He didn't know where she'd had it hidden on her, but somehow he wasn't surprised that she had been armed after all.

"Get him!" Ramirez roared. "But do not kill him!"

Half a dozen men surged at him. Some were Mexican, some gringos, but all of them were hard-bitten bandits who swarmed around him throwing punches. Frank fought back as best he could, blocking some of the blows and lashing out with hard fists of his own.

Many of the punches landed, though, and despite trying to ignore the punishment he was absorbing, Frank's reactions began to slow and he wasn't as steady on his feet. A fist slammed into his side, which was still sore from the kicks back in Tucson, and another man clubbed his hands together and drove them into the back of Frank's neck like a sledgehammer. Frank tried to stay on his feet but felt himself falling. More weight descended on him, forcing him to the floor.

The men rolled him over and pinned him down by hanging on to his arms and legs. Bracken leaned over him, shaking his head dazedly from the rap against the floor it had gotten. The gun in his hand was steady enough, though, as he swung it up and pointed it at Frank.

"No!" Ramirez snapped as he stepped alongside Bracken and caught hold of his wrist, pushing the gun back down. "I still want him alive."

"Why?" Bracken said. "You already sent that photograph of him to his kid. He's no good to us now."

Ramirez glared, clearly not liking the way the gunman had stood up to him.

"I am in command here," he said. "Browning may insist on seeing his father alive before he cooperates and turns over the ransom."

"Hell, once he brings the money to Saguaro Springs, what's it matter? Just take it away from him and kill him."

"I do not trust him. Browning has a reputation as a canny businessman. He may try some trick." Ramirez shook his head. "No, we will keep Morgan alive . . . for now."

Antonia moved up beside her father and didn't look

nearly as beautiful as before as she said, "Alive, perhaps . . .
but I want him to suffer for daring to lay hands on me!"

Ramirez nodded in response to that, willing to give his
strong-willed daughter what she wanted, and ordered his
men, "Take him to the dungeon."

As the guards hauled him to his feet, Ramirez added,
"For your sake, Señor Morgan, I hope your son has more
sense than you do."

# Chapter 12

*Tucson*

The tall young man in dark clothes and hat swung down from the train as clouds of smoke from the locomotive's diamond-shaped stack rolled over the depot platform. The only bit of color in his outfit was the turquoise-studded silver band around his flat-crowned hat. The Colt .45 that rode in a black holster on his right hip was strictly a tool for work with nothing flashy about it, no ivory grips or anything fancy like that.

The young man didn't have any baggage with him, only a pair of saddlebags slung over his left shoulder. He planned on traveling light. He strode easily through the crowd of passengers coming and going, to the other end of the long platform where the door of a boxcar had been slid open and a plank walkway put in place. A hostler led a fine-looking buckskin stallion out of the boxcar. Another man carrying the horse's saddle and blanket followed them to the platform.

The hostler said, "Here you go, Mr.—"

"Morgan," the young man interrupted him. San Francisco

was far behind him now, and so was Conrad Browning. He held out his hand for the reins. "I'll take it from here."

Taking the reins in one hand and carrying the saddle in the other, the Kid led the buckskin down the ramp at the end of the platform to the open ground beside the depot building. He got the saddle on the horse and cinched it into place, then attached the saddlebags.

He had studied several maps and knew that the small settlement of Saguaro Springs was southwest of Tucson, on the edge of the great Sonoran Desert, where it merged with the more hospitable rangeland to the east. The town was only a few miles from the Mexican border. The Kid would be able to make it there in a day on horseback, more than likely, but he intended to pick up a few supplies before he set out anyway, because you never knew what might happen along the way.

He swung up into the saddle and rode around the depot, then started along the street in search of a general mercantile where he could buy those supplies. He had gone only about a block when he passed the open doors of a livery stable and heard a dog bark inside.

Something about the sound made the Kid pull back on the reins and bring the buckskin to a stop. He looked through the open double doors of the livery stable and saw a big, shaggy, wolflike cur standing there. As the two of them looked at each other, the dog barked again.

"Dog?" the Kid said.

The big cur loped out of the barn. The Kid dismounted, and as his boots hit the ground, the dog reared up and rested his front paws on the Kid's chest. Most men would have been at least a little shaken to have such a scary-looking animal in his face, but the Kid just rubbed Dog's ears and scratched the top of his head. Dog's tongue lolled out in pleasure, revealing his mouthful of sharp, danger-ous teeth.

A short, mostly bald old-timer in overalls came out of the barn and stared at the Kid and Dog in obvious surprise.

"Would you look at that?" he said. "That critter barely tolerates me, but he acts like you're his long-lost friend, son. I reckon the two of you must know each other."

"We've met," the Kid said. "He must remember me. I sure remember him."

The liveryman took off his battered old hat, pulled a bandanna from his pocket, and wiped sweat from his fore-head. He said, "It'd be hard to forget a varmint like him who looks like he's first cousin to a wolf and acts like one, too." He put the bandanna away and stuck out his other hand. "I'm Pete McRoberts. This is my stable."

"Name's Morgan. Some call me the Kid."

McRoberts's bushy eyebrows rose.

"Morgan," he repeated. "Like Frank Morgan? Are you and him kin?"

"Distant." That wasn't true when it came to the blood relationship, but for most of his life the Kid hadn't even known that Frank Morgan existed, so he supposed it wasn't too much of a stretch.

"That's how come you know Dog, then."

"Yeah, he's been with Frank a few times when the two of us crossed trails."

The Kid took hold of Dog's front legs and put them on the ground again. As he did, he noticed the healing wound on the side of the big cur's head.

"What happened to him?" he asked sharply.

"He got walloped." McRoberts still had his hat off, so he pointed to a fading bruise with a scabbed-over cut in the middle of it, above his left ear. "Like me. Somebody pistol-whipped us both, knocked us out."

"Who'd do a thing like that?"

"Dunno," the old-timer replied with a shake of his head. "I never got a look at the no-good scoundrel. Dog probably did, but he ain't talkin'." McRoberts clapped the hat back on his head and scratched the silvery stubble on his jaw. "I'm bettin' that whoever was responsible for attackin' us had somethin' to do with Frank Morgan's disappearance, though."

"Morgan disappeared?"

"Yeah. I was expectin' him to pick up Dog and his horses the mornin' somebody sneaked up and buffaloed me, but he never showed up, at least not while I wasn't out cold. Both horses are still here. One of my other customers came in and found me layin' in one of the stalls and went hollerin' for the law. The town marshal and the county sheriff both investigated, and neither of 'em found hide nor hair of Frank. He ate breakfast that morning at Sorensen's Café—old Sorensen knew him and talked to him—but after that he plumb dropped outta sight."

The story didn't surprise the Kid. He knew from the ransom note that Frank had been kidnapped, and from the sound of what Pete McRoberts was saying, it must have happened here at the stable, early enough in the morning that not many people were stirring around.

"Did Frank tell you where he was going from here?"

"Nope, not that I recall." McRoberts frowned at the Kid. "You seem a mite more inquisitive than a distant relation might be, if you don't mind me sayin' so."

"Frank and I have helped each other out on occasion. If something's happened to him, I wouldn't mind knowing what it is. Maybe he needs help."

"Maybe so, but you'd have to find him first. The law hasn't been able to do that."

"The law has other things to tend to," the Kid pointed out. "They might not be able to devote the time and attention to the chore that somebody like me could."

"Yeah, I reckon that's true. I can't tell you much more'n I already have, though. The sheriff asked around and found out that Frank had dinner the night before he vanished with some good-lookin' Mexican gal, but nobody seems to know who she is. She checked in at the hotel under the name Antonia Escobar. Whether that was her right name or not, there ain't no tellin'. And she's gone, too. Nobody's seen her since the night she ate at the Ruby House with Frank."

That was quite a bit of information to take in at once, but the Kid's brain was keen enough to do it. He saw instantly that the woman who called herself Antonia Escobar had to be connected with Frank's kidnapping. She had gotten to know Frank somehow. She might have asked him for help. He never would have turned down such a request from a woman.

Questions remained, however. Was Antonia Escobar also the victim of a kidnapping? Was she being held for ransom somewhere near the settlement of Saguaro Springs, as Frank was?

Or had she been responsible for what happened to him? The Kid couldn't believe that one woman would ever be able to capture Frank Morgan, but she could have had help.

"Are you thinkin' you might go lookin' for him?" McRoberts continued.

"I'm just drifting," the Kid said. "I don't aim to get sidetracked."

From what McRoberts had told him, he didn't believe the old-timer could have any possible connection to the kidnappers, other than having been knocked out by them, but if anybody was hanging around and keeping an eye out to see if someone was looking for Frank, he didn't want to tip them off.

"Seein' as how you're related to him, you wouldn't want to take those horses and Dog off my hands, would you?"

"It's not my place to do that," the Kid said. "Frank might come back and expect them to be here." He paused. "If you need some money to keep looking after them, though, I reckon I could give you some."

McRoberts waved away the offer and said, "Oh no, that wasn't what I was thinkin'. Frank and me are old friends. I don't mind keepin' his trail partners here." A wistful note entered the man's voice as he added, "I hope he does come back for 'em one of these days. I'd sure hate to think that somethin' really bad has happened to him."

"That's not likely," the Kid said. "I don't know him all that well, but I know if there's anybody who can take care of himself, it's Frank Morgan."

"That's the plumb truth."

The Kid thanked McRoberts for the information and moved on down the street, walking and leading the buckskin now. Dog started to follow him, but McRoberts called the big cur back. Dog returned to the livery barn and sat down beside the old-timer, but the Kid heard some whining from Dog as he walked away. Dog wanted to come with him . . . and in a way the Kid wanted to take him along. Dog was a formidable ally in a fight, as well as being a connection to Frank Morgan.

The Kid knew he couldn't risk it, though. Frank's kidnappers were bound to recognize Dog if they saw him again, and if Kid Morgan drifted into Saguaro Springs accompanied by the big cur, members of the gang might spot him and know right away that the Kid and Frank were connected.

No, he thought, if he was going to win his father's freedom, he was going to have to do it on his own.

# Chapter 13

A few years earlier, Frank had read *The Count of Monte Cristo* by Alexandre Dumas, the novel of imprisonment and revenge being one of the volumes he had carried in his saddlebags and read by the flickering light of a campfire along lonely trails. So he knew about dungeons.

As far as he could recall, this was the first time he had ever actually *been* in one, though.

When Ramirez's men had hauled him down here, he had seen six doors along the side of the stone corridor, so he assumed six cells lay behind those doors. A single lantern burned, hanging on a peg on the wall at the bottom of the stairs. Some of the wavering light from it spilled through the tiny window in the door, so as Frank's eyes grew accustomed to it, he was able to look around at his surroundings . . . not that there was really anything to see.

It was much like what he would have expected from a dungeon: a small, cramped cell with stone walls, floor, and ceiling. No windows, since it was below ground level. A wooden door several inches thick, reinforced with bands of iron nailed into place around it. A six-inch-square window in the door with two iron bars in it, even though the opening was much too small for anyone to get through it.

Unlike most dungeons authors wrote about in books, however, this one was dry, with no water trickling down the walls to create a dank, oppressive atmosphere. Instead, the air smelled of ancient dust and the buckets in each cell that prisoners had used for sanitary purposes over the years—or decades. The stench had permeated everything.

The bucket in the corner was the only furnishing in the cell. No bunk or stool, so Frank had to sit or lie on the floor. The hard surface was pretty uncomfortable on his aging hip bones, not to mention his leg with the still-healing stab wound, but he tried to ignore the discomfort. That was just one more score to settle with his captors, and until he actually had a chance to do that, he didn't see any point in dwelling on it.

As he sat with his right leg stretched out in front of him, he drew his knee up and then extended the leg again, flexing the muscles so they wouldn't get too stiff. He had been doing that with both legs, but especially the right one since that was where Antonia Ramirez had stabbed him with the dagger. The wound had still been bleeding when he was thrown into the cell, but after an hour or so the door was unlocked and a Mexican woman came in carrying a pan of hot water and some rags.

Kern followed closely behind her with a shotgun. As he pointed the weapon at Frank, he had said, "The boss has given me permission to shoot you if you cause any more trouble, Morgan, so don't try anything."

"You can't fire that Greener in here without killing this innocent woman, too," Frank had said.

"As for innocent, I couldn't say one way or the other.

But there's plenty more like her where she came from, so one old señora more or less doesn't make any difference."

The callous comment made anger well up inside Frank, but he settled for saying quietly to the woman, "I'm sorry."

"*De nada*," she murmured as she knelt beside him with the water and the rags. Working by the dim light from the lantern, she tore the rip in his bloodstained trouser leg wider, exposing the wound, which she began to clean.

While she was doing that, Frank said to Kern, "Where's your partner, Bracken?"

That brought a laugh from the bearded man. He said, "General Ramirez won't let him come down here. I reckon he doesn't trust him not to just go ahead and shoot you, the first chance he gets. The boss is willing for you to die as long as there's a good reason for it, but believe it or not, Morgan, he's not just a wanton killer."

Frank grunted and said, "Next thing you'll be telling me that he really does want to lead a revolution for the good of Mexico, instead of just using that as an excuse to get his greedy hands on all the loot he can."

"It's not my job to tell you anything," Kern said with a shrug, "just to make sure you behave yourself while you're getting that leg patched up."

The woman used a wet rag to wipe away the dried blood. The wound had just about stopped oozing crimson by now. The woman reached down inside the neckline of her blouse and brought out a clump of moss. She got it wet in the pan of water and mashed it against the hole in Frank's leg. His jaw tightened slightly against the pain she caused by doing that. The ache didn't last long before receding. She bound the moss in place with a long strip of cloth that she tied securely.

When she was done with that, she motioned for him to push his trousers down far enough for her to examine the wound on his hip. The bullet burn had bled very little, so all she did was clean it and then nod to him to indicate that it would be all right.

Frank could see now that she was the same woman who had brought him one of his meals in the room on the second floor. He said, "*Gracias, señora.*"

"*De nada,*" she said again. *It is nothing.* But not to Frank. It was something, all right, the only bit of kindness he had encountered since being brought to this bandit stronghold, and he wasn't going to forget it.

Kern had ushered her out then and relocked the door.

Night and day meant nothing down here. Time passed without Frank knowing how much of it had gone by. Every so often, somebody brought him a meal, sometimes one of the guards, sometimes the older woman or one of the two younger ones he had seen before. The food was simple, just beans and tortillas and an olla of water, but it kept Frank alive.

Every time the older woman came, she checked his wound and replaced the moss. He knew the stuff was drawing out any poison and dulling the pain. When he was alone in the cell, he worked the leg, carefully enough to keep it from starting to bleed again, but what he was doing would also keep it from stiffening up. He did the same thing with his arms and shoulders. He wanted to be able to move quickly if he needed to.

He was up on his feet, shuffling around as much as he could in the close confines of the cell, when he heard footsteps in the corridor on the other side of the door. He wasn't surprised when they stopped, since as far as he'd been able to tell by listening, he was the only prisoner down here.

A man looked through the window, saw Frank standing there, and ordered, "Back against the wall, Morgan."

Frank moved away from the door. The guard unlocked it and came in wielding a shotgun, then kept Frank covered as he backed into one of the front corners. Another shotgunner came in and took up a position in the other front corner.

That made four loads of buckshot staring at Frank. At this range, if both guards emptied their weapons at him, there wouldn't be much left. They weren't taking any chances.

Because of those extra precautions, he wasn't surprised when Diego Ramirez appeared in the doorway. Today the man was wearing a blue uniform with a red sash around the waist and gold braid on the shoulders. Frank smiled as he looked at Ramirez and remembered a song from a comic opera he had seen a while back. He drawled, "You look like the very model of a modern major general . . . General."

Ramirez's features tightened with anger. He said, "Mock me if you wish, Señor Morgan, but you will be singing a different tune when I am the ruler of Mexico . . . if you are still alive. So far there has been no sign of your son with the ransom money."

Serious now, Frank shook his head and said, "He won't bring it. You've made a mistake. Conrad is stubborn as all get-out, and tight with a dollar, too. Besides, the boy doesn't give a damn about me. He never knew I was his pa, never even heard of me, until a few years ago. And he didn't like me when he met me and found out."

"If this is true, why have the two of you come to each other's aid on numerous occasions?"

"You've really studied up on us, haven't you?" Frank shrugged. "Sure, there have been times when we've found ourselves on the same side in a fight, but that doesn't mean anything. And you've overlooked one very important point, Ramirez. If I wind up dead, the whole shooting match belongs to the boy."

For a second, alarm flickered in Ramirez's eyes, too strong a reaction for him to conceal completely. Frank saw it and knew his thrust had gone home. Ramirez really *hadn't* considered the fact that Conrad would profit by Frank's death.

Ramirez was too convinced of his own infallibility to doubt his plan for long, though. He shook his head and said, "You should hope that you are wrong, Señor Morgan. Otherwise, things will go very badly for you."

"My stay here hasn't been all that pleasant so far. I've been shot and stabbed and beaten up."

"That is no one's fault but your own. I made it clear that I would be happy to cooperate with you, if you wished to cooperate with me." Ramirez squared his shoulders in the gold-braided uniform. "To that end, I am here to make one more effort to enlist you in our cause. It would greatly simplify matters, and I feel that a man such as yourself would be a most welcome addition to our forces."

Frank studied the bandit leader for a moment, then said, "Suppose I agreed to join up with you. You'd just believe that I was telling the truth and give me the run of the place?"

Without hesitation, Ramirez laughed and said, "I think you know better than that, amigo. A number of my close associates, including my daughter and Señor Bracken, have advised me not to trust you at all, now or ever. As you know, Señor Bracken feels that you should be killed. My daughter would not be upset if you were tortured, although not to the point of death. Neither of those things is necessary. However, to answer your question, if you proclaimed your allegiance to our cause, you would be watched at all times until I was satisfied that you were sincere. There would be no chance for you to escape, if that is what you're thinking."

"I guess that's plain enough," Frank said. "I won't be joining up."

Ramirez frowned and then jerked his head in a curt nod.

"So be it. There will be no third offer. Your only value to me now, Señor Morgan, is as a bargaining chip. If I get what I want, you live. If not . . ."

His shrug was eloquent, but Frank didn't believe what Ramirez said. He knew that even if Conrad paid the ransom, Ramirez planned to kill him. Conrad had to know that, too.

And that was one more reason Frank hoped that Conrad had a few tricks in store for Diego Ramirez and his band of cutthroats and thieves.

# Chapter 14

The young man who rode into Saguaro Springs on a tired buckskin horse was covered with trail dust and had a couple of days of beard stubble on his lean cheeks and jaw. He was dressed in black from head to foot, although the dust gave the shirt, trousers, boots, and hat a grayish cast. The dust also dulled the gleam of the hat's turquoise-studded silver band. The young man gave the impression of having ridden a lot of lonely trails for a long time.

That was exactly what the Kid wanted anybody who saw him to think, especially anybody working for whoever was responsible for Frank Morgan's kidnapping.

Saguaro Springs consisted of one main street that stretched for three blocks with a couple of small cross streets lined by adobe dwellings. The false-fronted business buildings along the main street were frame structures, for the most part. The only buildings that actually had two stories, as far as the Kid could see, were the Cactus Saloon and the Chuckwalla Hotel. He smiled faintly as he noted the names of both establishments.

He could see why the owner of the saloon had chosen that name. About half a mile northeast, at the base of a small hill, several springs bubbled out and formed a narrow stream that twisted its way south past the settlement and then curved west to disappear into the desert. Towering saguaros grew along the banks of that stream, their spiny fingers reaching high for the Arizona sky. The springs and the cactus gave the town its name, and the distinctive vegetation must have impressed whoever owned the saloon.

But why would anybody name a hotel after an ugly lizard? There had to be a story behind that, the Kid thought, but he wasn't sure he was curious enough to find out.

The rest of Saguaro Springs looked like a dozen other little Western settlements the Kid had visited in his wanderings. Even though the twentieth century had arrived, a person would never know that by looking around here. Saddled horses were tied to the hitch racks, and wagons with teams of mules or horses attached to them were parked along the street. No telegraph or telephone wires stretched into town, and no railroad spur ran this direction.

A few ranches could be found in the rangeland to the east, as well as mines in the mountains that rose in the distance to the south, on the other side of the border. The Kid was sure the settlement had been established as a supply point for those ranches and mines. It would probably never grow any larger than it was right now, and if the mines petered out, the ranches might not be enough to support it. Saguaro Springs led a precarious existence and one day might turn into a ghost town like hundreds of others scattered all across the West.

Those thoughts flashed through the Kid's keen mind as he studied the settlement from under the pulled-down brim of his hat. He noticed something else, too.

Hard-looking men wearing holstered guns lounged here and there or strolled along the dusty street. The other inhabitants of the town kept casting nervous glances in their direction. A tense, expectant atmosphere hung over Saguaro Springs, as if trouble might erupt at any second.

The Kid had his doubts that it would, though, since the settlement's ordinary citizens seemed scared to death and wouldn't start anything. Those hardcases had Saguaro Springs buffaloed.

The Kid angled the buckskin toward the saloon. As far as anybody could tell by looking at him, he was just another hardcase himself, so he ought to fit right in here.

He swung down from the saddle and looped the buckskin's reins around one of the hitch rails in front of the Cactus Saloon. To the left of the batwing doors as he faced the building was a large window with gilt-painted curlicues in the corners and fancy lettering spelling out the name of the place. To the right of the entrance were a couple of smaller windows, and in front of those windows a bench was placed on the building's low porch.

Two men sat on that bench with legs outstretched and booted feet crossed at the ankles. One was a beefy Mexican in a tall sombrero. He was busy rolling a cigarette, while the other man, a lanky gringo in a brown tweed suit and brown derby, whittled on a block of wood. As far as the Kid could tell, the man in the derby was just carving slivers off the wood, because the block was a misshapen lump that didn't really resemble anything.

The Kid was stepping up onto the porch when the man in the derby whipped the knife toward him without any warning. It flashed through the air and struck one of the posts holding up the exterior balcony over the porch.

The throw was accurate and powerful enough that the blade's tip embedded itself into the post. The knife quivered slightly from the impact.

The knife was stuck into the post no more than two feet from the Kid's shoulder. He paused and looked at the man who had thrown it. A grin stretched across the man's angular face.

"You missed," the Kid said.

"Naw. If I'd've wanted to stick you, I would have." The man held out a hand. "How's about givin' it back?"

"Sure," the Kid said. He reached up and grasped the knife's bone handle. He pulled it free, and with a flip of his wrist he threw it back at the man. It stuck in the back of the bench between the man in the derby and the Mexican, who was licking the cigarette paper to seal it closed. He looked over calmly at the knife.

"Hey, señor, I did nothing to you," he said as he twisted the ends of the smoke. "Bracken is the one who decided to have some sport with you."

"Then maybe you should think a mite about the company you keep," the Kid said. He reached for the batwings to push them open.

"Hey," the man called Bracken said. He jerked the knife out of the bench and got to his feet. "I don't remember saying you could leave, mister."

"I don't recall asking your permission," the Kid returned coolly. Without waiting to see what Bracken would do, he moved the batwings aside and stepped into the saloon.

To his right, a couple of tables, empty at the moment, sat in front of the windows. Farther along that wall stretched the bar, gleaming hardwood with a brass rail along the bottom. At the back of the room were a staircase leading to the second floor and a small open area that would serve as a stage whenever the saloon had any entertainment booked. A piano sat back there with nobody to play it right now, looking a little forlorn.

A faro layout and a roulette wheel, also currently neglected, filled out the rear of the big room, and tables occupied the rest of the space. Four men stood at the bar nursing drinks, and two men had a bottle and glasses at one of the tables. Four men played poker at another table. Everybody in sight, including an aproned bartender behind the bar, was male. The Kid didn't see even one woman, but he supposed it was too early in the day for them. The ones who worked here were probably upstairs asleep.

The men at the bar and three of the poker players reminded the Kid of the two he had seen outside: hardcases who would sell their guns to the highest bidder. The other card player was a frock-coated gent with a thin mustache and dark hair parted in the middle. A professional gambler or the owner of the Cactus Saloon, or both.

The two men drinking at one of the tables looked more like merchants who owned businesses here in town. The glances they gave the men at the bar weren't too friendly, and the Kid got the same sort of wary frowns from the two men as he walked in.

The Kid was still moving as he took all that in with a glance. He stopped, though, as he heard the batwings slapped open behind him.

"Hey!" Bracken said. "Nobody talks to me like that and then walks off."

The Kid turned slowly and hooked his thumbs in his

gun belt. A faint smile curved his lips as he said, "Seems to me like I just did."

Bracken's stance—shoulders hunched a little, head leaned forward, right hand hovering near the butt of his gun—plainly showed that he was ready to hook and draw. The Kid didn't want to get mixed up in a gunfight this soon after riding into Saguaro Springs, but he wasn't in the habit of backing down from trash like this gun-wolf, either.

He wanted to catch the attention of whoever these men worked for, so he supposed killing one of them would do that. Assuming, of course, that the other seven hardcases in the room didn't fill him full of lead. He knew he could take down at least a couple of them before he hit the floor, but with seven-to-one odds, he had almost no chance to survive such a shootout.

And his death would leave Frank still a prisoner, the Kid reminded himself, so it would be better if he tried to avoid bloodshed . . . for now.

"But maybe we got off on the wrong foot," he went on to Bracken. "Let me buy you a drink and we'll call it square."

Bracken's lip curled in a sneer as he said, "I'm not gonna have a drink with you, you dirty son of a—"

"Bracken." The sharp, hard word came from one of the men at the poker table. "That's enough."

The Kid flicked a glance at the hombre who had spoken. His rounded face meant he was a little on the stocky side, and he had a close-cropped brown beard. He didn't look as much like a hired gun as the other men did, but the Kid had heard steel in his voice and decided he wouldn't want to cross this man unless absolutely necessary.

Bracken seemed to feel the same way, but he was too mad to back down completely. He said, "You didn't see what this stranger did outside, Kern, or hear the way he talked to me."

The Mexican who had been sitting on the bench with Bracken pushed the batwings aside and strolled into the saloon. With the now-smoldering quirley dangling in the corner of his mouth, he said, "This stranger is good with a knife, Kern. Bracken threw his at him, and he threw it right back. I think he could have given Bracken a close shave if he'd wanted to."

"Shut up, Enrique," Bracken snapped. "He was lucky, that's all. Lucky I didn't blast a hole in him first thing."

"Reckon you could have tried," the Kid said, "if you'd really wanted to."

He knew that comment might goad Bracken into drawing, and he still wanted to avoid that if he could, but Lord, the man was annoying! He had gotten under the Kid's skin like a burr under a saddle.

"Let it go, Bracken," Kern said from the poker table. "The boss won't be happy if you get yourself killed for no good reason, but I'm the one who'll get chewed out because of it."

"You think I can't take this stranger?"

"I don't know one way or the other, but I still say that's not a good enough reason to get yourself killed." Kern chuckled, although the sound didn't contain much actual humor, and nodded toward the bartender. "Besides, you don't want Mr. O'Reilly to have to spend a lot of time and energy mopping up blood from the floor, do you?"

Bracken's face was still flushed with anger, but with a visible effort, he controlled himself and walked over to the table where the two townsmen were sitting.

"Gimme a drink," he barked at them.

They didn't look happy about it, but one of the men picked up the bottle, splashed a couple of inches of whiskey into a glass, and pushed it toward Bracken. The gunman picked up the glass and tossed back the liquor.

The Kid turned toward the bar, figuring he would get a beer to cut some of the trail dust from his throat.

He could tell by the reaction of the men at the bar that something was about to happen. A split second later, the empty glass smacked into the back of his head and knocked his hat off. The heavy-bottomed glass thudded to the floor as the Kid stumbled forward a step. He heard rapid footsteps as he caught his balance. As he started to whirl around, he saw Bracken rushing at him, head lowered like a charging bull.

He tried to twist out of the way, but Bracken was snake-quick as well as snake-mean. He got an arm around the Kid's waist and drove him backward so that he crashed against the edge of the bar.

Pain shot through the Kid's body, but anger allowed him to ignore it. He brought up his right fist and slammed it against Bracken's head. That sent the derby flying through the air much like the Kid's hat had done a few seconds earlier.

Bracken pinned the Kid against the bar by leaning his body into him, at the same time hooking punches into the Kid's belly. After the first blow that the Kid landed, Bracken ducked his head down so the Kid couldn't get another good shot at it.

The Kid wasn't worried about fighting fair or clean, because the man he was pretending to be wouldn't have been. So in close quarters like that, he brought his knee up in a vicious thrust aimed at Bracken's groin.

Bracken must have sensed what was coming. He turned his body just enough to take the Kid's knee on his left thigh. It still hit him with sufficient force to knock him back a step, and with that sudden distance opening up, the Kid launched a straight, powerful right that landed cleanly on Bracken's jaw and drove him back even more.

Bracken fought to keep his balance but failed. He landed on his back on one of the empty tables. He didn't weigh enough to make it collapse, but it slid under him and toppled over, dumping Bracken on the sawdust-littered floor.

The Kid went after him. Again, it bothered him to kick a man when he was down, but he landed the toe of his boot in Bracken's ribs anyway, rolling him over onto his belly. The Kid reached down, got hold of the collar of Bracken's coat, and heaved him upright.

Then, while Bracken was still too groggy to put up a fight, the Kid rushed him toward the entrance, through the batwings, across the porch, and then flung him face-first into the street. Bracken landed hard, skidded a few inches in the dust, and came to a stop. He lay there mostly senseless, moaning softly.

The Kid turned, stepped back into the saloon, and looked around.

"That hombre have any friends who want to back his play?"

Kern laughed again. This time he sounded more genuinely amused.

"His play's already busted, mister. The rest of us have too much sense to back a losing bet."

"Speaking of backs . . . how likely is Bracken to try to put a bullet in mine?"

Kern shrugged and said, "I'd keep an eye out behind me if I were you. But you look like the sort of fellow who already does that."

"It's a habit I've gotten into," the Kid said.

"I'm not sure you have to worry *too* much, though. Bracken's pride is hurt worse than anything else, I expect, and shooting you in the back wouldn't salve it much. He'll want to take you head-on when the time comes, so he can prove something."

"Is he fast enough to do it?"

Kern's shoulders rose and fell again. He said, "*¿Quién sabe?* Maybe we'll find out."

"Maybe," the Kid said. He stepped up to the bar and went on, "I'll have a beer, Mr. O'Reilly."

The nervous-looking bartender nodded and picked up a mug from the backbar to draw the beer. Without being too obvious about it, the Kid walked off to the side as Kern gathered up his winnings and left the poker table. When O'Reilly set the beer in front of the Kid, Kern moved up alongside and dropped a half-dollar on the hardwood.

"It's on me," he said, "and I'll have one, too."

"Sure thing, Mr. Kern," O'Reilly said. Quickly, he drew the second beer.

"You picked up on my name, I reckon," Kern said as he lifted his mug. "What's yours?"

"Callahan," the Kid said. That had been his wife, Rebel's maiden name. He wasn't likely to forget it. He couldn't call himself either Kid Morgan or Conrad Browning, since it was likely Kern and these other hired guns would recognize both names.

Kern drank some of his beer and then said, "You can handle yourself all right, Callahan, that's pretty plain. Do you happen to be looking for work?"

The Kid swallowed some of his beer, smiled, and said, "I just might be."

# Chapter 15

The Kid's intentions had been to drift into Saguaro Springs, get the lay of the land, try to figure out where Frank was being held, and then come up with a plan to free him. Now, within an hour of him riding into the settlement, fate—along with the proddy gunman named Bracken—might have handed him a way of accomplishing those things.

He paused after his reply to Kern's question and then went on as if only casually curious, "What's the job?"

"One that pays well and might wind up being worth a hell of a lot more. What else do you need to know?"

The Kid took another drink of beer, then smiled and said, "I always try to get an idea of how likely it is that I'll be shot at."

"Oh, I reckon it's almost guaranteed that you will be, sooner or later. Is that going to bother you?"

"It never has so far," the Kid said with a slight shake of his head.

Kern seemed to like that answer. He laughed and drained the rest of his beer. As he set the empty mug on the bar, he asked, "Are you going to be around town for a few days?"

"Yeah. I've been on the trail for a while. My horse and I could both use some rest."

"I'll have to talk to some people and then look you up. Are you going to stay at the hotel?"

"I didn't see any other place in town to bed down, other than maybe the hayloft in the stable," the Kid said.

Kern nodded. "All right. Give me a day or two."

"I'll be around . . . unless Bracken manages to kill me before then."

"I've got my doubts about that happening," Kern said.

"If I do wind up having to kill him . . . will you be looking to settle the score for him?"

"Let's just hope it doesn't come to that."

With that noncommittal answer, Kern left the saloon. The Kid watched him go. Through one of the smaller windows, he saw Bracken sitting hunched over on the bench, slowly shaking his head as if trying to clear the cobwebs from his brain. His Mexican friend was with him and had probably helped him out of the street.

Kern stopped next to the bench and spoke to Bracken. After a moment, Bracken got to his feet unsteadily and he and the Mexican followed Kern out of sight.

The Kid figured he hadn't seen the last of any of them.

"Another beer, mister?" the bartender asked. "This one will be on the house."

The Kid turned to look at the man and asked, "Why's that, Mr. O'Reilly?"

The bartender glanced toward the table where the poker game was continuing without Kern. One of the men who had been standing at the bar had gone over and taken

Kern's seat. The other three hardcases were gathered at the far end, talking quietly among themselves. They didn't appear to be paying any attention to the Kid and O'Reilly at the other end of the bar.

"Bracken's caused trouble in here before," O'Reilly said, keeping his voice pitched low enough that only the Kid could hear him. "I've had to sweep up broken glass, mop up blood and spilled booze, and replace broken chairs. He's got a mean streak a mile wide in him, and he takes it out on townsfolk most of the time. It was mighty good to see him get his comeuppance for once."

"What would you have done if I'd killed him? Given me a whole bottle of whiskey?"

"It'd be worth it," O'Reilly answered fervently, then fear flared in his eyes again. "Oh, hell. I shouldn't be sayin' such things. I heard you talking to Kern about going to work for the general, and if you do, that means you and Bracken will be on the same side."

"We might draw wages from the same man," the Kid said, "but that doesn't mean we'll ever be friends. So you don't have to worry that I'll be telling tales." He paused, then added, "Who's the general?"

"Diego Ramirez. I, uh, don't think he was a real general in the Mexican army or anything. I don't think he was even *in* the Mexican army. But he likes the men who work for him to call him the general. He figures on replacing President Díaz down there."

The Kid raised his eyebrows. "You're saying he's a revolutionary?"

"So he claims."

"Sort of odd that a man like that would have a bunch

of gringo gun-wolves working for him, don't you think?" the Kid mused.

"General Ramirez hires anybody he believes can help him out, I reckon," O'Reilly said. He drew the second beer and set it in front of the Kid. "From what I just saw, I think he'll want to hire you, Mr. Callahan . . . if he decides he can trust you."

"So I reckon this fella Ramirez is north of the border right now?"

"He's got a place not far from here. An old abandoned rancho. He and his men moved in there a while back." O'Reilly's voice dropped even more. "Rumor is that the Rurales made it too hot for him across the line. That doesn't stop him and his men from paying a visit now and then, when their funds run low. There's a railroad that runs not too far on the other side of the border and a few settlements within a day's ride."

"So you're saying that he's really more of a bandit and train robber than a real revolutionary."

At that moment the three men at the far end of the bar pushed their empties across the hardwood, turned away, and started toward the entrance. O'Reilly picked up a glass from the backbar, plucked a rag from an apron pocket, and began industriously polishing the glass as he whistled, a low, tuneless sound.

The gunnies cast idly curious glances at the Kid as they walked past. None of them had stepped up to defend Bracken or try to settle the score for him. That didn't surprise the Kid. The gunman's code said a man was supposed to stomp his own snakes, and you never risked your life unless you were getting paid for it.

The Kid drank some of his beer while the three men

pushed through the batwings and departed. The poker game continued, but the men there were engrossed in their cards. The two townsmen weren't paying any attention to the Kid and O'Reilly, either.

"I reckon you didn't want those hombres to know you were talking about their boss," the Kid said quietly.

O'Reilly shook his head and said, "I just don't want to get in any trouble. I've said too much already. I got to live here."

"You own this saloon?"

"No, it belongs to Mr. Griffith over there." O'Reilly nodded toward the frock-coated man at the poker table. "But I've got a home. A wife and a kid. Just forget I said anything, all right? Just do me that favor."

"Like I told you, you don't have to worry about me, friend." The Kid set the half-empty mug on the bar. "Sure I can't pay you for this?"

"No, it's all right."

The Kid nodded and said, "I'll be seeing you, then."

O'Reilly still looked nervous as the Kid left. That was the permanent expression on the faces of the town's citizens. The ones who *didn't* work for this General Diego Ramirez, that is.

The Kid untied the buckskin from the hitch rack and led the horse along the street to a livery stable. The man who greeted him was tall and rawboned, with graying, rusty hair and a black patch over his left eye. He hooked his thumbs in the straps of his overalls and cast an approving eye over the buckskin.

"Fine-lookin' hoss, mister," he said to the Kid. "You lookin' for a place to put him up?"

"For now," the Kid replied. "Probably a day or two, maybe longer."

"Four bits a day, countin' feed."

The Kid nodded and handed over two silver dollars.

"That'll take care of the bill for a few days. My name's Callahan, by the way."

"Ezra Dawson." The liveryman cocked the brow over his good eye. "You got business in Saguaro Springs?"

"That remains to be seen," the Kid replied dryly. He took his saddlebags and Winchester and headed diagonally across the street toward the Chuckwalla Hotel.

It was a decent-looking place, not fancy, at least on the outside, but sturdy and probably comfortable. As he stepped up onto the low porch, one of the double front doors opened and a woman came out.

She was in a hurry, and she was agitated, to boot. She wasn't watching where she was going. The Kid stepped aside quickly and neatly to avoid being run into. Only then did she notice he was there. She stopped short and said, "Oh, I'm sorry."

"Don't worry about it," he told her. "No harm done." He smiled. "Even if you'd plowed right into me, I don't reckon I'd have had any cause to complain."

That was the truth. The woman was young, early twenties more than likely, and quite attractive. Her long blond hair was pulled back and tied tightly behind her neck to hang in a horsetail down her back. She would have been even prettier, the Kid thought, if she wore her hair loose around her face, so it would soften the rather stern lines of her features a little. She was dressed in a white, long-sleeved shirt and long brown skirt.

Her striking blue eyes looked over the Kid and she

didn't seem too impressed with what she saw. He couldn't blame her for that, since he knew he looked like a saddle tramp covered with trail dust.

"You're a bit forward, aren't you, sir?" she said. "Commenting on a . . . a physical collision between us is improper."

"Not my intention," the Kid drawled. "I just try to tell the truth as I see it."

She nodded toward his saddlebags and rifle and asked, "Are you planning to get a room here at the hotel?"

"That's what I figured."

"Then I'm sure we'll see each other again. Don't feel any necessity to engage in conversation on those occasions."

"Keep my improper mouth shut, eh?" The Kid shrugged. "If that's the way you want it, miss."

"It is," she said. She turned and headed off along the porch without looking back.

The Kid started to go inside, but he paused in the door to glance after her. As he did, he caught her looking back over her shoulder at him. He smiled, and she jerked her head around and walked quicker.

He couldn't help but wonder who she was.

He went into the hotel, looked around the lobby, and saw that his hunch had been correct. The furnishings weren't the newest or the most elaborate, but they were well cared for. Everything was clean, from the windows to the potted plants to the rugs on the polished floor. For a hotel in a settlement not far from the Mexican border, the Chuckwalla was a nice place, and that had to result from the pride of the people who ran it.

A handsome, middle-aged woman with graying blond

hair stood behind the registration desk on the other side of the lobby. As the Kid approached, he saw a resemblance between her and the young woman who had almost run into him outside. Given their ages, more than likely this woman was the younger one's mother.

She gave the Kid the same sort of wary look that the woman on the porch had and asked, "Can I help you?"

He set his saddlebags on the counter and tucked the Winchester under his left arm.

"I'd like a room," he said. "I'll probably be staying several days."

"Rooms are two dollars a night," she said, her tone indicating that she believed he wouldn't be able to afford that.

"All right," the Kid said as he took a ten-dollar gold piece from his pocket and slid it across the desk. "That ought to buy me five nights, if I'm doing my ciphering right."

The woman arched her eyebrows and said, "Yes, that's correct." The swiftness with which she made the gold coin disappear told the Kid that the hotel probably didn't do a great deal of business. The woman wasn't going to miss out on this chance to collect. She turned the registration book around. "You'll need to sign in."

He picked up a pen from a holder on the desk and wrote *John Callahan* on the next empty line in the register. In the space for where he was from, he wrote simply *Texas*. That was a big place, and nobody was going to question him claiming it as his home. He wasn't going to put Boston, where he had grown up.

The woman must have had experience reading upside down. She took a key from the rack on the wall behind the desk and placed it in front of him as she said, "All right, Mr. Callahan, you'll be in Room Nine. Turn right at the top of the stairs. The room is on the front of the hotel, so you'll have some breeze, at least part of the time."

"I'm obliged to you," he said as he picked up the key. He glanced around the lobby. "The hotel doesn't have a dining room?"

"No, but there's a good café in the next block. It's called Abuelo's. You should be able to dine satisfactorily there."

The Kid nodded and said, "I have one more question, if you don't mind." When she just looked at him and didn't say anything, he went on, "Why is this place called the Chuckwalla Hotel?"

For the first time, her serious expression eased slightly. She said, "My late husband named the hotel. He was a prospector, you see, and in the days before the settlement was here, he got lost in the desert and nearly died of thirst. Then he spotted a lizard scurrying along and decided to follow it, thinking that it might lead him to water. He wound up at the springs, and they saved his life. When he looked around, he thought it might be a good place for a town, so he gave up prospecting and started a little trading post and hotel."

"You're saying that he founded the town," the Kid said.

"For all intents and purposes, yes. He called it Chuckwalla Springs at first, after the lizard, but some of the other early settlers convinced him that Saguaro Springs sounded better. He gave up the trading post to concentrate on the hotel, and he said that he was going to name it after the chuckwalla that had saved his life, and no one was going to make him change his mind. I'd met and gotten married to him by then, and I knew how stubborn he could be, so I didn't even try. This place has been the Chuckwalla ever since."

The Kid had gotten more of a story than he had bargained for. The woman suddenly looked a little surprised and flustered that she had told him the whole thing, too.

"Listen to me ramble on like that," she said. "I'm sorry to have bored you, Mr. Callahan."

"You didn't bore me," the Kid assured her. "Anyway, I'm the one who asked the question."

"Yes, but my daughter, Peggy, says that I talk too much. I'm Henrietta, by the way. Henrietta Cole."

"I'm guessing your daughter left here right before I came in."

"That's right. How did you—Oh. You saw her on the porch, I suppose."

"Yep. And I can see the resemblance between you. I figured you had to be mother and daughter."

"At least you didn't waste your time and mine by pretending to think we were sisters." Mrs. Cole sobered again. "I run a clean, decent hotel, Mr. Callahan. I don't know your business here, and I don't want to know. As long as you don't cause any trouble, that's all I care about."

"I don't know exactly what my business here is, either," the Kid said. "I was just sort of drifting, but then a fella talked to me about a job. Man named Kern. You might know him."

The woman's lips thinned in disapproval. She said, "I know *of* him, and the other men who work for that self-proclaimed general. You didn't really strike me as the same type, Mr. Callahan, otherwise we probably wouldn't have had this conversation. I have no dealings with gunmen and thieves."

"Does that mean you don't want to rent me a room after all?" the Kid asked quietly.

Mrs. Cole hesitated, then said, "No, I wouldn't go that far. You didn't say you were actually working for General Ramirez yet. If you do, he'll probably want you to stay out there at that cursed hacienda of his, at least part of the time, so you may not want to keep your room here."

The Kid arched an eyebrow and said, "Cursed? What do you mean by that?"

Mrs. Cole drew in a deep breath and shook her head. "I've said too much already," she told him. "I have work to do. Room number nine," she repeated. "Top of the stairs and turn right."

With that she went through a door behind the registration desk and closed it behind her, leaving the Kid standing there to digest all the things he had found out since riding into Saguaro Springs . . . and wonder about the things he had just gotten hints of.

# Chapter 16

The room was comfortable, with a good bed, a chair and a table with a wash basin and pitcher on it, a woven rug on the floor, and sunny yellow curtains over the window that overlooked the street. The air in the room was a little stale, so the Kid pushed the curtains back and raised the window.

As he did that, he looked diagonally across the street at the Cactus Saloon. A couple of gun-hung hardcases who undoubtedly worked for General Ramirez pushed out through the batwings and slouched off down the street. The townspeople all stayed out of their way.

The Kid wondered just how many gunnies the general had working for him. They seemed pretty abundant in Saguaro Springs, and they had the settlement's citizens spooked.

He stretched out on the bed for a while but didn't sleep. Instead he stared toward the ceiling and pondered on the task facing him. It seemed obvious that this self-styled General Ramirez was responsible for Frank's kidnapping. The ransom he had demanded would go to fund his revolution.

Such a bold move told the Kid that maybe Ramirez was serious about trying to raise an army and overthrow President Porfirio Díaz. Other revolutionaries were content to use such political posturing as a cover for being bandits, plain and simple. Such men rose to prominence from time to time but always were crushed by Mexican government forces or else faded away for some other reason.

From what the bartender O'Reilly had told him, the Kid knew that Ramirez and his men sometimes held up trains and raided settlements below the border, but if they could get a quarter of a million dollars for Frank Morgan, they wouldn't have to do that anymore. Ramirez could buy enough guns and ammunition and recruit enough men to make a serious stab at unseating Díaz.

Honestly, the Kid didn't know if that would be a good thing or a bad one for Mexico. Sure, Ramirez was an outlaw, but Díaz had a reputation as a brutal dictator. Mexico had almost always been ruled by men who were bandits at heart. Ramirez might do just as good a job as any of the others.

None of that was his business, the Kid decided. Ramirez had kidnapped Frank and threatened his life, and that made him an enemy. Not only that, Ramirez's men were terrorizing this town. That was another good reason to make sure the general's plans didn't succeed. The Kid realized the odds against him were high—one man against several dozen hired killers and desperadoes, maybe more—but he planned to have the element of surprise on his side. And if things worked out the way he wanted, he would be striking at them from inside . . .

As evening came on, he went downstairs to the lobby, figuring he'd go look for that café Henrietta Cole had mentioned earlier. The older woman wasn't behind the desk, but Peggy was. The Kid couldn't resist sauntering over to talk to her.

"I see you help your mother run the hotel," he said to Peggy.

"That's right." Her chin jutted out a little. "I thought I told you it wasn't necessary for us to have any more conversations."

"People do a lot of things that aren't strictly necessary, just because they want to."

"But I *don't* want to talk to you, Mr. Callahan."

"You saw my name in the book, eh?"

"I keep track of whoever is staying here, yes."

Her chilly attitude was beginning to annoy him. He said, "Look, I don't know what I did to rub you the wrong way, Miss Cole, but it wasn't intentional. I'd just as soon call a truce and see if we can't be friends."

She glared across the desk at him and snapped, "You haven't *rubbed* me in any way. That's the sort of bold talk that I don't like."

"I didn't mean it like that, and you know it."

"Do I?" she asked coolly. "I've heard that you may be going to work for Ramirez. His men have a habit of swaggering around town and taking whatever they want, and nobody dares to try to stand up to them. Not after what happened to Mr. Jenkins—"

Her voice choked off and she looked down at the desk. After a couple of seconds, the Kid asked, "Who's Mr. Jenkins, and what happened to him?"

Her blue eyes lifted. Defiance flared in them. She said, "He owned one of the stores. A couple of Ramirez's men came in there, said unspeakable things to Mrs. Jenkins, and started to take some things without paying for them. Mr. Jenkins was already upset because of the way they had behaved toward his wife. He tried to stop them from leaving with his goods, and they beat him very badly."

"I'm sorry," the Kid said.

"That's not the worst of it," Peggy said. "He got the gun he kept under the counter and followed them into the street. When he brandished the gun at them, one of the men turned around and shot him. Killed him."

The Kid shook his head and said, "That's a shame, but if this fella Jenkins had a gun in his hand and was threatening to use it—"

"I know, I know," Peggy said bitterly. "It was a fair fight. That's what the law would have said—if we had any law in Saguaro Springs. But honestly, an elderly storekeeper like Mr. Jenkins against a cold-blooded killer like Carl Bracken . . . how could that possibly be fair, no matter who had a gun in his hand first?"

*Bracken. The Kid* wasn't surprised that he had gunned down one of the townspeople. More than likely, Bracken had gone into the store just looking for an excuse to kill somebody.

"Anybody else in town have a run-in like that?" the Kid asked quietly.

"Shot down in the middle of the street like a dog, you mean?" Peggy shook her head. "No, but Señor Hernandez at the blacksmith shop got into an argument with some of the general's men, and he disappeared that night. He hasn't been seen since. And other men who clashed with them have been beaten. It's only a matter of time before someone else is killed."

"I didn't have anything to do with any of that," the Kid pointed out.

"No, but you're talking about joining forces with those men. I heard that the one called Kern practically offered you a job."

"Word gets around fast," the Kid said.

"It's a small town. And we have to keep up with what's going on." She paused. "Our lives may depend on it."

"Well, I'm sorry for your troubles," the Kid said. "I'll try not to add to them."

"The best way for you to do that is to leave town and not come back."

"Maybe," the Kid said, "but I'm not ready to drift on just yet."

He nodded to Peggy, who just glared at him, her face pale with anger, as he turned and walked out of the hotel.

Abuelo's café was run by a middle-aged Mexican couple, and although they gave the Kid friendly smiles when he came in, he could see the tense wariness in their eyes. As Peggy Cole had said, Saguaro Springs was a small town, and nearly everybody knew what was going on almost as soon as it happened. The Kid was the stranger who had ridden into town and given the widely despised Carl Bracken what he had coming to him . . . but he was also a hardcase who might hire on with the same man Bracken worked for. The townspeople didn't know whether to regard him as a friend or an enemy.

The Kid was their friend, although he wasn't going to reveal that just yet. But he had already decided that if there was any way to do it along with rescuing his father, he was going to end the stranglehold that Ramirez's men had on this town.

That resolve grew stronger in the Kid as he spent the next day wandering around the settlement. He strolled into the various businesses and talked with the owners, the people who worked there, and the customers. They were afraid of him, no doubt about that, but their fear made them polite. His friendly conversation made more than one of them relax enough to admit that things had not been good in Saguaro Springs since Diego Ramirez and his men had moved into the abandoned hacienda.

When the Kid was at the livery stable checking on his horse, he mentioned something that had been puzzling him to Ezra Dawson.

"I heard somebody say that the ranch where General Ramirez is staying is cursed. Why would anybody believe such a loco thing?"

The liveryman, who had been forking hay into one of the stalls, paused and leaned on his pitchfork as he said, "Because it ain't loco. That place is jinxed. A pure hoodoo, if you ask me."

"Why do you say that?"

Dawson shifted a lump of chewing tobacco from one cheek to the other and went on, "Look what happened to Walt Creeger."

"I don't know who that is."

"The fella who started the ranch. Creeger had hisself a Mex partner name of Seguin. They built that hacienda sturdy enough to stand off attacks by Apaches or *bandidos* and started runnin' cows on the range around it. But then Seguin disappeared. Creeger told folks he'd gone back to where he come from in Mexico. This was before the town was here. Creeger wasn't around for much longer his own self. He fired all the vaqueros workin' for him and let the stock run wild. Onliest fella left on the ranch 'sides him was the old *viejo* who cooked for him. That fella claimed Creeger just walked off into the desert one day and never come back, but folks didn't know whether to believe him or not.

"Then, years later, after a sandstorm had blown through, some fellas found a skeleton out in the desert. A whole skeleton, mind you, which meant the fella it belonged to had been buried, otherwise the coyotes would've torn the body, and the bones, apart. The wind had uncovered the grave. And the poor varmint hadn't buried hisself, if you get my drift."

"Somebody killed him," the Kid said.

Dawson nodded sagely and continued, "The skull had what looked like a bullet hole in the back of it. Not only that, the right leg had been busted sometime in the past and had healed up a mite crooked, meanin' that whoever it was would've had a pretty bad limp."

"Creeger," the Kid guessed.

Dawson shook his head. "Nope. Old Seguin hisself. He's the one who limped. Folks got to figgerin' that Creeger and Seguin had a fallin'-out for some reason, and Creeger put a bullet in the Mex's head, then hauled him out into the desert and buried him. That's simple enough, but then things start to get a mite odd."

"The hacienda was cursed because of Seguin's murder," the Kid said.

"That's right. That old cook said Creeger took to actin' scared, lookin' over his shoulder all the time like somebody was fixin' to ambush him. He'd holler and ask anybody who was around, didn't they see him skulkin' through the house at night?"

"Seguin's ghost?"

Dawson shrugged and said, "I ain't sayin' the ghost was there . . . but Creeger *thought* it was. And eventually that drove him so mad he run ever'body else off and finally wandered into the desert to get away from Seguin's spirit."

"And then died out there himself."

"Nobody knows for sure," Dawson said. "Some say Creeger's still roamin' around, all these years later, crazy as a hydrophobia skunk. Some claim to have seen somethin' at night, nothin' but bones and rawhide skin and long white beard, howlin' like a coyote . . . but *not* like a coyote, too, if you know what I mean."

The Kid looked at the old liveryman for a long moment, unsure whether to laugh. He didn't want to hurt Dawson's feelings, so finally he just said, "That's a good story. I don't know whether to believe it or not, though."

"If it's true, it don't matter whether somebody believes it. And if it ain't true, that don't matter, neither."

"I suppose you're right about that," the Kid said. "I wonder if Ramirez knew about the rancho's background when he and his men moved in."

"No tellin'. Maybe he figgered forty or fifty gunwolves was enough to handle any ol' ghost. Or maybe he just ain't the superstitious sort. How about you, youngster? I heard talk about you goin' to work for him, but maybe you'd rather stay away from that hoodoo ranch."

"Ghosts don't scare me, either," the Kid said.

And that was a good thing, considering all the death and tragedy lurking in his past.

By evening, he hadn't seen Kern, which came as no real surprise because the gunman had said it might be a couple of days before he looked up the Kid again.

After another meal at Abuelo's, the Kid walked over to the saloon to pass some time. He chatted with the bartender, O'Reilly, while he nursed a beer. The slick-haired gambler came over, and O'Reilly introduced him to the Kid as Harold Griffith, the owner of the Cactus. After shaking hands with the man, the Kid said, "I suppose you named the saloon after those saguaros growing along the creek."

"That's right," Griffith said. "They're very distinctive. Since the town was already called Saguaro Springs, I just used *cactus* in the saloon's name when I took it over. That was a considerable improvement over what the original owner called it."

"What was that?" the Kid asked, mildly curious.

"Hoolihan's," Griffith said.

"That was the name of the gent who owned it," O'Reilly added. "I worked for him, too." He smiled. "He never had much sense, otherwise he never would've sat down to play poker and lost the place on a busted flush. Say, that would make a good name for a saloon. The Busted Flush."

"We'll stay with Cactus," Griffith said. To the Kid, he went on, "I appreciate you not killing Bracken in here yesterday. That would have brought a lot of attention that I don't need. Actually, the less attention that bunch pays to anything in town, the better." Griffith lit a cigar and regarded the Kid coolly as the smoke spiraled up from its glowing tip. "I'm a pretty good judge of character, and honestly, you don't strike me as the sort of man who'd be likely to throw in with them, Mr. Callahan."

Something inside the Kid stirred uneasily. Everybody he'd talked to in Saguaro Springs seemed to have warmed up to him, albeit reluctantly. Except for Peggy Cole, of course. But he didn't *want* these townies taking a liking to him. That could interfere with his plans.

He put a flinty mask over his features and said in a chilly tone, "As long as the payoff is good enough, I don't care who I work for. Never have."

"Then I guess I was wrong about you," Griffith said. He put the cigar back in his mouth and clenched his teeth on it. "It happens now and then."

"Does that mean you don't want me to drink here anymore?" the Kid asked.

"I didn't say that. Your money's as good as anyone else's."

"And you don't want any trouble, in case I *do* go to work for the general—"

Before the suddenly unfriendly conversation could continue, a loud clatter of hoofbeats came from the street outside. A man called out. Curious, the Kid left his half-full mug of beer on the bar and turned to saunter over to the entrance. He put both hands on the tops of the batwings and looked out. The sun was down, but enough of a glow remained in the sky for him to see what was happening.

A wagon had pulled up in front of the Yates General

Store, two doors down from the hotel. Several riders had accompanied the vehicle into town. Judging by their outfits, they were a mixture of gringos and Mexicans. As the Kid watched, they reined in and dismounted to tie their horses to the hitch rack.

One of the men caught the Kid's eye immediately. The tall, lean form and the derby hat were unmistakable. The gunman Carl Bracken had returned to Saguaro Springs.

However, one of the other riders swung down from the saddle with such grace that the Kid couldn't help but notice. The rider was dressed in black, like he was, but these garments were leather and the trousers clung to undoubtedly female calves, thighs, and intriguingly curved hips.

She didn't climb to the loading dock that served as the store's porch. Instead she spoke to the driver, a burly, bearded man in a sombrero, and then turned to stride toward the hotel. She pushed her low-crowned black hat off her head and let it hang by its strap behind her neck, where her long, raven hair was woven together in a braid. Light from a window she passed spilled over her lovely features.

From the bar behind the Kid, O'Reilly called, "Mr. Callahan, you want the rest of your beer?"

The Kid ignored him, pushed through the batwings, and started across the street toward the hotel, where the beautiful young stranger had disappeared through the front doors.

# Chapter 17

By the time the Kid stepped into the lobby, the young woman had crossed to the desk, where she stood with a visibly tense attitude. On the other side of the desk were Henrietta and Peggy Cole. Peggy wore an angry glare on her pretty face, but her mother just looked worried.

The Kid came in as the newcomer was saying, "So you don't want me to stay here?" Her voice was cool and controlled but held an undertone of hostility as she went on, "You *are* in the business of renting rooms, aren't you?"

"Not to the likes of you," Peggy snapped.

The dark-haired young woman reacted as if she'd been slapped.

"And just what is it you think I am?" she demanded.

"The daughter of an outlaw," Peggy responded. "You're probably no better than an outlaw yourself."

Henrietta said, "Please, there's no need for this—"

The two young women ignored her. They were about the same age, but otherwise they were a striking contrast, one dark, one fair. And both very attractive, the Kid thought, that was another thing they had in common. He stood just inside the lobby. None of the three at the desk had noticed him. They were too intent on their own confrontation.

"I can pay, if that's what you're worried about," the newcomer said with a sneer in her voice.

"Blood money, no doubt, taken off the body of some poor victim your father robbed and killed," Peggy said.

"Our money has been good enough for everyone else in this primitive little town."

Peggy started around the desk as she said, "Just because everybody else is too scared to stand up to you, that doesn't mean we are. You're not welcome here, Señorita Ramirez. Can't you get that through your head?"

Well, that confirmed who the dark-haired girl was, the Kid mused, although he'd already suspected that from the things Peggy had said.

"I go where I please!" Señorita Ramirez said.

"Not here!" Peggy responded, equally hotly.

"Peggy, please—" her mother tried again.

Peggy was in no mood to listen. She was standing only about a foot away from Señorita Ramirez now, and without warning, she lifted her hands and gave the dark-haired girl a hard shove that made her stagger backward a few steps.

Señorita Ramirez caught her balance, said, "Oh!"—and went at Peggy. Peggy tried to block her, but she pushed the blonde just as hard, causing Peggy to fall back against the desk. Peggy rebounded from the impact, lunged at Señorita Ramirez, and a second later both of them were wrapped up in each other's arms, slapping and clawing and letting out shrill, furious cries as they battled.

Henrietta hurried around the desk and said, "Stop it! Peggy, no!" She paused, took a step toward the two young women as if she wanted to separate them physically, then stopped again, clearly unsure what to do.

The Kid could have intervened and put a stop to the fight, but he wasn't sure he wanted to get between two wildcats like that. If he did, he stood a good chance of getting clawed, too.

Then Peggy changed her tactics. She balled one hand into a tight, compact fist and brought it up and around in as pretty a punch as the Kid had seen lately. The fist smacked cleanly into Señorita Ramirez's jaw. She flew backward from the force of the blow.

The Kid took a quick step, put out his arms, and caught her under the arms before she could fall. She hung there against him for a second, shaking her head, then twisted her neck to look around at him. No flicker of recognition appeared in her dark eyes, but she did look grateful for a second.

Then she straightened and threw herself at Peggy, who wasn't able to get out of the way in time. Señorita Ramirez tackled the blonde and both of them went down, landing on one of the rugs that slid a little underneath them.

Wearing trousers gave Señorita Ramirez a slight advantage as she and Peggy rolled around on the floor and wrestled with each other. The long dress Peggy wore today tangled around her legs and hampered her efforts. Señorita Ramirez rolled her onto her back, straddled her, grabbed her by the neck, bounced her head on the floor, and started choking her.

So far the Kid had been content to be a bystander and just observe for the most part. But now it appeared that Peggy might be in actual danger of being injured seriously, so he moved forward lithely, bent and took hold of

Señorita Ramirez around the waist, and hauled her off the blonde. The dark-haired girl's booted feet dangled several inches off the floor. She kicked her legs furiously as she writhed in the Kid's grip and tried to get free. Curses in Spanish tumbled from her lips, followed by the haughty demand, "Let go of me!"

Numerous thudding footsteps sounded behind the Kid, and as he turned in that direction, he heard another sound with which he was very familiar: the metallic ratcheting of guns being cocked.

Several men had charged into the hotel lobby from outside and now held revolvers pointing at him. Carl Bracken was one of them, and as he saw the Kid, his eyes burned with an unholy fire from his desire to pull the trigger. The danger to Señorita Ramirez was the only thing that stopped him.

"Hold your fire! Hold your fire, damn it!" That order came from the big, bearded Mexican who had been at the reins of the wagon team. He bulled into the lobby behind the other men but realized quickly what was going on. He cursed some in Spanish, too, then looked at the Kid and said, "Let go of her, amigo, right now."

Señorita Ramirez had stopped struggling when she saw the gunmen, but she still hung there in the Kid's grip. He said, "If I put her down, you're going to shoot me."

"No, we won't," the bearded man promised.

"Speak for your own damn self, Valdez!" Bracken snapped. "He has been asking for a bullet ever since he rode into town, and I'm gonna give him one!"

"No!" The sharpness of Señorita Ramirez's tone made

Bracken, Valdez, and the rest of the gunmen look at her. "No shooting. Put your guns away."

"But, señorita—" Bracken began.

"You heard me." Her voice was like ice, a thing that wasn't common in this hot, arid country. "Valdez is right. There will be no shooting . . . for now."

With obvious reluctance, Bracken and the other men pouched their irons. The Kid lowered the señorita until her feet were on the floor, then let go of her and stepped back. He glanced toward the desk and saw that Peggy had gotten up and retreated behind it, along with her mother. Peggy appeared shaken but all right. Henrietta had an arm looped protectively around her daughter's shoulders and looked determined but frightened at the same time.

Señorita Ramirez turned to face the Kid.

"Do you always involve yourself in things that are none of your business?" she asked.

She was even more attractive close up like this, so that he could see the fire in her dark eyes. But her father was the man behind Frank's kidnapping, so he reminded himself not to let her good looks distract him too much.

"I'm staying here at this hotel," he said. "Figured you murdering Miss Cole right here in the lobby might cause the place to close down, and then I'd have to hunt up other accommodations."

"She attacked me! If I had killed her, it would have been self-defense."

"Not once you had her down like that. She wasn't a threat to you anymore."

From behind the desk, a still-angry Peggy said, "I wasn't defenseless. I could have taken care of myself."

So both of the young women were mad at him, the Kid thought. That was all right. It distracted them from wanting to tear into each other again.

Bracken said, "This fella needs to pay for laying his hands on you, señorita. Why don't you let me and some of the boys give him a good stomping?"

"Make sure you have plenty of help if you try," the Kid said with a cool smile. "When you went after me by yourself, Bracken, you wound up being tossed out into the street like a sack of garbage, as I recall."

Bracken had lowered his gun, but he started to lift it again as his face contorted with hate. The burly Valdez put a hand on his arm to stop him, much like Kern had done in the saloon. It appeared that some of General Ramirez's men had their hands full just keeping Bracken from flying off the handle.

Señorita Ramirez said, "Valdez, take the men back over to the store and get those supplies loaded up. I'll be along in a few minutes to pick up the things I want. Then you can go ahead and drive back out to the rancho tonight."

"I don't like leaving you in town by yourself, señorita," Valdez rumbled.

"I can take care of myself just fine," she snapped as her chin lifted in defiance. "Besides, several of the men will stay and ride back with me tomorrow." She glanced at Bracken. "Not him."

Bracken's face flushed with anger, but he didn't say anything. He must not have wanted to argue with his boss's daughter.

Señorita Ramirez was a young woman accustomed to getting her own way, the Kid thought.

After a moment, Valdez nodded and said, "*Sí*." He

gestured curtly to the other men and told them in Spanish to leave. They filed out of the hotel, several of them in addition to Bracken casting hostile glances toward the Kid.

He hoped to be one of them soon, so he wished circumstances would stop conspiring to put him on the other side.

When they were all gone except Valdez, he frowned and said, "Señorita, you are sure—"

"Go," she said. "I will be there shortly, as soon as things are settled here."

"There's nothing to settle," Peggy told her as she turned toward the desk again. "You're not staying here." Peggy jutted her own chin out. "We're full up."

"You have no empty rooms?"

The Kid knew that wasn't true, but he said, "The señorita can stay in my room."

The dark-haired girl turned her head and arched a finely curved brow at him.

"I'll go down to Dawson's and see if he'll let me sleep in the hayloft, of course," the Kid went on. "I don't mind giving up my room for a lady."

"She's not a lady," Peggy said. "She's a—"

Her mother stopped her by squeezing the arm that was still around her shoulders. Henrietta said, "We can find a room for you, Señorita Ramirez. Don't worry about that. And you don't have to give up your room, Mr. Callahan."

Señorita Ramirez regarded the Kid through narrowed eyes for a moment, then said, "Callahan. You are the man I overheard Bracken ranting about earlier. I thought as much from the way he acted just now. He's carrying around a great deal of hatred for you."

"I know," the Kid said. "I'm not overly fond of him, either."

"Given the chance, he will kill you."

"I'll try not to give him the chance."

"That may mean killing *him*."

The Kid shrugged as if that possibility wouldn't bother him. To tell the truth, it wouldn't.

"You are also the man Señor Kern spoke about to my father," the señorita went on. "He believes you would be a good addition to our forces. What do you think of that, Señor Callahan?"

"Nobody's actually said yet what the job pays," the Kid replied.

"And that is the most important consideration? You would not fight for the liberty and dignity of the Mexican people?"

"I'm an American," he said. "The Mexican people have to look out for themselves . . . unless, of course, the money's right."

She studied him again, then shook her head.

"You are not a good man, Señor Callahan."

That was exactly the impression he was trying to convey. He smiled and said, "I never claimed to be."

She turned away then, clearly dismissing him, and faced the desk again.

"I am tired, and I still must visit the store. I will stay here tonight and ride back out to the rancho tomorrow. Is that acceptable?"

Peggy made a disgusted sound and stomped out through the door behind the desk. Her mother summoned up a smile, though, and said, "The room is two dollars, señorita."

The dark-haired girl laid a gold eagle on the desk, five times the rent for one night.

"I do not haggle," she said. "I want the best room you have."

Henrietta said, "They're, ah, all pretty much the same . . ."

"Mine's mighty comfortable," the Kid said.

"And again you insinuate that I should share your room, Señor Callahan," Señorita Ramirez said. "You are a bold caballero. Men who are bold often win great treasures."

The Kid smiled.

"But more often, they wind up dead, because a very fine line exists between boldness and foolishness," she went on. "Which side of that line do you fall on, señor?"

"I only know one way to find out."

"That discovery will not be made tonight." She turned back to Henrietta. "My room, señora?"

"Fourteen," Henrietta said. She took a key off the rack and laid it on the desk. "It's already all made up, so it'll be ready for you whenever you're ready for it."

Señorita Ramirez picked up the key and nodded. "*Gracias. Buenas noches, Señor Callahan.*"

The Kid touched a finger to his hat brim, then watched as the señorita turned and walked out of the hotel. Her braid bounced a little with each step.

"I hope you remember that I run a decent place here, Mr. Callahan," Henrietta said. "Anyway, you want to steer clear of that girl. If trouble ever got up and walked around on its own two feet, it would look just like her."

The Kid had to laugh. He didn't doubt that at all.

# Chapter 18

The Kid lingered in the hotel lobby, sitting in an arm-chair next to a potted plant and reading a three-week-old copy of the *Tombstone Epitaph* that someone had left behind, until Señorita Ramirez came back half an hour later. By now, both Peggy and her mother had disappeared into their living quarters at the back of the hotel's ground floor.

The dark-haired young woman carried a few small packages. She stopped a few steps into the lobby as she spotted the Kid. He folded the newspaper and set it aside, then stood up.

"Señor Callahan," she said, "I sincerely hope you are not about to make another improper suggestion."

"I don't recall making any improper suggestions," he said as he smiled. "I wanted to be sure you made it back from the store without any trouble. And now that you have, I'd be happy to walk you to your door." He held up a hand to fore-stall any protest. "And no further. Just being a gentleman."

She regarded him intently for a moment, then said, "I believe under certain circumstances, you might wear the disguise of a gentleman, Señor Callahan, but your true face is that of a barbarian."

"Now, señorita—"

"I did not say that being a barbarian is a *bad* thing, señor. Such men know who they are, they know what they want, and when the time comes, they take it. And anyone who attempts to stop them will regret it. Such men often accomplish great things. Bloody things, to be sure, but great as well."

"Is this leading to anything?" the Kid asked. The impatience in his tone wasn't entirely feigned.

"You may walk me to my room, but remember, señor . . . a woman can be a barbarian, as well."

"With you around, I'm not likely to forget it."

He saw what he thought was a flicker of pleasure in her eyes when he said that, but she covered up the reaction quickly. With a faint smile, she turned toward the stairs and he fell in step beside her.

"I'm a little surprised your father lets you come into town by yourself," he said as they started up.

"I am not by myself. Valdez and the other men accompanied me. Besides, my father knows I can take care of myself."

"You're not packing a gun," the Kid pointed out. "As tight as those trousers are, there's no place for one. Sorry for being so bold, but that's just a fact."

"I doubt that you're really sorry," she said, "but I forgive you anyway. And as for being armed . . . a person can carry other weapons besides guns."

She extended her left arm so that the sleeve of her black shirt pulled up over her wrist. The handle of a small dagger peeked out from under the sleeve. The sheathed dagger was strapped to her forearm.

"I carry one on each arm, and I am very good with

them," she said. "Whether throwing them, or fighting close up. I can demonstrate . . . ?"

"No, I'll take your word for it," the Kid said. "I suppose I'd be wasting my time if I offered to carry those packages for you."

"Indeed. I am no . . . what is the expression? No shrinking violet. No hothouse flower. I am desert born and desert raised, Señor Callahan. Hardy. A survivor."

"I believe it," he murmured.

They reached the landing. The señorita's room was to the left, the Kid's to the right. They both turned left. When they stood in front of the door to her room, she balanced the packages in her left arm and took the key from a pocket in the tight trousers with her right hand.

"Good evening, Señor Callahan," she said.

"Are you leaving early in the morning?" he asked.

"What business is that of yours?"

"Who knows what a barbarian's business is?" he countered.

She smiled and said, "I believe I will see you again."

"More than likely," he said.

Deftly, she unlocked the door, then favored him with a last glance over her shoulder as she went inside. The door closed, leaving him standing alone in the dimly lit corridor.

As he turned toward his own room, he thought about the odds facing him. As if General Ramirez and his dozens of hired killers hadn't been enough to contend with, now he had to worry about this beautiful young woman who might become a dangerous enemy as well. At the same time, she fascinated him. He sensed that her sultry looks concealed a savage, fiery streak.

A man might burn his fingers—or worse—if he ever got close enough to find out.

But he might have to do that in order to rescue his father.

Señorita Ramirez hadn't answered his question about how early she was leaving the next morning, so the Kid made sure he didn't sleep too late. Even so, he was still well rested when he came downstairs and found Peggy in the lobby, dusting the plants and the furniture. She heard his footsteps on the stairs and smiled as she turned to greet him, but the smile disappeared when she saw who he was.

The Kid tried to be pleasant anyway. He said, "Good morning, Miss Cole."

"Good morning," she replied, but with a noticeable lack of enthusiasm. "Did you sleep well?"

"I did."

"You probably dreamed about Antonia Ramirez."

"Antonia? Is that her name? I don't believe I've heard it until now."

Peggy sniffed and said, "That's her name. Now you can go ahead and talk about how pretty it is."

"Well . . . Peggy's a pretty name, too. And it suits you."

She just gave him a scornful look and went back to her dusting.

The Kid knew the question risked arousing her wrath even more, but he asked, "Has the señorita come down yet this morning?"

He wasn't sure at first if Peggy was going to answer, but after a moment's hesitation, the blonde said, "Just a few minutes ago. She left carrying some packages."

"She's probably down at the stable getting ready to leave town, then."

"I'm sure I wouldn't know."

The Kid figured he shouldn't push things any further with her, so he just smiled, pinched the brim of his hat politely, and left the hotel. When he reached the street, he turned toward Ezra Dawson's livery stable, the only one in town. Antonia's horse and those belonging to her father's men had to be there.

As he approached the stable, he spotted Antonia standing in front of the open double doors with a couple of men. He was a little surprised to recognize one of them as Kern, who hadn't been with Antonia's party the night before. He must have ridden into Saguaro Springs separately, the Kid thought.

Three men, two Mexicans and an American hardcase, led a group of horses out of the barn, including the magnificent black stallion Antonia had been riding when the Kid first saw her.

Even though the hour was early, the sun was up and a number of people moved around town already. One man wearing a long duster walked toward the livery stable on the same side of the street. The Kid frowned slightly as he noticed something odd about this man's gait. The hombre moved stiffly, and as the Kid looked closer, he saw a tense, fixed expression on the man's face.

He had seen looks like that before and knew what they usually meant. With swift steps, the Kid angled his course to intercept the man.

He might not have enough time to do that, he saw. The man brushed the duster back and started to lift the double-barreled shotgun he had been holding down alongside his right leg.

The Kid could have drawn and fired, but if he did, he might kill the man and since he wasn't sure exactly what was going on here, he didn't want to do that. It was clear who the shotgunner's targets were, though. His wild-eyed gaze was fixed on Antonia and her companions in front of the livery stable. None of them had noticed the man striding toward them.

The Kid yelled, "Hey!" and broke into a run. The shout distracted the man with the shotgun. Instinctively, he stopped walking and swung the weapon toward the Kid. Seeing those two barrels looming like a cannon would unnerve most men, but at a moment like this, the Kid's nerves were ice.

He covered the ground between the man and himself in a hurry. He lashed out with his left arm and hit the shotgun's barrels, knocked them skyward just as the man pulled the triggers. Both barrels discharged with a thunderous roar that pounded the Kid's ears like giant fists, but the double load of buckshot blasted harmlessly into the air.

The Kid lowered his right shoulder and rammed into the man, knocking him backward. Momentum carried the Kid forward, and both he and the shotgunner sprawled in the dirt at the mouth of the alley beside the livery stable.

"You son of a—!" the man screamed. He tried to ram the butt of the shotgun's stock into the Kid's face. The Kid jerked his head aside, but the blow landed on his left shoulder and numbed that arm.

The Kid's right arm still worked just fine. He grabbed the shotgun's barrels and wrenched them to the side, twisting the weapon as he did so. The man couldn't hold on to it. It slipped out of his hands, and the Kid slung it away.

Unarmed now, the man hammered at the Kid with his fists. The Kid slashed at the man's neck with the side of his right hand. The stroke landed where the neck and shoulder came together and seemed to stun the man for a second. That was long enough for the Kid to roll to the side and come up on one knee.

A shot roared somewhere close by. A bullet smacked into the ground near the would-be shotgunner's head and kicked dirt into his face. He choked and coughed and rolled onto his side. Before whoever had fired the shot could trigger another one, Antonia Ramirez cried, "No! Don't shoot!"

The man in the duster lifted his head, rapidly blinked his eyes clear, and focused on the Kid, kneeling a few feet away. The man's face was narrow and foxlike, topped by curly brown hair. He was probably in his late twenties. Breathing hard, he glared at the Kid with pure hatred blazing in his eyes.

"Hold on," the Kid said as he extended a hand. "Just stay where you—"

The man didn't listen or let the Kid finish. He pushed himself onto hands and knees and launched himself into a flying tackle aimed at the Kid.

The impact drove the Kid over backward. He landed awkwardly with one leg twisted under him and couldn't get any leverage to throw his opponent off. The man dug at his belly with a knee and flailed wild punches.

The Kid clubbed his hands together and shot them straight up at the man's chin. His teeth clicked together loudly, and his head rocked so far back it seemed like it was about to come off his shoulders. That took the fight right out of him. The Kid grabbed the duster's lapels and heaved the man to the side, freeing himself.

The man lay huddled in the dirt, moaning softly, while the Kid clambered to his feet. One of Ramirez's men shouldered the Kid aside. The three gun-wolves who had stayed in town to ride back out to the hacienda with Antonia today crowded around the fallen man and pointed their guns at him. Their stances made it clear they were ready to blow the man full of holes.

"Wait," Antonia commanded sharply.

"That's right," Kern added. "Can't you tell that hombre's not a threat anymore?"

"He was going to kill us, Kern," one of the Mexican gunmen said. "We cannot allow him to get away with that."

The fallen man stopped moaning, but he still gasped for breath. He managed to push himself up on one elbow. He lifted his head and glared toward Antonia.

"No," he said hoarsely. "I . . . I was going to kill *her*."

Ezra Dawson came up and said, "Harley? Good Lord a'mighty, boy, is that you?"

Antonia turned to the one-eyed liveryman and asked, "Do you know this man?"

Dawson nodded and said, "Yeah, he's Harley Jenkins. His pa was Fred Jenkins, used to run one of the stores here in town. Last I heard, Harley was cowboyin' over in New Mexico." Dawson's voice took on a grim note as he added, "I reckon he heard about what happened to his pa and just got here to try to do somethin' about it."

The Kid recalled Peggy telling him that Bracken had gunned down a storekeeper named Jenkins.

Coolly, Antonia said, "I had nothing to do with the death of this man's father."

"One of your pa's men done it!" Harley Jenkins cried

from where he lay on the ground. "I lost my pa, but since I couldn't get to yours, I figured it was only fittin' he knows what it's like to lose a daughter."

"Harley, you durn fool," Dawson said. "If you'd fired that scattergun, these fellas would've killed you a second later."

Harley grimaced and said, "Not if I'd cut 'em all down."

"Then I would have killed you," the Kid said.

"I thought all of you scoundrels were together," Harley said sullenly. "I didn't know I wasn't gonna have all of you in my sights."

The Kid shook his head and said, "I'm not one of the general's men. I just won't stand by and watch someone commit murder if I can do something about it."

"Now, that's an interesting thing," Kern said. "Because the general sent me into town to fetch you back out to the hacienda, Callahan. He wants to talk to you, and if he likes what he hears, I'm pretty sure he'll ask you to throw in with us."

"That sounds like a fine idea to me," the Kid said. "Maybe the way things have gone, he ought to make me the señorita's personal bodyguard."

"Keep on dreaming, Señor Callahan," Antonia said. "But you would be wise not to suggest such a thing to my father."

"You're probably right," the Kid said with a smile and a shrug. "I'll go back to the hotel and fetch my gear, then get my horse saddled."

"Do not waste any time," she told him. "If you are not ready, we ride without you!"

# Chapter 19

When the Kid came down the stairs in the hotel with his saddlebags over his shoulder and his Winchester in his left hand, Peggy asked from behind the desk, "Are you leaving?"

"That's right," the Kid replied.

"I heard the shooting a little while ago. When I stepped out onto the porch and looked down the street, I saw that you were right in the middle of the trouble . . . with that woman. I wasn't surprised."

The Kid could tell that she was curious about what had happened, despite her chilly manner, so he told her. The news that Harley Jenkins had been involved caused her eyes to widen.

"Poor Harley wasn't hurt, was he?" she asked. He heard the fear in her voice.

"Not to speak of," he replied with a shake of his head. "A little banged up, but so was I." The feeling had returned to his left arm, but his shoulder still ached where Harley had hit him with the shotgun. "That's a lot better than catching a load of buckshot or a slug from a .45." He had heard something else in her voice. "You know Jenkins?"

"Of course. He's several years older than me, but we went to school and church together. I think he was . . . sweet on me for a while . . . before he went off to be a cowboy."

"I can see why he would be."

Peggy's chin lifted. "I'm not interested in flattery from anyone who's chasing around after a woman like Antonia Ramirez. I assume that *is* where you're going, out to that old hacienda?"

"The cursed hacienda."

"If it wasn't cursed before, it is now, since that bunch of bandits moved in there."

The Kid didn't see any point in arguing with her, so he just said, "There's no need to hold my room, even though I paid for several nights."

"I wasn't planning to," Peggy responded.

When he reached the livery stable, he found that Dawson had already saddled the buckskin. The Kid checked the cinches and harness anyway, even though he didn't doubt Dawson's ability. He never mounted up and rode without having a look for himself. Precautions like that helped keep a man alive.

The others were still there. Despite Antonia's acerbic warning, she and her party hadn't gotten in any hurry to ride out of Saguaro Springs. The Kid wasn't sure if they had taken their time so he would be able to depart the settlement with them, but when they pulled out, he was riding beside Kern.

Not surprisingly, Antonia took the lead as they headed southwest. She would always want to be out in front, no matter what she was doing, the Kid mused. Her three watchdogs spread out behind her, one to each side, one riding directly in her wake. Kern and the Kid brought up the rear, rocking along side by side in their saddles. Antonia set a fast pace, moving out twenty yards ahead of all the others.

"Her pa's got his hands full with that one, doesn't he?" the Kid said quietly.

Kern chuckled. "If you think I'm going to talk about the señorita behind her back, you'd better think again, Callahan. I'm not that fond of gossip to start with, and sometimes it can be downright dangerous."

"Then tell me about the general. Does he really plan on leading a revolution south of the border, or is that just an excuse for holding up trains and such?"

Heavily, Kern said, "I'd tell you to ask the general that question, but he'd probably kill you if you did."

"The only reason I'm curious is that I don't really give a damn who's in charge down there in mañana-land."

Kern scratched at his bearded jaw and then said, "Neither do I. But the general pays well, and I reckon he really *does* want to help his country. *And* if that makes him a mighty rich man, to boot, then that's all to the good, isn't it?"

"I just want to know what I'm getting into, that's all."

"Join up and you'll be going along on jobs with the rest of us. That means trains, sometimes a mule train loaded with gold or a mine payroll, maybe a bank now and then. You have objections to any of that?"

The Kid shook his head and said, "Nope."

"Do you have *experience* with any of those things?"

"I've helped hold up a few trains," the Kid lied. "And I've stuck up more than one bank. I can carry my share of the load, Kern."

"You'll get along just fine, then," the bearded man said with a nod. "If the general decides you're trustworthy." He paused. "I've got to admit, you pitching in to stop him from shooting us this morning is going to help your case, and so is the fact that the señorita likes you."

"She does?" The Kid grinned. "I thought you said you weren't going to gossip."

"Damn it. Just forget I said that, all right?"

"Sure," the Kid said easily.

He wasn't going to forget it, though. Antonia Ramirez might wind up playing a large part in his efforts to rescue Frank Morgan. Already, a rudimentary plan had begun to form in the Kid's brain. Outfighting such a large force as the general's would be almost impossible. He would have to get Frank free some other way, maybe by forcing a trade for another hostage.

Diego Ramirez would turn over Frank in order to save his daughter, wouldn't he? The Kid had already had chances to grab her, but he needed to know more first. He had to find out as much as he could about Frank's situation and come up with a way for both of them to get away without being killed.

And when he thought about that plan, something stirred uneasily in his belly. If he kidnapped Antonia and threatened her life, would that make him just as bad as Ramirez? The whole idea rubbed him the wrong way. Yet facing such overpowering odds, he had to use every weapon at his command. He couldn't afford to discard any option.

For now, all he could do was wait and see how the hand played out . . . and see which cards were dealt next.

\* \* \*

They came in sight of the hacienda by the middle of the day. The Kid saw it looming up from the arid landscape when they were still several miles away. At first just a dark, irregular mass showed on the horizon, like some sort of rock formation, but as they rode closer, it took on a more definite shape. A little shock went through him as he realized it was built like a European castle. He and his mother and stepfather had traveled on the Continent when he was young, and he had seen such structures with his own eyes.

Now he was seeing one again, although in a strange mixture of styles, this "castle" was surrounded by outbuildings like those found on a typical border country rancho, as well as an adobe wall with wooden gates that reminded the Kid of a military outpost.

Walt Creeger, who had built this place, hadn't just gone mad out of the blue, the Kid mused. He must have been a little touched in the head to start with. Or maybe, to be generous, he was just . . . eccentric.

"Mighty impressive," the Kid commented to Kern as the group rode closer.

"The general's got it in his mind that after he takes over, he'll negotiate with the government in Washington to make this part of Mexico. Says he'll trade 'em some other territory somewhere else for it. That way he can make it his presidential estate and run the country from it whenever he's not in the palace in Mexico City."

"I don't know how well that would work. This is a long way from anywhere else. Hard to govern a country from the middle of nowhere."

Kern shrugged and said, "Maybe, maybe not. If he's the president, he can have a telegraph line run up here, so he can stay in contact with Mexico City all the time. Hell, he could even have a spur line built from the railroad. It's only about thirty miles south of here, across the border."

The Kid thought about it and slowly nodded. Kern was right. The idea sounded ludicrous at first, but Ramirez actually might be able to make it work . . . if he overthrew Porfirio Díaz and took over the country. That was going to be a lot harder. But a quarter of a million dollars in ransom money would make it easier.

Ramirez would never get his hands on that money. Not if the Kid had anything to say about it.

Antonia turned her horse and fell back so that she rode beside the Kid and Kern. She nodded toward the looming edifice in front of them and asked, "What do you think of it, Señor Callahan?"

"Mighty impressive," he admitted. "But I heard stories back in town about it being haunted."

"You mean the tale about the madman who built the place and then murdered his partner?" Antonia scoffed. "A story for parents to frighten their children with, nothing more. We have been here for several months, and I have seen no ghosts, nor any lunatics wandering in the desert. I am too practical to believe in such things."

"I'm not all that superstitious myself. It looks like the place would be easy to defend against an attack. I imagine that's why your father chose it as his headquarters."

Antonia nodded and said, "We were fortunate to find it when we left Mexico."

*When the Rurales ran you out of Mexico, you mean*, the Kid thought, but he was smart enough not to say it.

Sentries had probably had spyglasses trained on them for quite a while as they approached the stronghold. The heavy wooden gates swung open so the riders could pass through. The Kid looked around, took note of the parapet along the wall and the guard tower at each corner of the compound. Artillery could knock that wall down, but short of that, even an army would find it difficult to conquer the place.

A man was posted in each of the guard towers, and several other riflemen paced along the parapet. An air of readiness for trouble hung over the compound. The Kid wasn't the sort to give in to despair, but under the circumstances, he could have been forgiven if his spirits had sagged. Any rescue attempt would face almost insurmountable odds.

He wouldn't give up, though. He would never abandon his father, not after all he and Frank Morgan had gone through together.

The three hardcases who had been given the job of watching over Antonia while she was in Saguaro Springs peeled off from the group and rode toward a long, low, open-fronted building being used as a stable. The Kid supposed they regarded Antonia as being safe enough, now that they were back in the compound.

With the Kid and Kern flanking her, Antonia rode toward another adobe building that seemed to guard the entrance to the castle. A door opened as they came up to it, and Valdez emerged from the building.

"*Hola, señorita*," he greeted Antonia. He cast a wary eye toward the Kid and added, "You brought this man with you."

"My father summoned him," Antonia said. "It wasn't my decision." She swung down from the saddle and handed the black's reins to Valdez. "Where is my father?"

"About to sit down to dinner. He told me to bring you to him as soon as you arrived."

Valdez held out a hand and with a sweeping motion ushered them toward the castle.

The Kid felt a little like someone in a fairy tale walking into an ogre's castle. His masquerade was a precarious one. If anyone here tumbled to his real identity as Conrad Browning, his rescue effort would be a spectacular failure. He had to continue convincing all the members of this band of killers that he was really John Callahan, drifting hardcase and gun-wolf for hire.

An oversized steel door led into the looming hacienda. It would take a cannon to knock it down, too. But it swung open easily enough, albeit with creaking hinges, as a short, fat, bald Mexican in a swallowtail coat and frilly shirt pushed on it. More than likely, he was the general's majordomo, the Kid thought. A would-be dictator needed a majordomo.

The man stepped back out of the doorway and came to attention. Antonia smiled and patted him on his smoothly shaven cheek.

"You are always respectful, Regalberto," she told him. "I like that about you."

"Of course, señorita," he said. "It is only proper."

Antonia glanced toward the Kid and murmured, "Some should learn how to be so proper and respectful."

"Where I come from, people have to earn respect," he said, unwilling to let her little dig pass without comment. "They're not born to it."

"We come from very different places, Señor Callahan."

"And yet we're on the same side."

"Not yet," she said. "Not yet."

She turned and strode across a large, marble-floored entrance hall toward a pair of open double doors. Kern nodded for the Kid to follow her, and then he fell in behind the Kid as Valdez went out. The door clanged as Regalberto closed it.

Antonia led the way into a room dominated by a long, gleaming dinner table. A man sat at the far end, sipping from a glass of wine as he lounged in a chair with a tall, ornately carved back and equally fancy arms. A place setting of china and crystal was in front of him, but no food yet. He set the glass aside and said, "Ah, Antonia, my dear! You have returned from your little outing." He looked past her at the Kid and added, "And you have brought a guest with you."

"That was your idea, Papa," she said. "You sent Kern to fetch him."

The man stood up, came toward the Kid with a stride like that of a stalking tiger, and extended his hand.

"*Buenos días*," he said. "I am General Diego Ramirez . . . soon to be *presidente* of the great nation of Mexico!"

# Chapter 20

The general cut an impressive figure. As the Kid shook hands, he noted the tight blue trousers, flared out at the bottom over polished black boots, the short red jacket with lots of gold braid and trim, and the green silk shirt with pearl buttons. Ramirez was something of a peacock when it came to his clothes.

His face reminded the Kid more of a hawk, though, with a prominent, bladelike nose and the snapping black eyes of a predator. A rumpled thatch of graying dark hair, a mustache that drooped over his wide mouth, and lean, weathered cheeks gave him a touch of dignity. He looked like a man who had packed a great deal of living into his years. Surprisingly enough, the Kid felt instinctively drawn to him. Ramirez had the sort of natural leadership ability that created armies . . . and overthrew governments.

Unfortunately, his face also had lines of rakish cruelty stamped into it. Once he set out to gain something, he wouldn't allow anyone or anything to stand in his way until he had his objective in his grasp. Any blood spilled in the process was just too bad.

The Kid gathered those impressions in a split second

as he grasped Ramirez's hand in a tight grip. He knew it
was considered impolite in Latin cultures to look directly
into a man's eyes when meeting him, so he lowered his
gaze slightly and said, "It's an honor and a pleasure to
meet you, General. I've heard a great deal about you."

Ramirez chuckled and said, "Very little good, I expect,
if you have been in Saguaro Springs."

"On the contrary, your daughter seems to think quite
highly of you."

"You and my daughter are . . . well acquainted?"

"Not really," the Kid said. "We only met briefly a couple
of times in town." He smiled as he thought about the way
he had manhandled Antonia as he broke up the fight between her and Peggy Cole. He wondered if she would tell
her father about that. "And then of course we rode out
here together today, but she was usually well out in front."

That got an actual laugh from Ramirez. He turned to
Antonia, cupped her chin with his hand, and said, "Yes,
that is where she likes to be! Your . . . shopping trip . . .
went well, little one?"

She pulled back a bit so he had to drop his hand from
its caress. "I got the things I needed," she said. "But there
was trouble. Señor Callahan may well have saved my life,
and the lives of your men."

Ramirez's bushy eyebrows rose in surprise.

"What happened?" he asked with a harsh note of anger
in his voice. "The men I ordered to stay with you were
supposed to protect you!"

"It was an unfortunate situation, General," Kern said.
"The son of a man Bracken had to kill a while back returned to Saguaro Springs looking for revenge. He was

about to open up on us with a shotgun when Callahan stopped him."

Ramirez drew in a deep breath, causing his nostrils to flare. He regarded the Kid intently and said, "You have my deepest gratitude for saving my daughter's life, señor, as well as those of my men."

"It seemed like the thing to do at the time," the Kid said.

"I will not forget it. You have my word on that. I owe you a great deal . . . and a Ramirez always pays his debts." The resplendently dressed *bandido* gestured toward the table. "As a beginning, I would like for you to have dinner with me and Antonia."

"I'd be happy to."

"You stay as well, Kern," Ramirez snapped.

"Of course, General," the stocky gunman said. It was becoming obvious to the Kid that Kern was Ramirez's *segundo*.

The majordomo stood stiffly just inside the dining room. Ramirez glanced at him and said, "Regalberto, tell the women to set two more places, and then we will be ready to eat."

Regalberto bowed slightly and said, "Of course, Excellency." As far as he was concerned, Ramirez was already the supreme leader of Mexico.

Or of this little piece of Arizona Territory, anyway, the Kid thought wryly.

The majordomo bustled out. Ramirez waved the others toward the table and said, "Let us sit."

"I would prefer to freshen up after the ride from the settlement, Papa," Antonia said.

"Nonsense. You look fine. A little trail dust is nothing to concern yourself with. Is that not so, Señor Callahan?"

"I'm used to it, myself," the Kid said. "Been on the drift for quite a while now."

"I would like to learn more about you." Ramirez motioned toward the chairs again. "Please."

Antonia rolled her eyes, but she took her seat to her father's right. The Kid sat to Ramirez's left, with Kern on his other side. A female servant appeared from somewhere and poured wine into glasses for them.

Ramirez lifted his glass and said, "To Señor Juan Callahan, for his service in saving my daughter's life."

"You honor me, General," the Kid said.

They all drank, Antonia with a bit of ill grace, and then Ramirez went on, "I know it is not considered polite to inquire too much about a man's background, but I am curious about you, Señor Callahan. I can tell by looking at you that you are a fighting man."

"I wasn't always," the Kid said. "In fact, when I was a youngster, I wasn't much good to anybody. But then my folks died, and I had to learn how to make my own way in the world."

That response actually had a good deal of truth in it. Ramirez nodded and said, "Life can be a very hard teacher. But the lessons we learn serve us well, eh?"

The Kid took another sip of his wine. It had a raw bite and wasn't very good, but out here in the middle of nowhere, you couldn't expect anything else.

"I learned that I'm good with a gun," he said. "It seemed to come natural to me." That was true, as well. "So I figured if I had a talent, I ought to put it to good use. That's what I've been doing ever since."

"Where?" Ramirez asked sharply.

"Texas, Colorado, California," the Kid answered with a shrug. "All over the Southwest, really. I've never been the sort to stay in one place for very long at a time."

"I hope that if you join our cause, you will consider remaining with us after we are victorious. Every man who supports me will have a place waiting for him."

"Are you asking me to throw in with you, General?"

"Not just yet, perhaps," Ramirez said. "But everything I have heard so far makes me believe that you would be a good addition to our ranks. But for now . . ." He nodded toward the two servant women, one older, one younger, who had just come into the room and were carrying platters of food. "Let us enjoy our dinner!"


During the time Frank had been down here in the dungeon, he had learned the names of the older woman and the two younger ones. Not that they ever talked to him when they brought him his meals and the older woman checked his wounds, but sometimes the guards called them by name. The older woman was Juana; the younger ones were Beatriz and Florita. Frank was pretty sure that Beatriz was Juana's daughter, and Florita was her niece.

Knowing their names didn't help him, but thinking about it was something to do. He also thought about ways to escape from his imprisonment, but so far he hadn't come up with anything even remotely workable.

His hip still ached a little from the bullet graze but was healed for the most part. His right leg was stiff at times from the stab wound, but it no longer bothered him much, either. The moss that Juana had used to treat it had been quite effective.

Feeling better meant that he was more restless than ever, and pacing back and forth as best he could in the close confines of the cell didn't do anything to relieve that feeling.

He was pacing like that when he heard footsteps approach and then a key rattled in the lock. He backed to the far side of the cell, knowing at least one shotgun-wielding guard would cover him when the door opened.

It swung back, and sure enough, an American gunman named Hardy stepped into the cell and leveled a short-barreled coach gun at Frank. Hardy moved aside, out of the doorway, to allow Florita to enter the chamber. She carried a wooden tray with a bowl and a cup on it that she placed on the stone floor between her and Frank.

"You fellas sure must be scared of me," Frank drawled as he grinned at Hardy. "You never come in here without a scattergun."

Hardy grunted and said, "And I don't mind pullin' the triggers if I need to, so don't get any ideas, Morgan."

"No ideas," Frank said. "*Gracias, Florita.*"

The girl didn't acknowledge the thank-you. She just turned and went stiffly out of the cell. Hardy backed out, never lowering the shotgun as he did so.

Frank chuckled as the key turned in the lock again. They acted like he was the most dangerous man alive.

He hoped he would get a chance to demonstrate to them that they'd been right to be so cautious.

He sat down cross-legged on the floor beside the tray. The bowl contained some sort of stew, probably *cabrito*, and he saw now that a chunk of bread sat beside the bowl.

He could use it to sop up the liquid from the stew. The cup was full of weak coffee. The meal wasn't much, but it would keep him alive.

He used his fingers to pick out the lumps of goat meat, which were tough but nourishing, along with pieces of potato and wild onion. Sips of coffee washed down the food. He dipped the bread into the stew and ate it, too, but it wasn't a big enough piece to soak up all the liquid. Some was left in the bottom of the bowl. Frank picked it up to drink the last of the savory juice.

But before he did, he saw something shiny lying on the tray. The bowl had been sitting on top of it, concealing it.

Frank picked it up and brought it closer to his face to study it in the dim light. He held a thin piece of metal, half an inch wide and four inches long, pointed on one end. He ran a fingertip along the edges to test them. The metal wasn't sharp, but it was sturdy despite its thinness.

A man could use just this sort of tool to open a lock . . . if he knew how.

Frank didn't, but he thought he could figure it out.

He knew from listening that no guards were posted directly outside his door. They always came down the corridor from the bottom of the stone staircase. He had heard their footsteps approaching often enough. He had also heard faint snoring coming from that direction at times, so he believed they had a chair down at the end of the corridor and would doze there while they were making sure he didn't escape.

He would have to deal with that problem later. Getting the cell door unlocked was the first obstacle to overcome.

He drank the rest of the coffee, then stood up and moved to the door. Bending over to work on the lock was awkward for a man of his height, so he went down on one knee and began to probe in the keyhole with the little metal strip. He put his other hand against the door to steady himself.

Frank had seen men pick locks before. He knew it was as much an art as a science, and he possessed no such artistry. But he had sensitive hands and nerves, and keen hearing as well. He turned his head and put his right ear close to the lock as he explored inside it with the metal strip.

Every time he felt the tip catch on something, he applied gentle but steady pressure to see if he could move the lock's mechanism. When it resisted, he eased off. He didn't want to break the metal.

Long minutes of maddening trial and error went by. He began to worry that Florita and the guard would return so she could pick up the bowl, cup, and tray before he was able to unlock the door. If that happened, he would have to hide the metal strip in his pocket and try again later. That might even be better, he decided. His chances of escape would be better if he broke out of here in the middle of the night.

After being locked up in this cell for long, miserable days, though, he wanted to be *out*. He would try for a few more minutes.

Just as he told himself that, he heard a faint scraping sound inside the lock as he twisted the metal strip.

Frank paused, made sure the tip was still caught securely on whatever it had caught on, then applied pressure again. Once more something scraped. Little by little, he worked it to the left until finally, with a whisper-quiet thud, whatever was moving came free.

That was just the first step. A handle still had to be turned in order to open a latch. Frank had heard the guards doing that every time they had come to the cell. Could he reach it by sticking his arm between the bars on the little window?

He stood up, put his face to the opening, and listened. He didn't hear anyone talking or moving around. From the window, he could see part of the corridor, but not the end by the stairs. He didn't know if a guard was posted there around the clock.

"Hey!" Frank called quietly. "When's that pretty little señorita coming back?"

No answer. The corridor might be empty . . . or the guard might be ignoring him.

He took a deep breath and thrust his left arm between the bars.

No alarmed shout, no rushing footsteps. He pressed his shoulder against the bars as hard as he could to get as much reach as possible and felt around for the handle. After a moment his fingertips brushed against it. He strained harder as he tried to get a grip on it. The first time he attempted to turn the handle, his fingers slipped off. Frank clenched his jaw and tried again.

This time the handle turned a little. Frank was able to get a better grasp. He twisted.

The latch clicked. The door moved toward him slightly. He withdrew his arm from the window and eased the door open, going slow so the hinges didn't creak as much. He leaned forward and peered along the corridor toward the stairs. No guards were in sight. Two ladder-back chairs sat on either side of a table where the guards could play cards or put a whiskey bottle and some glasses, but at the moment those chairs were empty.

Frank was out of the cell, but he was a long way from freedom. A small army of cold-blooded killers blocked his way out of this castle and the compound beyond.

This was the necessary first step, though. He hurried along the corridor toward the stairs.

Before he got there, he heard footsteps echoing through a hallway somewhere up above . . . and they were coming nearer with each passing second.

Florita and the guard were on their way back to the cell.

# Chapter 21

Frank could have turned and gone back inside the cell, but if he did, Hardy would realize the door was unlocked and know that something had happened. That wouldn't help Frank, and it might cause a great deal of trouble for Florita.

Faced with that choice, he did the only thing he could. He hurried forward, dropped to hands and knees, and crawled under the table next to the chairs. He was a big man and it wasn't easy, but he managed, pressing his body against the wall to conceal himself as much as possible. Now he had to hope that Hardy wouldn't spot him under there. The man wouldn't be expecting trouble, so he might not. One thing about hired guns: they tended to get a little lax when they weren't in the middle of a fight.

The footsteps were louder now as they descended the stairs. Frank listened closely. He believed only two people were headed down here to the dungeon. That was good. An extra guard would have just increased the odds against him.

He held his breath as they reached the bottom of the stairs and moved past the table. He saw two sets of feet, one clad in sandals with bare ankles above them and a long skirt swishing around the calves, the other crammed into well-worn boots.

Then he stood up, grunting a little as he grasped the edges of the table and lifted it on his bent back. His leg nudged one of the chairs and made it scrape on the stone floor. The guard heard that and started to turn quickly, but Frank raised the table higher and crashed it down on top of the gunman.

The impact drove Hardy to his knees and made him drop the shotgun. It clattered on the floor. He recovered enough to make a lunge for the shotgun, but Frank kicked him in the jaw and knocked him sprawling on his back. A lot of the anger and frustration that had built up inside Frank since he was captured went into that kick. When he looked at the guard, who was now out cold, he could tell that the man's jaw was broken.

Frank didn't figure he was going to lose a second of sleep over that.

He bent and picked up the scattergun, then plucked the unconscious man's revolver from its holster and stuck it behind his belt. Only then did he look at Florita, who stared at him in shock. She tried to speak, but it took her a moment before she was able to.

Finally she said, "Señor, you . . . you freed yourself . . ."

"And I reckon I've got you to thank for that," Frank said. "You took a mighty big chance, smuggling that piece of metal to me so I could pick the lock. It wouldn't have gone well for you with the general if you'd been caught."

"I trusted to *el Señor Dios* to protect me and grant you your freedom," she said.

"We're a long way from that. How many men are upstairs?"

Florita shook her head and said, "I do not know. Seven or eight, at the very least. Two pistoleros, Señor Kern and another man who is new here, dine with *el General* and Señorita Antonia right now."

Frank had known all along that he couldn't shoot his way out of the hacienda. But if Ramirez and Antonia were his prisoners, the general's men wouldn't dare harm him. He needed to get to some horses and put some distance between himself and this unholy place.

"You stay here," he told Florita as he turned toward the steps. "*Muchas gracias* for what you've done—"

"Wait," she said. "Let me come with you."

"It's too dangerous—" Frank began.

She bent and picked up the guard's hat, which had fallen off when Frank brought the table crashing down on him. As she punched the broad-brimmed black hat into shape, she said, "Wear this and keep your head down."

"I can't pretend to be that hombre," Frank said as he nodded toward the guard. "I'm a heap bigger than him."

"But it might fool the others for a moment, especially if I am with you acting like nothing is wrong, and that moment might be important."

She had a point there, Frank thought. With the odds so high against him, any advantage, however slight, was worth pursuing.

"All right," he said as he took the hat from her. It was too small, but not by much. The hired gun was slightly built but had a big head.

"Drag this dog into the cell," Florita suggested. "I know where he keeps the key. I should get the things I brought down for your meal. It will look better if I have them when we go back up."

"You're right, señorita," Frank agreed. He got hold of the unconscious man's collar and hauled him along the corridor. Florita hurried ahead of him and went into the cell to fetch the tray, bowl, and cup.

Once Frank had Hardy laid out on the floor, the young woman delved inside one of his trouser pockets and came up with the key. They stepped out, and she locked the cell behind them.

"It would be all right with me if no one ever found him and he rotted in there," she said in a low, vehement voice. "He is a pig!"

Frank wasn't going to ask her what the guard had done to cause her to hate him so much. He didn't figure that was any of his business.

"Are you sure about this?" he said to her. "You can stay down here where it's safe while I go up."

She shook her head. "You must get away from here, Señor Morgan. When you do, go to the café in Saguaro Springs run by Julio Hernandez. He is my uncle, and he will know what to do."

Frank wasn't sure what she meant by that, but he nodded and said, "All right. Let's go."

They returned to the bottom of the stairs, where he paused long enough to set up the table, which was lying on its side where it had fallen after he used it to knock out the guard. It was sturdily built and hadn't broken apart.

Then they started up out of the dungeon. That felt mighty good to Frank.

No matter what happened from here on out, he had a

fighting chance again. That was all he had ever asked out of life.

He heard voices before they reached the top of the stairs. Florita, who was beside him, said quietly, "There is a room up here where the guards sometimes sit and drink and amuse themselves. It was empty when Hardy and I went down to the dungeon."

"It's not now," Frank said. "Sounds like a couple of men."

"Let me go first," the girl suggested. "That is the way it would be if Hardy were with me."

Frank nodded and let her move up a couple of steps above him. He lowered his head, so anyone looking down the stairs at them would see Florita for the most part, as well as the black hat on the man behind her.

"Here she is now," a man's mocking voice said as Florita neared the top of the stairs. "Hey, sweetheart, how about you put on another little show for us, like you did the other day? I never saw a gal dance quite like that before."

"It was somethin', all right," another man put in. "C'mon, darlin', put that tray down and shake them hips for us. I always liked you hot-blooded Mex gals."

"I must take these things back to the kitchen," Florita muttered with her head down. She was off the stairs and in the guardroom now, with Frank close behind her.

"Hell, your *tía* won't mind if you ain't back right away. I want to watch you dance—"

"Hey!" the other guard interrupted. "That ain't—"

Florita swung the tray before the man could finish warning the other one that it wasn't Hardy with her. The cup and bowl went flying. The tray smacked across the man's face.

Frank leaped at the other man and brought the coach

gun up. He didn't want any shooting to alert the rest of the hacienda that something was going on, so he slammed the shotgun's butt into the guard's jaw. Bone shattered, just as Frank's kick down in the dungeon had broken Hardy's jaw. The guard dropped to the floor, senseless.

The other man was more surprised than hurt by Florita hitting him with the tray. He staggered back a step but stayed on his feet and clawed at the gun on his hip. His mouth opened to shout for help.

Before he could make a sound, Florita hit him again, this time slashing the edge of the tray against his throat. He stumbled against the wall, suddenly gasping for air, his fast draw forgotten for the moment as he choked. That gave Frank enough time to swing the coach gun one-handed. The twin barrels struck the man on the side of the head and knocked his hat off. He sagged, slid down the rough stone, and wound up on the floor making a gro-tesque gurgling sound as he instinctively struggled to drag breath through his ruined windpipe. He went still and his eyes began to glaze over as he lost that struggle.

Florita glared down at the guard's body with a look of primitive hatred on her face. She might have been an ancient Aztec in that moment, glorying in the death of an enemy.

Then she took a deep breath and came back to herself. She turned to Frank and said, "We must hurry. We can go through the kitchen. There is a hall where the guards seldom go. From there you can reach the stable and get a horse—"

Frank stopped her with a shake of his head.

"That's not going to do me much good," he told her.

"I'd have to shoot my way past the guards at the gate and all the men on the wall."

"There are men here, brought from Saguaro Springs and forced to work, who will open the gates for you."

"Maybe so, but they'll get gunned down while they're doing it. And then the riflemen on the wall will shoot me out of the saddle anyway. You said the general and his daughter are eating dinner right now?"

She gave him a wary look and said, "*Sí.*"

"Take me to the dining room."

Her dark eyes widened as she said, "You are mad! Two of those killers are with them—"

"That's still better odds than out in the compound," Frank said. "And with the general and Señorita Antonia as my prisoners, the rest of the bunch will think twice about sending a lot of lead in my direction."

She stared at him for a long moment, then finally nodded and admitted, "You are right. That may be your best chance."

"If we run into any guards, I'm going to grab you around the neck and put this shotgun to your head. That way it'll look like I forced you to help me. So if I don't make it out of here, nobody will know about your part in getting me loose."

"Hardy and the other man whose jaw you broke might tell."

Frank shook his head. "I reckon it all happened fast enough they won't be sure. You just deny everything."

She nodded again and said, "*Sí.* We will go this way."

She led him through a corridor, turned along another one, then another. Frank had a frontiersman's sense of direction when he was outside, but inside a building, in a maze of hallways like this, he was soon lost. He couldn't have retraced their steps to the dungeon if he'd tried . . . not that he had any desire to return to that hellhole.

They didn't run into any guards, but they did encounter a couple of female servants who started to back away, wide-eyed with fear, when they recognized Frank. Florita spoke to them in rapid, urgent Spanish, though, and they didn't flee. Instead they came to Frank, touched his arm, and babbled prayers in Spanish, asking *el Señor Dios* to aid and protect him.

Florita turned to him and said, "Ramirez and his men are all cruel. We would be free of them."

"If I can get out of here and take the general and his daughter with me, you will be," he told her. "All those hired guns won't hang around very long with nobody to pay them. They'll take off for the tall and uncut when they realize the so-called revolution is a bust."

"I pray that you are right. Come."

They resumed their twisting-and-turning journey to the hacienda's dining room.

"We are almost there," Florita said in a low voice, turning her head to speak over her shoulder to Frank as they went along a corridor with several doors on each side and a partially open door at the far end. They weren't far from their destination when the last door on Frank's right opened and a man stepped out into the hallway.

He stopped short, looked at Florita, and grinned. Frank recognized the angular face, the brown tweed suit, the derby hat. *Bracken.*

And Bracken recognized him, too. The gunman's startled face as he glanced over Florita's shoulder testified to that. Bracken's hand dived for the gun on his hip as his features contorted.

Frank's plan to grab Florita and pretend that she was his prisoner if they were confronted was useless here. He knew that Bracken would just shoot *through* the girl to try to get him. The gunman was every bit that vicious and ruthless.

So Frank's left arm swept Florita to the side, out of the line of fire, as he lunged forward and slashed downward with the coach gun's barrels. They cracked across Bracken's wrist just as his gun cleared the holster. He howled in pain as his hand sprang open involuntarily. The revolver fell to the floor.

Frank bulled forward, rammed his shoulder into Bracken, and drove the man backward against the door at the far end of the corridor. Wood splintered and the door flew open. Bracken's feet tangled together and he fell, but Frank's momentum carried him forward and he tripped on the gunman's flailing legs. The too-small hat came off Frank's head as he toppled forward.

He landed on his knees and his left hand but had managed to hold on to the coach gun with his right. He looked up, saw the long dining table several yards away with several people standing at one end of it where they had just jumped up from their chairs. General Ramirez, not surprisingly, was at the head of the table, with his daughter, Antonia, to his right.

Two men had been seated at the general's left. They turned now to see what the commotion was, and Frank recognized one of them as Kern, the gunman who had been with Bracken in Saguaro Springs.

The sight of the other man sent a shock through Frank as he gazed into the eyes of his son, Conrad.

# Chapter 22

The food that the servant women brought into the dining room was very good: grilled chicken cooked with onions and peppers, fresh tortillas, and beans. They kept the glasses full as well, and even though the wine wasn't outstanding, it went well with the food.

"General" Diego Ramirez was clearly a man in love with the sound of his own voice, the Kid thought as he ate. All through the meal, Ramirez talked about his plans once he ousted el Presidente Díaz and took over Mexico. To hear him tell it, the place would become a paradise on earth, with everyone taken care of from the lowliest farmer to the aristocrats in Mexico City.

Of course, most of those aristocrats would have their wealth stripped from them so that the poorer people could be taken care of. He never really explained how that was going to work, and the Kid was willing to bet that the privileged class wouldn't really go away. It would just consist of different people . . . people who had found favor with the new *presidente*.

Those who did not find favor would wind up standing

in front of a wall, facing a firing squad. That was always the way it happened in Mexico.

"Some say this vision of mine is only a dream, but I will make it a reality," Ramirez declared. "Once I am in power, I will change Mexico forever, my friends. Change it for the better!"

"I am sure you will, Papa," Antonia said, "but first there is still the little matter of seizing that power."

"The day will come!" Ramirez said with a scowl as he thumped his fist on the table. "Mark my word, it will come." He turned his head to smile at the Kid and Kern. "How can it not, with such stalwart fighting men lending us their support?"

He had guzzled down more wine than any of them, and the Kid thought he was starting to show it. His voice was a little louder and more slurred than it had been.

Kern said, "I hate to mention it, General, but not all of your men have joined up with you for political reasons. I support your cause, of course, but a lot of those fellas . . . all they care about is the payoff."

The general's scowl returned. "You mean they want money."

"They're as loyal as anybody you'd ever want on your side . . . as long as they're getting paid," Kern said with a shrug. "And I really do hate to bring it up . . ."

"But we are running low on funds." Ramirez sounded like the words tasted bitter in his mouth. "This I know, Señor Kern. I know it all too well."

And that was why they had kidnapped Frank, the Kid mused. Ramirez didn't just need the ransom money to expand his army. He needed it to keep many of the men he already had from deserting him. But so far that money hadn't been forthcoming, so he was going to have to take other steps.

Ramirez gulped down the wine that was left in his glass and thrust it out for one of the servant women to fill. While she was doing that, he went on, "That is why some of you will be riding south tomorrow."

"Across the border?" Kern said. "To the railroad?"

"I have received word that a shipment of gold will be on its way by train from Monterrey to the West Coast so that it may be put on a boat and taken to a bank in San Diego." Ramirez threw back his head and let out a raucous bray of laughter. "It seems that a group of wealthy men have decided that Mexican banks cannot be trusted. They fear that Díaz will seize their riches. So they believe their gold will be safer in an American bank!"

"Maybe it would be," Kern said with a smile, "if it ever got that far."

"Truer words were never spoken, *mi amigo*." Ramirez seized his refilled glass and downed more wine. He leaned forward and narrowed his eyes at the Kid. "I am thinking, Señor Callahan, that if you wished to prove yourself to us—"

Before he could go on, something slammed into a door at the side of the room. The impact made the door fly open, and as that happened, all four people at the table leaped to their feet. Ramirez staggered a little because of all the wine he had consumed. The Kid turned to see two men lying on the floor, where they had landed after falling through the opening. He recognized the one closest to the door as the gunman called Bracken.

The other man, holding a short-barreled coach gun, was Frank Morgan.

As the Kid stared at his father, he knew without having to think about it that Frank was trying to escape. That didn't surprise him at all. Locked up in this isolated, castlelike stronghold, Frank wouldn't have had any way of knowing that the Kid was going to try to rescue him. He would have taken on the job of obtaining his freedom for himself.

But as Kern, standing beside him, reached for his revolver to deal with the threat of the shotgun, the Kid realized he would have to step in to save his father. And that would blow his masquerade as a drifting gunman all to hell.

Before that happened, Bracken recovered enough to throw himself on Frank from behind. Kern's gun slithered out of its holster, but he held his fire because of the chance he'd hit Bracken. The Kid stood there tensely with his hand on the butt of his own Colt as he waited to see how this was going to play out.

Frank was bigger and heavier than Bracken, but the gunman fought with a maniacal intensity. He reached over Frank's shoulder with his left hand, got hold of the coach gun's twin barrels, and forced them toward the floor. At the same time he looped his right arm around Frank's throat and hung on. Bracken's weight was enough to drive Frank the rest of the way to the floor. The shotgun's barrels struck the stone. That jarred the weapon out of Frank's grasp.

Frank tried to roll over on Bracken, but Bracken writhed out of the way like a snake. He spun on the floor and swung his leg around in a kick that drove his boot toe into Frank's solar plexus. Frank hunched over, and the Kid knew that the kick had just knocked the wind out of his father.

As Frank struggled up onto his knees, Bracken bored

in on him and swung bony fists. Normally, Frank would have shrugged off such punches, but they had more of an effect because he was gasping for air. His head rocked back under the blows. But he reached out with one hand, snagged Bracken's coat, and went over backward, hauling the hardcase with him. Frank's right foot came up. He planted it in Bracken's belly and levered the man up and over. Bracken waved his arms and legs wildly as he flew through the air. Then he crashed down on the floor with stunning force.

By now Ramirez had started bellowing for help. Three of his men charged through another door into the dining room. They bristled with guns, and the barrels of those weapons swung swiftly toward Frank. Kern was ready to fire as well, but the Kid, acting in the split second he had, leaped toward Frank, blocking Kern's shot. The Kid palmed out his Colt, reversed it faster than the eye could follow, and smashed the butt against Frank's head just as Frank started to turn toward him. The Kid saw the instant of bafflement in Frank's eyes before unconsciousness dulled them. Frank pitched headlong to the floor.

The Kid flipped the gun around and stood there over his father, covering him with the Colt.

"Hold your fire, hold your fire!" Ramirez ordered as Kern and the other three men surrounded Frank as well.

The Kid kept his face and voice cool and impassive as he asked, "Who the hell is this hombre?"

"You do not recognize him?" Ramirez said.

"Never saw him before in my life."

"That is the notorious gunfighter Frank Morgan. The one called the Drifter."

"Huh," the Kid grunted as if mildly surprised. "I've

heard of him, but we never crossed trails before. What's he doing here, and why's he on the warpath?"

"That is none of your business, señor," Ramirez snapped. The flurry of violent action seemed to have sobered him. "What is important is that you have prevented him from escaping, or at the very least, threatening harm to my daughter and myself."

"Glad I could lend a hand," the Kid said dryly. He stepped back and pouched his iron.

Inside, he was cursing bitterly at a fate that had robbed him of a perfect opportunity. He and Frank could have gotten the drop on Ramirez, Kern, and Bracken, then used Ramirez and Antonia as hostages while they got out of here. The quick arrival of those other gun-wolves, all of them ready to blast holes in Frank, meant that the Kid had had only an instant to save his father's life. His swift action had the added benefit of preserving his ruse, of course . . . but he would have traded that for a way out of the stronghold and some fast horses.

No point in worrying about something that luck hadn't provided, he told himself.

He sure hoped he hadn't hurt Frank too badly by clouting him like that. Better to have a sore head than be full of bullet holes, he supposed. Frank had a thick skull, the Kid reminded himself.

Ramirez flapped a hand toward Frank in a dismissive gesture and told the men who had rushed into the dining room, "Drag him back down to his cell." He turned to Kern and went on, "Go down there and find out how Morgan got loose and made it all the way up here. Whoever is responsible, I want them punished. I think . . . five strokes of the whip."

Kern looked doubtful about that. He said, "General, I'm not sure—"

"Five strokes, I said! See to it."

"Yes, sir," Kern said resignedly. He nodded toward the Kid. "What about Callahan?"

"I am not finished speaking with Señor Callahan. I believe he has established his trustworthiness by subduing Señor Morgan . . . at least for now."

Well, that was *some* good news, anyway, the Kid thought.

One man took hold of Frank's arms and lifted his torso while the other two got a leg apiece. They carried him out of the dining room. Kern went over to Bracken, helped him to his feet, and said, "You come on with me, Carl."

Bracken shook his head groggily and said, "Wha . . . what the hell happened? How'd Morgan get loose?"

"That's what we're going to find out."

As the two hardcases left the room, Ramirez gestured for the Kid to take his seat again and told Antonia to sit down, too.

She did so, then said, "Perhaps it would be best if we ridded ourselves of Morgan, Papa. Keeping him alive has been nothing but a nuisance."

The Kid managed not to look shocked by the casual way she suggested murder. He supposed he couldn't expect anything else from her, since she'd been raised by a bandit and a cutthroat. He picked up his wineglass just to be sure his expression didn't give him away.

"Until we have the ransom money—" Ramirez began.

"There has been no indication that we will *ever* receive the ransom money," Antonia broke in. The Kid figured she was the only one in the stronghold who would dare interrupt the general. "The Browning whelp will either pay or not. He has no way of knowing whether Morgan is still alive."

She would be mighty shocked if she knew that the "Browning whelp" was sitting right across the table from her, the Kid thought.

"Morgan can be killed anytime," Ramirez said. "As long as there is a chance he may prove useful to us, he will stay alive . . . *if* he does not force us to kill him by trying to escape or threatening to harm either of us." The general's voice hardened. "Then his usefulness will be at an end."

His expression eased as he turned again to the Kid.

"But your usefulness is just beginning, Señor Callahan. You are still free to go on your way if you choose to do so, but surely you see just how well you fit in with our group."

The Kid nodded slowly. He didn't believe that he was free to go on his way at all. If he didn't agree to join forces with Ramirez, the general would have him killed out of hand. He was certain of that.

So for more than one reason, he said, "I think you're right, General. I'd be mighty pleased to support your cause and help you achieve your goals any way I can." He grinned. "And if it puts some dinero in my pockets, well, I support *that* cause, too."

Ramirez laughed and hit the table with the side of his fist again.

"I can promise you dinero, my friend, *mucho dinero*. Remember the train I mentioned to Señor Kern a short time ago?"

"The one carrying those aristocrats' gold to the coast?"

"Exactly. Tomorrow you will ride south with my men, and by tomorrow night a portion of that gold will belong to you. Even though I trust you, it will be a good test for you, no? A profitable test for both of us." Ramirez picked up his wineglass. "Let us drink to gold!"

"To gold," Antonia said as she raised her own glass.

The Kid didn't hesitate in reaching for his glass. He had been a lot of things in his life, he told himself . . . and now, if he wanted to have any chance of saving his father, he was going to have to be a train robber, too.

"To gold," he said as he raised his glass.

# Chapter 23

Three thoughts crawled through Frank Morgan's brain as consciousness oozed into it like molasses on a cold morning.

He was lying on something hard, which more than likely meant the floor of his old cell in the dungeon.

His head hurt like blazes, throbbing with every beat of his heart.

And his own son was the one who had walloped him and put him back here.

Frank was well aware that when he and Conrad first met, the boy despised him. Had no use for him at all. But that had changed over the years, as they fought side by side and pulled each other's fat out of the fire numerous times. At least, Frank had believed it changed.

Conrad had been quick to spring forward and knock him out cold with a gun butt, though, just as those other fellas rushed in with drawn guns . . .

Frank stiffened as understanding burst on his brain. He had still had Hardy's revolver stuck behind his belt, but it was underneath him where he'd have had a hard time getting to it fast, and he had lost the shotgun. In another second or two, a hail of lead would have torn into him, and he wouldn't have been able to do a thing about it.

The only one who'd been able to prevent that from happening . . . was Conrad.

Frank heaved a sigh of relief. He was still in a mighty bad fix, but his son didn't hate him after all.

And if Conrad was here, dressed like a hardcase instead of a businessman and packing iron, it could only mean one thing.

Kid Morgan was back, and he had come to this outlaw stronghold to free his pa.

A grin tugged at Frank's mouth as he lay there. He hadn't been around to raise Conrad when the boy was growing up, but he still came by his stubborn, contrary nature honestly. Frank had hoped all along that Conrad wouldn't give in and pay the ransom.

Instead, he was infiltrating Ramirez's outfit. That was the only explanation for him being there having dinner with Ramirez, Antonia, and Kern. Frank suspected that quite a story was behind that. He looked forward to hearing it.

While those thoughts were going through Frank's brain, the ache inside his skull had subsided somewhat. He risked opening his eyes. He had been in the darkness of unconsciousness long enough that even the lantern's faint glow coming through the window in the door was enough to make him squint. A few fresh throbs of pain boomed inside his head, but then his eyes adjusted and the discomfort eased off again.

He was definitely inside a cell. It looked like the same one, but more than likely, they were all pretty much alike, so it was difficult to be sure. At any rate, he was locked up . . . and he didn't like it.

Slowly, he pushed himself up into a sitting position, rested his back against the wall. He had no idea what Conrad's plan was and no way of communicating with his son.

But he had confidence. He had seen Conrad come through all sorts of great danger and greater tragedy. Honestly, there was no one he would trust more to help him get out of this mess.

So for now he would wait, and rest up from what had happened today, and when the time came for Kid Morgan to make his move . . . Frank would be ready.

After the excitement in the dining room, Ramirez led the Kid to what he called his study, another chamber on the ground floor of the castlelike structure. Bookshelves covered one wall, and on them were leather-bound volumes dusty and moldy with age. They must have belonged to loco old Walt Creeger, the Kid thought, although everything he had heard about Creeger so far wouldn't have caused him to think that the man was much of a reader.

The study was furnished with shabby gentility. The furniture had been good at one time, but now it was worn and rotten and sported places here and there where something had gnawed on it. And this was going to be Ramirez's presidential "palace," the Kid told himself wryly. That was suitable, he supposed, for dreams founded on lawlessness, cruelty, and butchery.

Antonia had gone up to her room after the toast they

had made to gold, and this time Ramirez hadn't tried to stop her. He and the Kid weren't alone in the study, however. Valdez had appeared from somewhere, and as the burly Mexican stood leaning against one of the walls, he idly caressed the wooden handle of a machete thrust behind the sash at his waist. The intent way in which he watched the Kid made it clear that he wouldn't mind using that machete on the newcomer if it became necessary.

"Cigar?" Ramirez asked the Kid as he took a thin black cheroot from a wooden box on the desk.

"No thanks. I don't use 'em. But I'm obliged for the offer."

Ramirez clamped the cheroot between strong-looking white teeth and snapped a lucifer to life. He held the flame to the cheroot and puffed until it was burning well. Then he dropped the match to the stone floor and ground it out under his bootheel.

He blew out a cloud of smoke and said, "You are a man of quick reactions. My men would have killed the prisoner in another heartbeat, had you not knocked him out." Ramirez regarded the Kid with what was apparently genuine curiosity. "Why would you do that? Why did you not just allow my men to shoot him?"

"Surely that would have disturbed your daughter, to see a man gunned down like that," the Kid suggested.

Ramirez looked at him a moment more and then laughed.

"You do not know Antonia well. Did you not hear her say that we would be better served by Morgan's death?"

"Well, yeah, she did say that," the Kid admitted.

"So do not claim that you saved Morgan's life in order to spare my daughter's . . . delicate sensibilities."

"To be honest with you, General, I didn't even think about it. I just saw a threat and acted to put a stop to it. I didn't consider what your men might do, because I'm used to dealing with problems myself. And that was a quick and easy way of doing it."

Ramirez slowly nodded.

"I understand. Swift action . . . it is a habit with you."

"That's right."

"And yet, if you join forces with me, you will be expected to obey orders. You cannot do whatever your impulse tells you to do, whenever you want to do it."

"I know. And I've worked together with other folks before. Those trains I said I held up, I didn't do that by myself. Whoever's in charge, I'll do what they say."

"Tomorrow," Ramirez said, "that will be Señor Kern."

"He's the boss, then," the Kid said.

Ramirez nodded again, apparently satisfied with the Kid's answer.

The little majordomo, Regalberto, bustled into the study and spoke quietly enough to Ramirez that the Kid couldn't make out the words. Ramirez's face darkened with anger, though, so evidently he didn't like what he had heard.

"Señor Kern has his orders," Ramirez snapped. "Tell him that I intend for him to carry them out . . . personally."

Regalberto nodded and scurried out. Ramirez turned to the Kid and went on, "You must be curious why such a notorious gunfighter as Frank Morgan is our prisoner."

"It does seem a mite strange."

Ramirez puffed on the cheroot for a moment, then

said, "I offered him a chance to join us, to help make my dream a reality, but he refused. So he serves us in another way. Did you know, amigo, that Frank Morgan is a very rich man?"

"An old gun-wolf like him? Hell, they say he never even sold his gun, never got involved in a scrape unless he believed it was the right thing to do," the Kid scoffed. "That's no way to get rich."

"Once, Señor Morgan was married to a very wealthy woman. When she died, he inherited half of her riches. Their son inherited the other half and has made the businesses even more valuable. I learned this from an agent in San Francisco who supports our cause."

The Kid wondered who that agent might be, but it didn't really matter. The relationship between him and Frank wasn't exactly a secret, nor was the fact that the Browning holdings were worth a lot of money. Anybody could find out those things with a little digging.

"I sent a letter to Morgan's son explaining that he will be killed unless we receive a payment of two hundred and fifty thousand dollars," Ramirez went on.

The Kid let out a low whistle of admiration.

"A quarter of a million. That's one hell of a fortune, General. You think you can get it for that old pelican?"

"It is my fervent hope that I do. Not only does my revolution need the money, but I feel a certain admiration for Morgan. He has survived many years of a very perilous life. He is like an ancient wolf, gray and scarred, not as strong and fast as he once was, perhaps, but still dangerous."

"Well, I hope you get that loot, too. Put that together with the gold we're taking from that train tomorrow, and your revolution will be set, won't it, General?"

"Indeed, a new day will dawn in Mexico, my friend, a new day!" Ramirez puffed on the cigar and then said around it, "Now, come with me. I wish you to see something."

The Kid had no idea what Ramirez had in mind next, but after everything that had happened, he didn't think anything would surprise him.

Ramirez led the way from the study out to the hacienda's main entrance, where he and the Kid stepped into an open area between the castlelike building and the flat-roofed adobe structure that stood in front of it. Valdez followed them.

Ramirez pointed at the adobe building with his cigar and said, "When I rule Mexico, my government will be headquartered there while I am here at my palace. A second capital, you could say."

The Kid nodded. The general was as loco as old Walt Creeger, but it wouldn't do any good to tell him that. It would just get the Kid dead in a hurry.

Kern walked out of the hacienda. He didn't look happy.

"Report, Señor Kern," Ramirez snapped. "Did you find out how Morgan was able to escape?"

"I found out a few things," Kern said. "He had a servant with him when he ran into Bracken, a girl called Florita. She was the one who took Morgan his meals today. Hardy was supposed to be standing guard. But Hardy was locked up in Morgan's cell with a busted jaw. Two more men were in the guardroom at the top of the stairs to the dungeon. One of *them* had a broken jaw, too, and the other one was dead."

"This Florita, she turned Morgan loose?"

"I don't know how she managed it, but she had the key

to his cell in the pocket of her skirt. And even though
Bracken didn't get a real good look, he says she wasn't
acting like she was Morgan's prisoner when he ran into
them." Kern grimaced. "I hate to say it, but it sure looks
like she's responsible."

"Then you know what must be done," Ramirez said.

"General, I'm just not sure it's a good idea." Some of
the frustration Kern had to be feeling came through in his
voice. If he hadn't been frustrated, he never would have
risked talking to Ramirez like that.

The general's jaw tightened. He glared at Kern and
said, "You have your orders, señor. Where is the girl?"

"Bracken found her," Kern replied as he gestured
vaguely toward the hacienda. "He's got her."

"Bring her out." Ramirez looked toward the adobe
building. "I think one of those vigas will do nicely."

Something stirred uneasily inside the Kid. He wasn't
sure what Ramirez had in mind, but he didn't like the
direction this was headed.

Kern stepped into the hacienda, and a moment later
he reappeared along with Bracken. They held a young
Mexican woman between them, each of them tightly gripping one of her arms. She bore a resemblance to the servants who had served them dinner, the Kid realized, but
she wasn't one of that duo. Her face was defiant, but she
looked frightened, too. Probably with good reason.

Kern and Bracken marched her across the open space.
Valdez followed. Around the compound, men seemed to
realize that something was going on and drifted in this
direction.

Valdez stepped through a door into the adobe building
and came back with a coiled lasso. He shook out one end

of it and tossed it over a viga, one of the wooden beams that protruded from the adobe wall just below the roofline. Kern and Bracken grabbed Florita's wrists and thrust her arms above her head. They slid their grips down enough that Valdez could wrap the lasso around her wrists and tie it tightly.

Then Valdez stepped back and put some pressure on the rope, pulling hard enough on the other end that Florita cried out and was forced to go up on her toes.

Kern looked over his shoulder at Ramirez, who said calmly, "Continue."

Bracken grinned, licked his lips, and said, "Let me do this part, Kern."

Kern didn't argue. Bracken gripped Florita's shirt at the back of her neck, under her tumbled mass of raven hair, and savagely ripped it apart. It tore all the way down her back. Bracken shoved the ruined garment aside to expose the long, smooth, brown expanse of skin. He ran the fingertips of his right hand along her spine and laughed when she tried to flinch away from his touch. With Valdez putting so much pressure on the rope, though, she couldn't move much.

Bracken turned and said, "General, can I—"

"No," Ramirez said. "Kern."

With his face set in stony lines, Kern stepped into the adobe building and came back holding a whip. He shook it out, and to the Kid, it seemed to coil and hiss like a snake. It took all of his iron self-control to keep his face impassive and not reach for his gun. He wanted to let out a furious yell, yank his Colt from its holster, and start shooting.

More than two dozen men had gathered to watch this

grim spectacle, though, and the Kid knew that if he gave in to that urge, he would be dead in a matter of seconds and no longer able to do anything for Frank. He felt a little muscle jump in his jaw, but that was the only sign he gave of how horrified he was.

"Five lashes, Kern," Ramirez said. "Now."

# Chapter 24

Kern positioned himself about ten feet behind Florita. The Kid could tell by the way Kern handled the whip that the gunman wasn't an expert at its use. However, in a situation such as this, a man didn't have to be an expert.

Just brutal . . . or pragmatic enough to know that he didn't have a choice.

Kern took a deep breath. Florita didn't sob or beg for mercy as she hung there by her wrists. She held her head up. From where the Kid stood, he could see the defiant set of her jaw. He hoped that defiance would be enough to carry her through this ordeal.

Kern drew his arm back, then brought it forward quickly. The whip struck at an angle across Florita's back with enough force to make her jerk forward. It left a red stripe that began to ooze blood in a few places.

Ramirez said, "That was hardly enough to count as a lash, Kern. The girl still has five strokes coming to her for her treachery. Make them good strokes, or you will only increase her pain."

Bracken began eagerly, "General, I can—" but Ramirez cut him off with a curt gesture.

Kern dragged in another deep breath. This time when he wielded the whip, he put more force behind it. Florita jerked again, and although she didn't cry out, the Kid heard a sharp hiss of breath. When the whip fell away from her back, it left a long, diagonal cut in the smooth skin. Blood trickled from it in a few places.

"Much better," Ramirez said. "Four more."

The Kid had wondered before if Ramirez was genuine in his desire to improve things in Mexico. This grisly display answered that. Anyone who could stand there watching so calmly, so self-satisfied, while a young woman was brutally whipped, had no real compassion, no desire for justice. If by some bizarre twist of fate Diego Ramirez ever ruled Mexico, he would rule by blood and fire and terror. It would be a new age for that country, all right . . . a dark age.

Florita managed not to show much reaction to the next two lashes, but she couldn't hold back cries of agony as the final two strokes fell. She jerked and spasmed as the whip struck her. Small drops of blood flew in the air from the impacts. Her back was crisscrossed by crimson welts. As Kern stepped back after the final stroke, Florita sagged. The way her weight pulled on her wrists had to hurt, but she probably didn't even notice it because of the fiery torment of her back. Her head drooped forward. The Kid knew she hadn't passed out because he could hear her muttering something. It would have been better if she had lost consciousness.

While the whipping was going on, the general's men who had gathered to watch had been laughing and talking and making bets among themselves on when or if Florita would pass out. Their callousness infuriated the Kid, but he couldn't do anything about it right now. All he could do was pretend to be one of them, which made him sick to his stomach. He was overwhelmingly outnumbered, but somehow, some way, he would bring a reckoning to these animals, he vowed.

The crowd began to disperse as Valdez eased the pressure on the rope. Florita's knees buckled. Valdez let go of the rope completely. It slithered over the viga and Florita crumpled to the ground. Blood had splattered around her, forming small, circular splashes in the dirt that were now drying in the heat.

Movement to the Kid's right caught his eye. The two women who had served the meal hurried forward with distraught looks on their faces. They must have been watching from the hacienda and now wanted to go to Florita and try to help her.

Bracken stepped into their path and said, "Hold on there, you two. The general hasn't said you can be out here."

"Step back, Bracken," Ramirez ordered. "Let them do what they will."

Bracken shrugged and said, "Sure thing, General," but he glared at the two women as they took hold of Florita's arms and carefully lifted her to her feet. Tears shone in their eyes, the Kid saw as they turned back toward the hacienda with the bloody, half-conscious girl between them, but fury burned there as well.

Ramirez hadn't learned the lesson that ultimately led to the downfall of all tyrants, the Kid mused. You can only push people so far before they turn and fight.

The three women disappeared into the hacienda. Ramirez turned to the Kid. He had smoked the cheroot down to a butt, which he dropped on the ground and stepped on.

"So it will be in Mexico when I govern," he said. "Justice for those who transgress my rules will be swift and stern but fair. And the people will learn what is best for them."

"Because you'll tell them?"

Ramirez spread his hands and said, "Who better to do so?"

The Kid didn't have an answer for that. Actually, he thought anybody would be better to set up the rules of a society than a bloody-handed bandit, but Ramirez wouldn't want to hear that.

"Valdez will show you to your quarters," Ramirez went on. "Your horse has been cared for."

"*Gracias*, General."

"Welcome to the revolution, Señor Callahan!"

Ramirez didn't offer to shake hands when he said that, and the Kid was glad. He would have rather shaken hands with a rattlesnake.

Ramirez went inside. Valdez came over and jerked his head in an indication for the Kid to follow him. As he started to turn away from the hacienda, the Kid glanced up at the looming structure and saw a curtain move in a window on the second floor. It was falling closed, but as it fell he caught a glimpse of the face behind it.

That face belonged to Antonia Ramirez. She must have been watching while Florita was whipped, he realized.

And she was smiling like a cat with a bowl full of cream, as if she had enjoyed every second of it.

\* \* \*

The adobe building that served as a barracks for the general's army had been the crew's bunkhouse when this was a rancho. The Kid could tell that. Someone had already brought his saddlebags and rifle to the barracks and dumped them on one of the bunks. Ramirez might have dined with the Kid, as if he were an honored guest, but evidently from now on he would be treated like any of the other men, just one more soldier in the general's army of rebellion.

That was all right. He didn't want to stand out . . . not yet, anyway.

The Kid was sitting on his bunk when a man came into the building, stretched out on the next bunk, and reached underneath it to pull out a guitar. An American with red hair and a scattering of freckles across his bony face, he looked more like he ought to be behind a plow on a farm somewhere instead of in the middle of an outlaw army.

As the man began to strum chords on the guitar, the Kid leaned over and extended his hand.

"John Callahan," he introduced himself. "I'm a new recruit to the general's cause."

The redhead sat up with the guitar still across his lap and grasped the Kid's hand.

"Howdy, Johnny," he said. "I'm Sam Woodson. And I reckon you're like me, more of a recruit to the general's money . . . which, speakin' plain-like, he ain't got a whole hell of a lot of right now."

"I thought you boys have been pulling jobs across the border."

Woodson plucked the guitar strings again and said, "We have, but it takes a heap of dinero to feed this many fellas and make sure they got ammunition. I ain't what you'd call a scholar, but I done figured out it's usually the side what has the most money that wins the wars."

The Kid laughed and said, "You're right about that."

"Once the general gets the ransom money for that ol' gunfighter he's got locked up in the dungeon, though, we'll all be in high cotton. For a little while, anyway."

"And I hear tell we're going after a shipment of gold on a train tomorrow, too."

Woodson's eyebrows rose. "Is that so? I hadn't heard that yet. I reckon Kern'll get the boys together this evenin', the ones who are goin' along, anyway, and tell us all about it."

"Kern runs the jobs?"

"Yeah. The general can't concern hisself with little details like that. He's got loftier things to think about. And Kern, well, he may look like your friendly cousin, but he bossed a gang of bank and train robbers for a while, back in Missouri and Kansas, so he knows what he's doin'."

"I'm glad to hear it. I'm supposed to be one of those riding along on this job, and there's a better chance of coming back alive with an experienced leader." The Kid paused, then risked some more talk. "What about that hombre Bracken?"

Woodson's lanky fingers hit a discordant note on the guitar.

"You don't want to get crossways with that varmint," he responded. "That's all I'm sayin'."

"*Loco en la cabeza*, eh?"

"You didn't hear that from me," Woodson insisted. "You'd best talk about somethin' else."

"Sure," the Kid said easily. "Where are you from?"

A grin spread across Woodson's face as he said, "I don't mind that question. I'm a Texan, born and raised. Come from down around San Antone."

"How'd you wind up helping to overthrow the president of Mexico?"

"Well, that's a long, borin' story that involves a whole *heap* of bad decisions! Let's just say that me an' hard work ain't ever been amigos. I always figured they was other ways for me to get what I wanted. Sometimes I been right, and sometimes I been wrong."

"What about this time?"

"I reckon we ain't settled that yet. Time'll tell."

Woodson started playing an actual song instead of just strumming at the guitar strings. He was pretty good at it, too, the Kid thought. He felt an instinctive liking for the jovial Texan, but at the same time, he thought there was a good chance Woodson would gun him down without hesitation if it ever came to a showdown.

Which it was going to, sooner or later.

And if Woodson tried to stop him from rescuing Frank, the Kid might have to kill him.

They were all following a grim trail.

One of the adobe buildings was being used as a mess hall. It wasn't big enough for all the men to eat at the same time, so they took their meals in shifts. The Kid was in the second shift that evening, and as he and eleven other men, including Sam Woodson, walked in and took their places on bench seats at a long table, a couple of women brought out fresh platters of food. The Kid was surprised to see that one of them was Florita.

Her face was set in stiff lines and seemed to be drawn in pain. She moved as if each step hurt her. But she did what she was supposed to do. When she turned her back, the Kid saw several places where blood had spotted her shirt.

Some of the men looked at her in apparent sympathy, but others didn't care about the agonizing ordeal she had gone through. More than one reached up to pat her on the rear end as she passed them, and a couple even landed outright slaps.

The second time that happened, Woodson said, "Here now, there's no call for that."

The offender, a skinny Mexican, bared his teeth at Woodson and said, "You really want to defend this *puta*, Texan? You want a sample of what my people gave yours at the Alamo?"

That was the wrong thing to say. Even the Kid knew that. Woodson sprang up and burst out, "How about what happened to you greasers at San Jacinto, huh? When ol' Santy Anny pissed his drawers and tried to pretend he was a woman so us Texicans wouldn't catch him and give him what he had comin'! Hell, to save his life, he'd'a prob'ly got down on his knees and—"

The Mexican was on his feet, too. He snarled, reached for the knife at his belt, and started toward Woodson, but a voice barked from the doorway, "Sit down, or I'll shoot both of you."

The two would-be combatants froze as Kern stalked into the room, followed by Carl Bracken.

"I said, sit down," Kern snapped.

Reluctantly, Woodson and the Mexican resumed their seats. The glares they traded showed their hostility hadn't really diminished, though.

Kern hooked his thumbs in his gun belt and went on, "All of you know the general's ordered that there'll be no fighting among ourselves. I intend to enforce that order. Now, I need to talk to some of you."

"We just sat down to eat, Kern," one of the Americans complained.

"So fill up your plates and bring them with you," Kern said. "I'm not going to stand around and wait for you." He jerked a thumb toward the door. "Woodson, Callahan, Martell, Benitez, Gonzales, Eagleton, Smith. Come with me."

The Kid filled a plate with stew, grabbed a chunk of bread to go with it, and picked up a cup of coffee to take along as well. He and the other men Kern had named followed the gunman outside and into the building that would be Ramirez's "second capital" if he ever became *presidente*.

More men were waiting for them there, passing around bottles of whiskey and tequila. Some of the men who had brought cups of coffee with them from the mess hall borrowed the bottles and splashed liquor into their coffee.

A map hung on the wall of the room where they were gathered. This train robbery really was being planned like a military operation, the Kid thought. Kern tapped a finger on the map and said, "The train will enter these hills right here. The approach is a long grade where the train will have to slow down enough for some of us to catch up to it on horseback and swing onto the platforms between the last few cars. The rest of us will be waiting at the top of the grade, where the tracks go between some cutbanks.

We're going to collapse one of those banks and block the tracks. The train will be forced to stop, and we'll already have control of the back end of it. We'll take the locomotive and work our way along the rest of the cars until we find that gold we're after."

"Are we gonna get what we can from the passengers while we're at it?" one of the men asked.

Kern nodded and said, "Yeah, as long as you don't let it distract you from our real mission. Any money and jewelry they have on them will likely be chickenfeed compared to that gold shipment."

"And if anybody gives us trouble?" Bracken asked. The Kid had a feeling the gunman already knew the answer to that question. The Kid had a pretty good idea himself.

"Kill them," Kern said. "But don't go out of your way to gun people down as long as they're cooperating."

Bracken grinned. He would find an excuse to kill somebody before the day was over tomorrow. The Kid felt certain of that.

He had been able to stand by and do nothing while Florita was whipped, even though it had been one of the most difficult things he had ever done. He didn't believe he would be able to do the same if some innocent person's life was in danger. Frank wouldn't want him to do that.

Maybe if he could come up with some way to keep the robbery from going off as planned . . . The wheels of his brain began to turn. Lost in thought as he was, he almost didn't hear Kern say, "Callahan, you'll be with me."

"What?" the Kid said.

"You're riding with me tomorrow." Kern smiled faintly. "The general trusts you, so I reckon I do, too. But it never hurts to keep an eye on a new man for the first few jobs. We don't know how you're going to react to things, after all."

The Kid shrugged and said, "Suit yourself. It doesn't matter to me. The only thing I care about is that gold."

"Then you won't have any trouble."

The Kid wasn't so sure about that. The task he had set for himself had just gotten harder. The task of keeping innocent blood from being spilled . . .

# Chapter 25

Twenty men rode out from the hacienda the next morning. The Kid was among them, riding in the middle of the pack next to Sam Woodson, who had brought his guitar along, carrying it on his back by a sling he had attached to it. Kern had glared at him but didn't tell him to leave the instrument behind.

"Where'd you pick up the habit of carrying that guitar?" the Kid asked as they rode.

"Oh, back in Texas when I was a kid. I was a mite on the wild side, y'understand, and strummin' on it sorta calms my nerves. Kern don't like it when I bring it along on a job. The first coupla times, he told me that if my geetar caused anything to go wrong, he was gonna take it and plant it where the sun don't shine. Then he'd kill me. But he figured out I just like to have it along. It ain't like I'm gonna start playin' while we're laid up somewheres waitin' to ambush somebody. That'd be plumb stupid. So he don't like it, but he puts up with it 'cause he knows I'm a good hand to have around on these jobs."

The Kid didn't doubt that. The walnut grips of Woodson's Colt showed enough wear to indicate that the gun had been used plenty of times.

Unlike in Texas, where the Rio Grande was a clear, unmistakable boundary between the two countries, here in Arizona it was possible to cross from the United States into Mexico without ever realizing it. After the outlaws had ridden for a couple of hours, the Kid was sure they had to be south of the border by now. When Kern called a halt to let them rest the horses, he stayed in the saddle long enough to take a pair of field glasses from his saddlebags and peer through them at the horizon.

"I can see the hills where we'll take the train," he said as he put the glasses away. "We should be there in plenty of time. The train's not due until the middle of the afternoon."

"You know these Mexican trains," Bracken commented. "You can't count on them being anywhere close to on time. No greaser ever kept to a schedule yet."

One of the Mexicans laughed and said, "And my people do not have the pains in the belly that plague you gringos, Bracken. That is because we know how to enjoy life and not worry all the time like you *norteamericanos*."

"Let your horses drink a little," Kern ordered. "But not too much. This is dry country."

He didn't really need to point that out. The landscape was arid as far as the eye could see. The only vegetation was scrub brush and an occasional clump of hardy grass.

The Kid took off his hat, poured a little water into it from his canteen, and let the buckskin drink. He rubbed the horse's ears. They had been down a lot of hard, lonely trails together. Before much longer, it would be time to put the buckskin out to pasture. But not yet. They still had some adventuring to do together.

The group set out again a short time later. It wasn't long

before the hills were visible to the naked eye. As usual out here in this region of mostly flat terrain and clear, dry air, they appeared closer than they actually were. The sun was directly overhead before the riders reached the rugged, brush-dotted slopes. A few stunted pines grew atop the hills, as well.

They pushed southward, keeping the hills to the west, the riders' right, and soon something else came into sight: a line of telegraph poles stretching off into the distance to the east.

The Kid said to Sam Woodson, "I reckon the telegraph line follows the railroad?"

"That's right. We've hit trains before, in different places than this. Kern always likes to cut the wires so nobody from the train crew can shinny up a pole with a telegraph key, tap in, and get word to the Rurales about what's happened."

"Speaking of the Rurales, don't they patrol this area?"

"Yeah, but they're spread pretty thin and the general's got somebody on the inside with 'em, so he usually has a pretty good idea when they ain't gonna be around."

"The general has agents who support him in a lot of places, doesn't he?" the Kid asked.

"Yeah, and that's why if he ever gets his hands on enough dinero, he stands a real good chance of topplin' ol' Díaz and takin' his place as king."

"President," the Kid said.

"King, president, emperor . . . it don't much matter what you call 'em. As long as they run things and got the power o' life and death over folks, they're the big boss, and that's all that matters."

The Kid couldn't argue with that logic.

The rails themselves were visible now, twin lines of

steel running parallel on the slightly raised roadbed. When Ramirez's men reached them, they turned and followed the rails west toward the hills.

A quarter of a mile from the base of the slopes, they came to an arroyo running north and south with a trestle spanning it. Kern reined in, and as the Kid followed suit, he lifted his eyes and traced the railroad's route up into the hills. The slopes pressed in fairly close on both sides of the tracks, but there was enough room for men to ride their horses alongside the train. They would need to be careful, though. If a horse tripped and fell, its rider might be thrown to a hideous death under those rapidly turning wheels.

Kern pointed to the top of the grade and said, "The ground levels out right on the other side of those cutbanks. That's why we'll stop it there. We don't want the engineer pouring on the steam and picking up speed." He looked around at the others and started pointing out men. "You, you, you . . ." He kept that up until he had picked nine men, including the Kid and Woodson. "You'll be with me down here in the arroyo. The rest of you head up to the cutbanks with Bracken and get to work caving in one of them and blocking the tracks. Cut the telegraph wire, too."

"We're going to wait in the arroyo until the train goes past?" the Kid asked.

"That's right."

"I'm assuming that the hombres who are shipping that gold will have hired guards to protect it."

An ugly smile twisted Bracken's face as he said, "Aren't you the smart one, Callahan." It was a gibe, not a question.

The Kid held on to his temper, which wasn't easy since Carl Bracken would rub a saint the wrong way.

"What I mean is, they're liable to be watching for trouble. They might spot us down in that arroyo."

Kern said, "That's why we're going to be under that trestle. They won't be able to see us under there."

The Kid nodded. The trestle was small enough that ten men on horseback might have a little trouble fitting under it, but he supposed they could manage.

"They'll have a man on the rear platform of the caboose, more than likely," Kern went on. "He's the first one we'll pick off."

The first man they would murder, the Kid thought. That idea gnawed at him. He was going to try to prevent that, but it wouldn't be easy.

He couldn't stop all the killing, he told himself bleakly. Not without warning the train crew and the gold guards that the holdup was about to take place, and if he did that, Kern, Bracken, and the other men would blast him full of holes. He had to wait until they were distracted, then in the confusion of the robbery he would gun down as many of them as he could and hope the guards would do for the others.

Then he could head back to the hacienda as the only survivor of the failed raid and resume trying to figure out a way to rescue Frank. It wasn't a bloodless solution, and he knew the general would be mighty suspicious of him, but he didn't see any other way to prevent as much slaughter as possible and keep that gold out of Ramirez's hands.

Now that Kern had split up the group of bandits, Bracken took his bunch and rode off up the railroad grade toward the top. Kern and the others let their horses pick their way down into the arroyo, which was about ten feet deep and maybe thirty feet wide. Flash floods had eroded the banks until they weren't too steep or sheer.

Kern told the men to dismount, then said, "Lead the horses under the trestle. Oscar, you and Timms will be responsible for holding them. The rest of you can take it easy until the train is about to get here. I'll keep watch."

He took out his field glasses and trudged back to the top of the arroyo, where he sat down on a low slab of rock to peer into the east, where the gold train would come from.

"We're lucky," Sam Woodson said to the Kid with his characteristic grin. "We get to wait in the shade while Bracken and them other boys are up there a-laborin' in the hot sun like poor farmers. I knowed the life of a desperado was for me."

He had pulled the guitar around in front of him, and now his fingers strayed over the strings, plucking them and sending a cascade of musical notes into the air.

"Nobody asked for a serenade, Woodson," Kern called down into the arroyo.

"Just passin' the time," Woodson replied. "If you want me to stop, Kern, just say so."

Kern shook his head. "No, I reckon there are worse things than that racket you call music."

"He likes it, really," Woodson said quietly to the Kid. "He just won't admit it."

If he got the chance, the Kid told himself, he would wallop Woodson over the head and knock him out, rather than killing him. More than likely it would end just as badly for him if he was caught by the gold guards and turned over to the Rurales, but the Kid couldn't take responsibility for the lawless life that had led Woodson to this juncture. He just didn't want to blow the hombre's lights out himself if he could avoid it.

An hour dragged by in the heat. Woodson got tired of playing the guitar and singing. He sat down in the shade underneath the trestle, leaned against one of the thick wooden pillars holding it up, tipped his hat down over his eyes, and went to sleep.

The Kid climbed up the bank to join Kern, who cast a suspicious glance at him and asked, "What do you want?"

"Just thought I'd help you watch for that train," the Kid drawled. "Not that that'll make it get here any sooner."

Kern grunted. "I don't need any help. But I guess you might as well wait up here as down there. Just don't start talking my ear off the way Woodson always tries to."

"Not likely." The Kid gazed off to the east. "I *am* a mite curious, though. You don't strike me as the sort of fella to get mixed up in a revolution. You're no firebrand like Ramirez."

"I'm not doing it out of any fondness for Mexico, if that's what you're thinking. I don't care who runs that bunch of bean-eaters. The general pays well when he's got money, though. And there's Señorita Antonia—"

Kern stopped short, glared, and looked away, as if he'd realized that he had said too much.

"The señorita *is* a mighty fine looker," the Kid said. He didn't mention the pleasure she had taken in watching Kern whip Florita, which made her considerably less beautiful in his eyes.

"Just forget I said anything," Kern grated. "The señorita's going to be parading around the palace in Mexico City like a princess one of these days, and I'll be either dead or long gone."

"Maybe. You never know how things will play out."

"I know how this will," Kern snapped. "Leave it alone, Callahan."

"Sure, amigo," the Kid said easily. "I didn't hear a damn thing . . . except maybe . . . a train whistle?"

"Damn it!" Kern jerked the field glasses to his eyes. "You got me distracted. That's why I didn't want anybody up here with me."

That wasn't what had distracted Kern, the Kid mused. Thinking about Antonia Ramirez had done that . . . and daring to hope that he might have a chance with her someday. The Kid didn't believe that would ever happen . . . but every man's dreams were his own private province, and no one else could set their boundaries.

"I don't see anything," Kern said after a moment of looking through the field glasses. "You must have imagined what you thought you heard—Wait. There's . . . Yeah, it's smoke from the locomotive." He lowered the glasses. "Here it comes."

He slid down the bank with the Kid right behind him and called to the other men, "Mount up! The train will be here in a few minutes."

An air of excitement gripped them as they swung up into their saddles. Shafts of sunlight slanted down through the gaps in the trestle and painted men and horses with a checkerboard pattern. They were pressed close together as they waited tensely.

The rumble coming through the rails overhead grew steadily louder as the vibrations increased. The Kid could hear the *chuff-chuff-chuff* of the engine as well. He didn't know why the engineer had blown the whistle a short time earlier—there wasn't anything out here in the middle of nowhere to get in the train's way—but the man was laying off it now.

The noise was tremendous as the locomotive reached the trestle and roared over it, blotting out those stray beams of sunlight. The earth itself shook underneath the horses' hooves. Having those untold tons of metal passing directly overhead, only a few feet away, was a discomforting thing. The Kid had never experienced anything quite like it before.

Beside him, Sam Woodson made a face and said something, but with that deafening racket going on, the Kid couldn't understand a word of it. He could tell that Woodson wasn't happy, though. None of them were. Even when the locomotive had passed beyond the trestle and started up the grade, the noise of the railroad cars traversing it was still tooth-rattling and nerve-racking.

Finally, the caboose cleared the trestle. The assault on the Kid's ears had been so fierce he wasn't sure he would ever be able to hear correctly again. But to his surprise, he heard Kern fairly well when the bandit bellowed, "Let's go!" and waved his men into motion.

The riders charged out from under the trestle, five to a side. Their horses lunged up the arroyo banks, and the chase was on.

# Chapter 26

The Kid rode to the right of the tracks with Kern, Woodson, and a couple of Mexicans whose names he didn't know. The horses' hooves pounded on the hard-packed ground. The train had gotten about a fifty-yard lead along the tracks while the men were getting out of the arroyo. The train was still moving fast because the lo-comotive hadn't quite reached the grade, which meant it was pulling away from the riders.

That didn't last long. The train slowed as soon as the engine started up the slope, and then the men on horse-back began to gain on it.

As the Kid expected, a man stood guard on the platform at the back of the caboose. Smoke wreathed from the cigar he was smoking. He hadn't noticed the pursuers right away, but now he did and he reacted violently. He threw the cigar away, raised a Winchester to his shoulder, and blazed away at the outlaws as fast as he could work the rifle's lever.

The riders were close enough to return the fire with their handguns, although the range was fairly long for a revolver. Their shots came closer with each swift stride of the horses, though. The Kid saw sparks flying as bullets ricocheted from the rear end of the caboose and the railing around the platform.

The hurricane deck of a galloping horse was no place for accuracy, but the Kid had experience making such shots. The buckskin had an uncommonly smooth gait, too. Instead of firing wildly at the caboose, the Kid raised his Colt and drew a bead on the guard, aiming low. He squeezed off two rounds and saw the man fling the rifle away and twist around as he fell to the platform. The Kid was pretty sure he had drilled the man through the thigh, a serious wound but probably not fatal.

The caboose's rear door opened and arms reached out. Hands caught hold of the guard's clothes and dragged him inside. The door slammed.

"Come on!" Kern bellowed as he urged his horse to greater speed. Now that they were no longer charging into a hail of bullets, they could close in on the train even faster.

By now the men in the caboose would have signaled the engineer to pour on the steam. Huge gouts of smoke billowed from the locomotive's diamond-shaped stack. But with the slope the train was climbing, it could go only so fast, no matter how hard the engineer pushed it.

Rifle muzzles poked through open windows in the caboose. Flame spurted from the muzzles. But the angle was bad and made it difficult for the men inside the train to get a good shot at the outlaws chasing it.

The Kid and the others were climbing now, too, riding single file at the edge of the roadbed while the hill crowded in close on the other side. Kern was in the lead, with the Kid right behind him, then the two Mexicans, and finally Sam Woodson bringing up the rear. The horses had to slow down because they were going uphill, too, but they still moved faster than the train.

Kern reached the caboose and drew even with the platform. He forced his horse even closer and leaned far to his left in the saddle as he reached for the railing. He caught hold of it, kicked his feet free of the stirrups, and leaped from the saddle as he grabbed for the railing with his other hand, too. He snagged it and was able to swing onto the platform with surprising agility considering his stocky build.

Kern's horse kept running and pulled ahead, which gave the Kid room to maneuver the buckskin alongside the platform. He repeated Kern's daring move, grasping the railing and plunging from horseback to railroad car. His heart seemed to catch in his throat during that split second when he hung in midair between the two.

Then his boots hit the platform and he stumbled a little as he caught his balance. He had holstered his gun to make the transfer, as had Kern. Both of them pulled their irons now. Kern waved the other men on. It would be their job to take control of the next few cars in line.

"I'll kick the door open," Kern said over the train's clatter. "You go in low and fast."

The Kid nodded, but he had no intention of following that order. Instead, when Kern stepped in front of the door and lifted his right leg to kick it in, the Kid struck first, slamming the gun in his hand against Kern's head. The other riders had galloped on past the caboose, so none of them saw what happened.

Kern's knees buckled from the unexpected blow. He sagged forward against the door and held himself up with one hand while the other tried to swing the gun around toward the Kid. He gasped, "You bas—"

The Kid batted Kern's gun aside and struck again with his own before the outlaw could finish the oath. Kern went down to the platform, out cold.

The Kid dragged Kern over to one side, then rapped on the door with his gun barrel and raised his voice.

"Listen to me in there! Hold your fire! I'm not an outlaw! Don't shoot when I open this door!"

Leaning over, he grasped the knob with his left hand, twisted it, and gave the door a hard shove. Just as he expected, despite his shout, as soon as the door flew open the men inside the caboose started shooting. Guns roared and lead stormed through the doorway. The Kid waited with his back pressed against the caboose's rear wall, feeling the train rocking along as it continued up the grade.

The guns fell silent. The Kid called again, "Hold your fire! You're in no danger!"

An American voice replied, "Mister, I don't know who you are, but if you think we're gonna let you waltz in here and kill us, you're crazy."

"They call me Kid Morgan," the Kid said. He didn't know if that would mean anything to any of them or not. "Those men with me are part of Diego Ramirez's bunch, but I'm not one of them. I've just been pretending to be. I'm trying to stop this holdup."

"Ramirez!" the man inside the caboose exclaimed. "He's after the gold!"

"Yeah, I'm afraid so. I know it was supposed to be a secret, but it wasn't a very good one. If you'll let me in there without ventilating me, we'll figure out some way to stop them."

"Throw your guns in here first, then step in!"

"And have you boys get spooked and shoot me full of holes?" The Kid laughed. "I don't reckon so, fella. I'm coming in, and if any lead comes my way, I'll answer it in kind."

"All right," the man said with obvious reluctance. "Hold your fire, men."

He might be saying that while motioning for the men with him to do just the opposite, but the Kid had to take that chance. With his Colt ready, he stepped through the doorway and took a long stride into the caboose.

Five men were in there, counting the wounded man who was lying on an old sofa and had a bloody rag tied around his leg. An elderly, blue-uniformed Mexican conductor with a stiff-billed black cap on his head stood next to a squat safe, looking scared. A burly, middle-aged American in a gray suit and cream-colored Stetson held a shotgun pointed toward the Kid. Flanking him were two Mexicans with rifles.

The American said, "Damn, son, for somebody who claims not to be an outlaw, you're doing a mighty good imitation of one."

"I had to play along with that bunch or get killed," the Kid said. "Why don't we all lower our weapons?" The Colt in his hand was leveled at the American.

The man shrugged and said, "Considering the odds, I suppose we can give it a try. I doubt you can kill more than one of us before the others blow you to hell."

The Kid wasn't so sure about that—he believed he could get at least two of them—but he wasn't going to argue the point. He lowered the Colt until it pointed at the floor. The other men did likewise with their weapons.

The wounded man, another American, said, "Colonel, I think he's the one who shot me!"

The colonel asked, "Is that true?"

"I figured he'd rather have a bullet through the leg than half a dozen in his guts and heart and head," the Kid said. "I was trying to save his life."

The colonel grunted, then said, "Odd way of doing it . . . but I reckon it worked. You mind telling me what's going on here?"

"Like I said, those men ride for Diego Ramirez. Since the Rurales chased him out of Mexico, he's found himself a stronghold not far over the border in Arizona Territory."

The colonel nodded. "I'm familiar with Ramirez. He's the main reason we have guards on this train. The men I work for were worried that he might come after their gold. My name's Haas, by the way. George Haas."

"That other fella called you Colonel?"

"Retired," Haas said with a slight smile. "I had my fill of the military."

"So now you work for Mexican aristocrats."

"I work for whoever pays my wages. How about you? If you're not an outlaw, how'd you get mixed up with that bunch of *bandidos*?"

"It's a long story," the Kid said. "The important thing is, this train is coming to a stop pretty soon. Do you have enough men to hold off Ramirez's bunch?"

"I've got what you see."

The Kid caught his breath in surprise. "Just three of you?"

"There were four, until you shot one of 'em," Haas said dryly. "The gold shipment was supposed to be a secret, remember? We didn't want to draw attention to it."

His eyes darted over toward the safe. The Kid saw that and said, "You mean that's where it is, not in an express car or something like that?"

"It's just as safe here as it would be anywhere on this train. The walls of this caboose are nice and thick."

"Thick enough to hold off an army?"

"I reckon we'll find out, because those bandits aren't getting that gold."

A shudder went through the floor under the Kid's feet. That was the brakes being applied, he thought. The train began to slow, and he knew the locomotive had reached the barrier at the top of the grade.

"You'd better get ready," he said. "You're about to be under attack."

"I don't think so." Haas turned toward the door at the front of the caboose. He reached under his coat to take something out of his pocket. The Kid caught a glimpse of a paper-wrapped cylinder.

"What the hell!" he said. "Is that dynamite?"

"Thought it might come in handy," Haas said as he opened the door. Shots immediately blasted from outside, coming from the platform of the next car in line. The Kid knew Ramirez's men must have captured it and were ready for the guards to try to defend the gold.

They probably weren't expecting dynamite, though. As bullets chewed at the doorjamb, flew into the caboose, and started ricocheting around, Haas calmly struck a match and lit the short fuse attached to the cylinder. With a quick, underhand flip, he threw the dynamite across the space between the cars and through the open door on the other side. The Kid heard shouts of alarm, then a blast shook the train as smoke and fire filled the space above the coupling.

Everything had happened too quickly for the Kid to stop it. He was thrown off-balance for a second as the caboose suddenly lurched backward. He caught himself, peered through the open door, and saw that the dynamite had blown the whole back end off the next car.

The explosion had busted the coupling loose as well. The caboose was no longer attached to the rest of the train, and gravity began to take effect. The caboose's weight pulled it back down the slope. It rolled faster and faster as its momentum built up.

"Well," Haas said. "I didn't think about that happen—"

Blood and brains flew in the air as a bullet sizzling in from somewhere blew off a good-sized chunk of his head. He stood there for a second, dead on his feet, before he pitched forward in a gory sprawl. The blood-splattered old conductor shrieked in horror as he quailed back against the safe that held the gold.

The two Mexican guards screamed curses and jerked their rifles toward the Kid. He knew that they somehow blamed him for what had happened to their boss, and in their panic, they opened fire on him.

Bullets whined around him. One of them struck him in the side and knocked him halfway around. He didn't know how badly he was hit, but bad enough to make him drop his gun as he fell to one knee. He was about to lunge after the Colt, knowing that he wouldn't reach it before the two guards killed him.

Before that could happen, shots slammed from the rear of the caboose. The Kid felt the wind-rip of slugs above his head. The bullets thudded into the chests of the guards and drove them back against the wall behind them. They still tried to bring their rifles to bear, but strength deserted them and they collapsed. The rifles clattered to the floor.

The Kid looked over his shoulder and saw Kern striding into the caboose with a Colt in his hand. Kern pivoted sharply and fired again. The wounded guard, who had been trying to struggle up from the sofa, fell back with a red-rimmed black hole in the middle of his forehead.

The Kid made a grab for his gun, but it had slid toward the rear of the caboose and Kern got to it first. He kicked it out of the Kid's reach and leveled the still-smoking revolver at him.

"The only reason I killed them, you double-crosser, is so I can kill you myself."

# Chapter 27

The door at the rear of the caboose was still open. As the Kid looked past Kern, he saw the tracks and the telegraph poles and the hillsides rushing past the train. It looked that way from his perspective, anyway.

"You'd better hold off on pulling that trigger, Kern," he said, raising his voice to be heard above the wind. With open doors at both ends of the caboose, air gusted through the car with a rising roar as it went faster and faster. "It may take both of us to stop this runaway before it jumps the tracks!"

Kern grimaced, but he didn't fire. One man might be able to turn the brake wheel on top of the caboose with enough force to slow it down, but there was a chance he couldn't. The elderly conductor wasn't likely to be of any help, either.

"The caboose will slow down once it's out on the flats again," Kern said.

"But will it stay on the tracks when it hits the bottom of this slope going full out?" the Kid countered. "You willing to bet your life on that, Kern?"

The gunman glowered darkly, but he gestured with his

revolver and ordered, "Get out there on that front platform. Don't make a try for any of those guns that got dropped, either, or I *will* shoot you and take my chances."

The Kid nodded as he got to his feet. His lips pulled back from his teeth as pain rippled through him.

"I'm wounded, you know."

"Just live long enough for me to put a bullet in your treacherous heart, that's all I care about."

"You don't make me want to help you all that much," the Kid said as he turned toward the front of the caboose.

"You'll do it anyway or die sooner."

That was a persuasive argument. And the Kid could already tell that he wasn't badly hurt. The bullet had grazed along his right side, just below the ribs. It hurt like blazes and his shirt was wet and sticky with blood, but he wouldn't die from it.

He stepped out onto the platform. The rest of the train was dwindling in the distance above him, where it had come to a stop. The explosion had derailed the last car, so the train wouldn't be able to move again until that car was cut loose, too.

But that was somebody else's worry. The Kid's main concern right now was staying alive for the next few minutes.

All his plans had been derailed as much as that railroad car had. If he could get away from Kern, he might be able to find the buckskin and ride away from here. Unfortunately, the rest of Ramirez's men would be headed back down the hill within minutes to find out what had happened. Dodging them on foot would be impossible. Even mounted, getting away would be very difficult.

The Kid wasn't the sort to give up, though. Right now

the very real danger of the caboose wrecking loomed over him and Kern and the conductor.

"Get up there," Kern said, motioning to the grab irons on the caboose's side. The Kid took hold of the crude ladder, swung out onto it, and began to climb.

Here on the outside of the car, the wind created by its runaway journey down the long hill was even stronger. It slammed at the Kid and threatened to tear him loose from his precarious position. He pulled himself up by the grab irons as quickly and carefully as he could and when he reached the top, he sprawled on it and spread his arms and legs for stability.

Kern poked his head and the gun above the level of the caboose's roof. "Get down there to that brake wheel!" he shouted.

The Kid lifted his head and saw the wheel sticking up on a metal post at the caboose's rear end. Still spread-eagled, he worked his way to the center of the car and then was able to get up on hands and knees and crawl. After a few feet, he trusted his balance to stand up and trot toward the brake. He hoped the caboose wouldn't give a particularly violent lurch and throw him off before he got there.

He reached his objective and grasped the wheel, feeling a little better once he had something to hang on to. By now, Kern had holstered his gun and climbed on top of the caboose, too. The Kid turned the wheel, putting his strength and weight into the effort, and he heard an unholy squealing like a million demons in the pits of hell as the shaft turned and forced the brake pads against the wheels.

The caboose slowed, but only barely. Kern reached the wheel, grabbed it, and threw his strength into the effort, too. The caboose slowed more. The bottom of the grade was coming up quickly. The Kid and Kern both grunted as they renewed their struggle with the wheel.

The caboose was still going fast enough when it reached the bottom that it thumped heavily, but it didn't come loose from the rails and crash. And Kern had been right: once on the level again, it began to slow down even more.

Now that they were safe, Kern's hand flashed toward his holstered gun, but the Kid moved first by a heartbeat. He tackled Kern around the waist, and both of them sprawled on the caboose's roof as it continued to roll along the tracks.

Kern smashed a fist into the Kid's wounded side. For a second, the pain was blinding. The Kid did his best to ignore it and rammed the heel of his hand under Kern's jaw, forcing the gunman's head back. Kern hit him in the side again. The Kid rolled so the wound would be out of Kern's reach and tried to bring a kick around.

Kern grabbed his leg and heaved up. The Kid had no choice but to go with it, but as he twisted, he looped an arm around Kern's neck and dragged him along, too. Both of them rolled toward the roof's edge.

The Kid slapped his other hand against the roof and pressed hard, trying to slow himself. He fought for any sort of purchase. But while he was doing that, Kern rammed an elbow into his solar plexus and forced all the air out of his lungs. Gasping for breath, the Kid slid off the roof and plummeted toward the ground. Kern was right beside him.

Luckily for them, the caboose had almost come to a stop, so they didn't have much momentum. They landed on the sandy ground beside the roadbed and each rolled over a couple of times. The fall was enough to stun the Kid. He lay there on his belly and tried to force his brain and muscles to obey his commands.

His ears worked all right. He heard a swift rataplan of hoofbeats thudding closer, then stopping, and when he was finally able to lift his head and look around, he saw Carl Bracken, Sam Woodson, and a couple more of Ramirez's men sitting on horseback beside the railroad tracks. Woodson was leading the Kid's buckskin.

"Kern, what the hell happened?" Bracken demanded. "We heard some sort of explosion, and then the caboose was flying back down the hill."

Kern was breathless, too. He gasped for air and said, "Cover . . . cover him! Callahan! Damn . . . traitor!"

That was enough for Bracken. He whipped his gun out, and the lust to kill was bright in his eyes.

"Double-crossed us, did he? I'll take care of him, Kern—"

"Wait just a damn minute!" Woodson's gun was out, too, but it pointed at Bracken. "Don't go pullin' that trigger until we know for sure what's goin' on here."

Bracken snarled. "You don't want to do that, you damn ridge runner—"

Kern pushed himself up into a sitting position and said, "Both of you . . . take it easy. Keep Callahan . . . covered. What about . . . the rest of the train?"

"Nobody's going to give us any more trouble," Bracken replied. "We had to shoot the fireman and a couple of passengers, and that was enough to convince everybody else they'd better cooperate. I left enough men up there to keep an eye on things. We need to get back and look for that gold, though. Funny thing, we didn't run into any guards."

Kern pointed to the caboose, which had come to a stop about twenty-five yards to the east. He said, "It's in there. They put it in a safe in the caboose and tried not to draw attention to it by not sending along a bunch of guards. Damn fools."

He motioned to one of the other men, who dismounted and helped him to his feet.

"I heard them talking about it," Kern went on. "Callahan, or whatever the hell his name is, thought I was still knocked out. Reckon I came to sooner than he expected me to."

He should have busted Kern's skull wide open when he had the chance, the Kid thought bitterly.

"Get him on his feet and back on his horse," Kern ordered.

"We're not gonna kill him?" Bracken wanted to know. "Maybe find a nice ant hill and stake him out on it, like the Apaches do?"

Kern shook his head and said, "No, I was going to kill him at first, too, but I've decided we're going to take him back to the hacienda. The general can figure out what to do with him. I've got a hunch, though, that before it's over he may be wishing we'd gone ahead and found those ants."


By the evening of Frank's failed escape attempt, his headache had subsided to the point that he could ignore it. Conrad had done a good job of hitting him hard enough to knock him out without doing any permanent damage. Frank *hoped* he had suffered no permanent damage, anyway; he reckoned it might take a while to be sure about that.

He figured that under the circumstances, Ramirez

might order that he didn't get any supper, but footsteps sounded in the corridor about the usual time. When the door was unlocked and opened, though, it wasn't one of the girls who brought him his meal. Instead, one of the Mexican revolutionaries carried in the food, and two more gun-wolves accompanied him. All three of them stood there and watched him eat a plate of cornbread and beans and drink a cup of the watery coffee. Two pointed shotguns at him, while the third leveled a long-barreled Remington .44.

"You fellas must be really bored if you think this is an interesting way to pass the time," Frank said around a mouthful of cornbread.

"Shut up and eat, gringo," one of the Mexicans said.

When he was finished, they collected his plate and cup, then one of the shotgunners grinned and said, "You ought to be real proud of yourself, Morgan, considerin' what you caused to happen to that gal."

Frank's head snapped up. "What are you talking about?"

"Florita. The general had her punished for tryin' to help you escape."

Frank couldn't stop himself. He surged to his feet. The men stepped back and trained their weapons on him as their faces got intent . . . and a little bit nervous.

"That poor girl didn't do anything—" Frank began.

"Don't bother lyin' about it. Bracken found the key to this cell in her pocket. She wouldn't have had it on her if she hadn't unlocked the door for you."

Frank had never been a man who cursed a lot, but he bit back an oath now. The guards didn't have the straight of things, exactly, but it didn't matter. Ramirez had found out that Florita had done *something* to help Frank, and that was enough. He supposed that after she had locked the cell door when they stashed Hardy in here, she had slipped the key into her pocket and forgotten about it, what with everything else that had happened.

"What did the general do? Is Florita all right?"

"She's alive, if that's what you're worried about. The general decided she had five lashes with a whip comin' to her. Kern dealt 'em out. He put his back into it, too."

Kern would die for that, Frank vowed. But someone else was even more to blame than the gunman.

*Diego Ramirez.* The debt the so-called general had to pay just kept growing larger.

"You settle down now, Morgan, and hope that boy of yours comes through with the ransom," one of the men said as they backed out of the cell. "I suspect the general is startin' to get a mite impatient."

Another man added, "Maybe he should start cutting pieces off Morgan and sending them to the boy to convince him, no?"

That gave all of them a good laugh as the door clanged shut.

Anger seethed inside Frank the rest of that night and, after a few hours of restless sleep, into the next day. Another trio of armed men brought him his breakfast, but in the middle of the day, Beatriz came into the cell carrying a tray, accompanied by two of the bandits.

Frank stood up to take it from her and asked quietly, "Your cousin Florita, how is she?"

Beatriz looked down and didn't reply.

"I'm sorry," Frank said. "I never meant for anything—"

"Step back, Morgan," one of the guards snapped. "Girl, you get out of here."

Beatriz started to turn away, but as she did, Frank said, "The time's coming, Beatriz. This isn't going to stand."

Both guards chuckled at that. One of them said, "Sure, Morgan. Make promises you can't keep. Convince all those peons to get their hopes up. We'll just see what happens when our boys get back with that gold."

"What gold?"

The other guard took hold of Beatriz's arm and pushed her out of the cell. He glared at the other man as if telling him to shut up. They both went out, and the door slammed behind them.

Frank settled down to eat. As he did, he thought about what he had just heard. Some of the men had gone somewhere to get some gold. Nobody would just turn over riches to them, so that meant a robbery of some sort. They had gone to hold up a bank or a train.

More than likely, Ramirez would have sent a decent-sized force to carry out such a raid. So the number of men here at the stronghold had to be smaller than usual. A good time to make a move against Ramirez, Frank mused. Maybe Conrad would realize the same thing.

If Conrad was still here. The wild thought crossed Frank's mind that Ramirez might have sent him with the others after that gold. He was convinced that Conrad was trying to work his way into the gang, and what better way to find out if a new man could be trusted than to send him along on a big job?

Unfortunately, locked in this cell, with his captors more alert than ever now, there wasn't a thing he could do except wait. And waiting for action was mighty hard on a man like Frank Morgan . . .

The rest of that day was long. Beatriz brought his supper but again wouldn't speak to him or even look at him. She and Juana probably hated him because of what had happened to Florita, even though it wasn't his fault.

The guards didn't turn down the lamp at the end of the corridor at night, so the dim yellow light stayed the same all the time. It didn't keep Frank from sleeping, so it didn't matter to him. After spending some time, as usual, moving around as much as he could in order to keep his muscles loose, he stretched out uncomfortably on the floor and tried to doze off.

He hadn't yet fallen asleep when he heard a hoot of laughter from one of the guards. The man said loudly, "Now, this is more like it! It's damn well about time the general did somethin' for us poor fellas stuck down here in the dungeon in the middle of the night."

Frank stood up and moved to the little window in the door. Something stirred his instincts, a feeling in his gut that he needed to listen to this.

"Keep your voice down, amigo," another man said, his accent marking him as one of the Mexicans. "Never draw attention to something good. Other men will just try to take it away from you."

"Nobody's takin' this," the gringo guard said. "Hell, I'm surprised they let you down here in the first place, girl."

A woman's voice said, "My cousins are upstairs with your friends, keeping them amused. But it was not fair to leave you two hombres with no tequila and no company."

"Your cousin's the one who got whipped, ain't she?"

That made the visitor Beatriz.

"I have more than one cousin," she answered. "But all of them are beautiful."

"I'll bet. Just like you. Gimme that jug, Paco."

Frank smiled in the semidarkness. You could buy a man's skill with a gun . . . but you couldn't make him less stupid.

He heard more bold talk and more laughter from the other end of the corridor, followed ten minutes later by raucous snores that came from a pair of throats. Then quick footsteps along the hall from a slender, darting shape and the scrape of a key in the lock.

"Señor Morgan," Beatriz said, "this time you are getting out of here."

Frank was about to reply to her when an explosion boomed through the hacienda.

# Chapter 28

He felt the vibrations from the blast through his boot soles. A second later Beatriz jerked the door open and said, "We must go!"

Frank knew she was right. He had a hunch the explosion was a distraction to help him escape. He charged out of the cell and ran with her toward the stairs.

The two guards sprawled in their chairs, sound asleep from whatever Beatriz had used to dope the tequila. She glanced at them, and her lip curled as she said, "They are lucky I did not put poison in the jug!"

"You don't want their lives on your conscience," Frank told her as he plucked revolvers from holsters and shoved them behind his belt. He grabbed one of the Winchesters that leaned against the wall.

"After everything they and their compadres have done, I believe I would sleep fine."

"Could be, but there's no need to risk it." Frank nodded toward the stairs. "I reckon the fellas up in the guard room are knocked out, too?"

"They should be by now. My cousins Estellita and Marietta are dealing with them."

Frank wondered briefly just how many cousins she had, then decided it didn't matter. He went up the stairs quickly with Beatriz following closely behind him.

Two attractive young Mexican women and three sleeping gun-wolves were in the guardroom. Frank glanced at the men and saw that they didn't look like they'd be waking up anytime soon.

The two young women's hair and clothing were a little disheveled. Frank supposed they had been pawed some before the drug took effect and knocked out the guards. One of them reached down and pulled a bowie knife from a sheath on a man's hip.

"Take Señor Morgan and go," she told Beatriz. "Estellita and I will take care of these dogs."

"You don't have to kill them," Frank said.

The girl's face was like stone as she said, "They will have to die now or later in order to break the general's hold on our town. Why leave them alive now to maybe kill more of our people later?"

Frank couldn't argue with her. Even though he knew there was a difference between murder and killing an enemy in battle, he hadn't suffered at the hands of Ramirez's men like these women and their friends and relatives had, either.

"Come on," he said to Beatriz.

Grim-faced, she took his left hand in her right and ran along the corridor, leading him out of the stronghold.

"What was that explosion?" he asked as they hurried through the twisting hallways.

"A man who has Apache blood was able to crawl up to the wall and place a keg of blasting powder at its base, then run the fuse along the wall so it would not be seen as it burned. Ramirez's men will rush to the spot to see what happened, so there will be fewer of them at the back of the compound."

"So that's the way we're going out, eh?"

"*Sí*. We will go through the kitchen."

A moment later, they did exactly that. No lamps were lit, but Beatriz knew where she was going. Frank trusted her to lead him to freedom . . . although he was still a little surprised that so many people who didn't even know him would risk their lives to rescue him.

"There's a new man here, tall, sandy-haired, dressed all in black when I saw him . . . Do you know who I mean?"

"Señor Callahan," Beatriz replied. "I helped serve when he dined with the general, Señorita Antonia, and Señor Kern."

"Do you know where he is?"

"Ramirez sent him across the border with Kern and some of the other men to hold up a train, I think. They are not back yet."

A pang of disappointment went through Frank. He had been hoping that Conrad was still here and they could team up. With Kid Morgan at his side, he knew he could fight his way out of here if he had to.

But he had other allies and they seemed determined to help him. They were going to quite a bit of trouble to do so, in fact. That was a little puzzling to Frank, but he wasn't going to question their generosity.

They emerged from the hacienda through a rear door and Beatriz immediately pressed her back to the wall and motioned for Frank to do likewise. They stood there silent and motionless for a long moment. Frank heard quite a bit of angry shouting coming from the front of the compound.

Guns began to bark. Beatriz whispered, "They are shooting at shadows. None of la Mariposa's people can be seen in the darkness unless they wish to be."

"La Mariposa?" Frank repeated, keeping his voice equally low.

"You will meet her . . . if we get out of here alive."

Frank certainly planned to do that. Because of the time he had spent in the dungeon, his eyes were used to dim light. Here behind the hacienda, the only illumination came from the millions of stars floating in the ebony sky. That was enough for him to see the top of a ladder that suddenly appeared on the other side of the wall.

Beatriz saw it, too. She touched him on the arm and said, "Now!"

They ran toward the wall. As they did, Frank saw movement at the top of the ladder. A man's head and shoulders poked over the wall. He dropped something, and as it unfurled, Frank realized that it was a rope ladder. It reached almost to the ground on this side. Frank didn't know what it was attached to on the other side, but he hoped it was something sturdy enough to support his weight. He was a good-sized hombre.

"Climb!" Beatriz panted as they reached the wall and the rope ladder. "Get out of here, Señor Morgan!"

"You first," he told her.

"I will slip out later in the confusion, with the others—"

"You've got a chance to get away right now," he broke in. "Ramirez will be loco when he finds out he's got some dead guards. No telling what he'll do. You need to be far away from this place, so get up that ladder."

She didn't waste any more time arguing with him. He was grateful for that. She scrambled up the ladder with the agility of youth. Frank held on to it to steady it, which allowed her to climb even faster.

She reached the top and swung over it onto the wooden ladder. The man who had dropped the rope ladder had disappeared. Frank supposed he was waiting at the bottom on the other side.

He couldn't climb very well and hang on to the rifle, too, so he propped the Winchester against the wall and took hold of one of the rungs. He reached up, got another one, planted his foot on the lowest rung, and pulled himself up.

The rope ladder swung back and forth. He was too big for this, he thought, but he didn't have any other way out of the stronghold. The ladder tried to twist and tangle. He forced it to twist back the other way.

A shout went up somewhere not far away. Running footsteps slapped against the ground.

"Stop him!" a man roared. "Shoot him!"

Gunfire crashed in the night.

As the ladder twisted again in Frank's grasp, he saw crimson flowers of muzzle flame blooming in the darkness. Slugs smacked into the adobe wall not far from him. The four men shooting at him charged toward the wall. In a matter of seconds they would be too close to miss.

Frank maintained his grip on the rope ladder with his left hand, but his right swooped down to his waist and plucked one of the guns from behind his belt. Hanging there, swaying back and forth, he called on all his skill to guide his shots as he thumbed off a rolling volley of lead. The guard who'd packed this iron had carried a full wheel in it, instead of letting the hammer rest on an empty chamber, so Frank fired six times as he emptied the weapon. Those bullets scythed through the bandits and tumbled all four of them off their feet. They didn't shoot at him anymore.

Frank stuck the empty gun in his waistband and resumed climbing. Men were shouting all over the compound now, and he knew that in seconds, some of them would run back here to check on the fierce exchange of lead that had just thundered through the night. Frank grunted with effort as he hauled himself up the rope ladder.

"Come on, Señor Morgan! Hurry!"

He glanced up and saw that Beatriz was at the top of the ladder now, extending a slender arm down toward him. He didn't think she would be of much help in lifting his bulk, so he called to her, "Get back down there, señorita, before—"

Beatriz cried out as a pair of shots roared nearby. Frank swung around again and used his left hand this time to palm out the loaded Colt. Two more men had appeared and were pointing rifles at him. Three shots slammed from the gun in his hand before either of them could fire again. They went over backward as if they'd been slapped down by a giant.

Frank turned and climbed the rest of the way up the rope ladder. He didn't see Beatriz at the top of the wall and was afraid she'd been hit by one of those last shots. First Florita had been whipped for trying to help Frank and now her cousin might have been hurt or even killed. One way or another, Frank was going to see to it that Diego Ramirez got what was coming to him. The misery he had brought to the innocent, peace-loving people of this area had to be paid for . . . in blood.

Frank swung a leg over the wall, found a rung on the wooden ladder, and paused long enough to pull the rope ladder up and toss it on the outside of the wall. He saw several people waiting in the shadows at the bottom, but he couldn't tell if Beatriz was one of them. He climbed most of the way down the ladder and then turned and dropped the last couple of feet to the ground. He'd wanted to jump sooner but knew his bones were a mite too old for that.

A man clutched at his arm and said, "Come, Señor Morgan. We have horses nearby!"

Frank was glad to hear that. He wasn't sure if they could have gotten away from Ramirez's stronghold on foot. He knew there was a settlement somewhere in the area called Saguaro Springs, but he had no idea how far away it was.

Another figure stepped up beside him and a familiar voice said, "Señor Morgan, you are all right?"

"Beatriz? Were you hit?"

She laughed and said, "No, but one of those bullets struck the wall so close to me that I jumped back and fell off the ladder! I am fortunate I did not break my leg."

"I'm mighty glad to hear it. They didn't hit me with any of that lead they were throwing around, either, but some of it came too close for comfort."

They didn't bother taking the ladder with them as they hurried away from the stronghold. Two men were in the group in addition to Beatriz. They led Frank over a small rise and into a wide depression where another man waited with five horses.

Beatriz grabbed the reins of one mount from the waiting man and pressed them into Frank's hand.

"This is the best horse," she told him. "If we get separated, ride northeast. You can find your way by the stars, can you not?"

"For about twice as long as you've been alive, señorita."

She laughed again. "You will be able to find the settlement, then. Go to the café of Julio Hernandez, my uncle."

"I remember the name. Florita told me to find him, too, when she tried to help me escape."

"Tío Julio will take you to la Mariposa," Beatriz went on.

"Who is this butterfly you've mentioned a couple of times?"

"You will find out. Now, we must ride!"

Frank knew she was right. Soon enough, if they hadn't already, Ramirez's men would realize that even though the explosion had surely damaged the wall, it wasn't a full-scale attack. They would start looking around for what was really going on, then they would find the dead men near the rear wall and the guards inside the hacienda and would know that the prisoner had made his escape, with help from the people of Saguaro Springs.

When he had swung up into the saddle and the others were mounted as well, he said, "Ramirez is liable to attack the settlement. He'll know that you folks are behind what happened tonight."

"He may," Beatriz said, "but not right away. With the men he lost tonight, he does not have enough left to attack the town. Not until the ones he sent to hold up the train return."

Among them, Kid Morgan, Frank thought. Conrad would find a different situation waiting for him when he got back.

The five riders galloped off, heading almost due west as far as Frank could tell. Gradually they began to circle back to the north. He figured they would take the long way around to return to Saguaro Springs.

After a hard run for a while, they eased off to let the horses blow. Frank listened for sounds of pursuit but didn't hear any.

"Could be we gave 'em the slip," he said.

One of the men said, "Or Ramirez was afraid to risk any more of his men by coming after us. He could think that an ambush might be waiting for him."

"He will wait for the others to come back," Beatriz said. "When he feels strong enough, he will come to the settlement to punish us for defying him. He will try to burn it to the ground."

"Then we'll be ready for him if he does," Frank declared. "You've got a whole settlement full of folks, and obviously you don't mind fighting back. Why have you let Ramirez run roughshod over you all this time?"

"We are not fighters, señor," said the man who had spoken before. "We are shopkeepers and cobblers and blacksmiths and farmers. We want only to be left alone to live our lives in peace." An eloquent shrug lifted his shoulders in the starlight. "We believed that if we cooperated with Ramirez, he would leave us alone for the most part. Some might be harmed, but not all."

"That didn't work out too well, did it?" Frank's voice was harsher than he intended, but he had seen such things happen time and time again. Folks thought they could bargain with evil, when that wasn't possible. The only thing to do with evil was wipe it out . . . or die trying.

"For a time, no one was killed," Beatriz said. "But his

men became more confident, more arrogant, more brutal. Some worse than others."

"Bracken, I'd bet."

"*Sí*, he was one of the worst. He beat men who displeased him and attacked any woman who struck his fancy, no matter how old or young. Many of the others were almost as bad, though." A shudder ran through Beatriz. "And yet Ramirez boasts that he will do good for Mexico with men such as that."

A shrill *yip-yip-yip* sounded off to the left. Beatriz jerked her head in that direction. One of the men chuckled and said, "It is only a coyote, Beatriz. Nothing to worry about. He is more afraid of you than you are of him."

"I am not so sure," she muttered. "Sometimes I saw strange things at night in the hacienda. Things that dart through the shadows and then disappear."

"You know those old stories about the *lunático* are just stories."

Frank didn't have any idea what madman they were talking about but didn't figure this was the time to be asking about it. Beatriz remained tense as they rode on, though, casting nervous glances over her shoulder from time to time. Frank didn't hear any more yipping or see anything.

There had been something just a little *off* about that coyote's cry, though, he thought.

They continued pushing on through the night at a good pace, walking the horses at times, urging them into a ground-eating trot at others. The gray light of false dawn was in the eastern sky before they came in sight of the settlement. Frank saw several lights and knew that some folks were up either mighty early or mighty late.

Beatriz said, "Since we all made it together we can go straight to the cantina."

"I'll go by the store and bring Julio," one of the men said. As they neared the edge of town, he veered off from the others.

Beatriz took the lead and rode to a good-sized adobe building where light spilled through the open front door. Enough of it reflected up onto the wall above the entrance for Frank to be able to read the word CANTINA painted in an arch of letters. Something else was painted on the wall above the word, and as they came closer, he realized it was a brightly colored butterfly.

He wondered, then, was la Mariposa the name of the cantina or of a person . . . or both?

He supposed he was about to find out, because Beatriz and the others had reined their horses to a stop and were dismounting to go inside.

# Chapter 29

The sounds of animated conversation came through the cantina's open door. Beatriz motioned for Frank to come with her and they walked in first, with the three men following them. Hazy smoke from hand-rolled quirleys, cigarillos, and pipes hung in the air inside, along with the smells of beer, tequila, spices, and peppers. A hush fell over the room as Frank's bootheels rang on the plank floor. Heads turned and gazes swung to the newcomers.

A woman who had been standing beside the bar rushed toward them. "Beatriz!" she cried. "You are all right?"

"*Sí*, Tía Luciana," Beatriz replied. "We were successful."

The woman turned to look Frank up and down, her large, dark eyes intent as she did so. She said, "Then you must be Frank Morgan, señor."

"And I reckon you're la Mariposa," Frank ventured.

She was as colorful as a butterfly, although considerably more substantial than one of those flittering creatures. A lush figure curved her hips under the brightly embroidered skirt, and her full, round breasts threatened to spill out of the crimson shirt's low neckline. Gold hoop earrings sparkled in the lamplight, as did the blue sapphire she wore on a gold chain around her neck. Her thick, curly hair was black as midnight except for a few silver strands that showed she wasn't a girl anymore, despite the air of youthful vitality she possessed. Frank thought she was strikingly beautiful, especially when she smiled and laughed at his comment.

"I am Luciana Hernandez," she said, "but some do call me la Mariposa."

"This is your place, I suppose. And you're Beatriz's aunt."

"*Sí.*"

"Florita's, too."

"Juana is my sister, *sí*," Luciana said. "And our brother Julio has a café here in Saguaro Springs. He will be here shortly. Meanwhile, many of the other good people of our community have gathered to greet you, Señor Morgan."

She waved a slender but strong-looking hand at the crowd inside the cantina, and Frank took a good look at them for the first time. Luciana Hernandez was such an impressive woman that he found taking his attention away from her to be difficult. He was somewhat surprised at what he saw when he did, though.

At least a hundred people had assembled here, many of them Mexicans but a significant number of whites, too. A tall, rawboned man wore a black patch over his left eye. Two blond women, one older and one younger, bore a strong enough resemblance to each other that Frank knew they must be mother and daughter. A squat, black-bearded man had such massive shoulders that Frank assumed he was the local blacksmith. Another man wore the canvas apron of a shopkeeper.

Luciana had called them "good people," and Frank

could tell by looking at them that they were. These were the law-abiding, peace-loving citizens of Saguaro Springs that one of his companions had talked about during the ride here, the settlers who simply wanted to live their lives and be left alone, something they had discovered was impossible when dealing with animals like Diego Ramirez and his men.

And yet they had turned out here, very early in the morning when most of them were usually still asleep, to greet him. Frank couldn't understand why.

So he asked the question that puzzled him, and he asked it bluntly.

"What is it you folks want from me?"

"The answer is simple, Señor Morgan," Luciana said. "We want you to lead us, and help us kill Diego Ramirez and all the men who work for him."

The bandits brought along two packhorses when they set out to hold up the train, but that proved not to be enough to carry all the gold bars they found in the caboose's safe, after the elderly conductor had been forced at gunpoint to provide the lock's combination. Once the safe was open, Bracken had put a bullet through the old man's brain anyway. The Kid hadn't witnessed that, but he had heard some of the other men talking and laughing about how Kern was annoyed with Bracken for killing the conductor.

The rich men from Monterrey had consolidated their wealth into gold bars so it would be easier to transport, but that also meant it was easier for thieves to carry away.

Once as many bars as possible had been loaded on the packhorses, the remaining bars were distributed among the men. Each would carry two or three in their saddle-bags. The horses couldn't move quite as fast with the added weight, but since the telegraph wire was down and the train wasn't going anywhere until the tracks between the cutbanks were cleared, the bandits weren't worried about anybody alerting the Rurales.

They tied the Kid's hands behind his back and lifted him onto the buckskin. Kern said, "Woodson, tie that horse's reins to your saddle horn. You're responsible for not letting Callahan get away."

"All right, Kern." Woodson gave the Kid a mournful look and shook his head. "I sure didn't expect you to double-cross us, Johnny. You seemed like a good hombre."

The Kid didn't respond. Right now, he didn't care whether he had disappointed some outlaw. He just didn't give a damn.

Now he had to worry not only about rescuing his father but also about escaping himself.

He found one ray of hope in this mess. Kern kept referring to him as Callahan, which meant the gunman had still been unconscious when the Kid told the men in the caboose that his name was Kid Morgan. If Kern had heard that, he would have made the connection with Frank right away and would have figured out that the Kid was there to rescue the prisoner being held at the stronghold. He might have even tumbled to the fact that Kid Morgan was really Conrad Browning, although that was less likely.

As long as they didn't know who he really was, they might believe he had double-crossed them in an attempt to steal all the gold for himself. That might mean they would be a little less alert about keeping him away from Frank.

But he was just fooling himself, he thought bleakly as the gang rode north toward Arizona Territory. As soon as they got back to the stronghold and Ramirez found out what had happened, he would have the Kid whipped to death or tortured in some other way until he was dead. And most of the men would look on and enjoy the spectacle.

More than likely, so would Antonia . . .

Because of the slower pace, they were nowhere near the border by nightfall. Kern called a halt and had the men make camp in a clearing amid a cluster of rocks. They would arrive back at the stronghold by the middle of the next day. Woodson and another man hauled the Kid down from the saddle and propped him up against a rock.

Woodson stepped back and said, "Sorry, Johnny, but I can't untie you. Kern gave orders that you was to stay tied until we get back with you."

"They may not untie me then," the Kid said. "The general might decide to have me stood up against a wall right away."

"A firin' squad, you mean?" Woodson shrugged. "That'd be a damned shame."

"Probably better than the whip or some other torture, though."

The other man had wandered off to take care of his horse. Woodson continued looking mournfully at the Kid and went on, "What in blazes were you thinkin', Johnny?

You shoulda knowed you couldn't make off with all that gold when there were so many of us around. You didn't really believe you could get away with it, did you?"

"Being around that much gold sometimes keeps a man from thinking straight."

"Well, I s'pose you're right about that." A grin stretched across Woodson's face. "I know I can't hardly stop thinkin' 'bout all that purty yellow gold we're carryin'. But I know I don't stand no chance of gettin' more than my share of it."

"And as long as you get it, you don't mind being part of murdering innocent people."

Woodson's expression became solemn again as he said, "That's one thing I figured out a long time ago, Johnny. There ain't no innocent people. Only them as ain't been caught yet."

He walked off, and the Kid let him go. He knew now he couldn't count on any help from jovial, guitar-playing Sam Woodson.

Kern ordered a cold camp, not wanting to draw any attention with a fire, and when Woodson started to strum his guitar and sing quietly, Kern shut him up in a hurry.

"You know how sound carries out here, especially at night," Kern snapped. "A Rurale patrol could be moving around somewhere out there, and we don't want to give them any reason to come looking in this direction. Everybody stay as quiet as possible, and keep the horses quiet, too."

He came over to the rock where the Kid was sitting a short time later and gave him some water from a canteen, then put a piece of jerky in his mouth.

"Gnaw on that for a while," Kern said as he hunkered

on his heels in front of the Kid. "It's the only supper you're going to get tonight."

"Probably my last supper," the Kid said around the tough strip of dried meat.

"That wouldn't surprise me a bit. I haven't known you long at all, Callahan, but still, I thought you had more sense than that. How were you planning to get away with that gold?"

"Woodson asked the same thing. I reckon I would've figured that out when the time came."

Kern just grunted in disbelief, stood up, and walked off.

The Kid could have used another drink when he finished the jerky, but nobody offered him one so he did without. His position leaning against the rock was uncomfortable, but eventually he went to sleep.

The small sounds of men moving around woke him early the next morning, before dawn. The bandits were getting ready to ride. Kern allowed a small fire to boil a pot of coffee. Caution was one thing, but doing without coffee was downright uncivilized.

Sam Woodson brought a cup over to the Kid and held it where he could sip from it. Woodson had a biscuit with him, as well, from the supplies they had brought along. He broke off pieces of it and fed them to the Kid.

"You're going to a lot of trouble for me," the Kid commented. "You could've just let me go hungry."

"Ain't no reason to do that," Woodson said. "Things ain't gonna go well for you when we get back, Johnny, but ain't no need for you to suffer until then."

"And you'll just stand by and let them kill me?"

"Dang, son!" Woodson said. "I ain't knowed you but

about a day. You expect me to get myself killed tryin' to help you, when it wouldn't do you no good anyway?"

"You could loosen these ropes on my wrists without anybody noticing," the Kid suggested quietly, "and you could make sure my horse's reins aren't tied as tightly to your saddle horn. Give me a chance to make a run for it. I'd rather be shot trying to get away than tortured once we get back to the stronghold."

Woodson straightened from where he was kneeling.

"Can't do it," he said with a shake of his head, "and if you keep askin', Johnny, I'm gonna get a mite annoyed. Hell, you know how this game is played."

He turned and stalked off. With him probably went the last chance to escape before they got back to the rancho, the Kid thought. But he was still alive, so he would just have to find some other way to get loose and rescue Frank.

The idea that he would be unsuccessful, that both he and his father would die at the hands of Ramirez and the rest of these murderous bandits, never entered his head. He wouldn't allow it to.

They pushed on before the sun was up. A chilly predawn wind swept across the arid landscape. That coolness disappeared quickly once the sun rose. The temperature climbed just like the blazing orb in the sky.

Men and horses alike wilted a little in the heat as Kern kept them moving at a fairly brisk pace. He explained that he wanted to get back across the border so they could stop worrying about the Rurales.

"What about American lawmen?" the Kid asked.

"They don't get down here in this part of the territory much," Kern replied. "The county sheriff and his men are spread too thin, and there's no army post nearby, so we don't have to watch for cavalry patrols, either. It's a good setup." He paused. "Too bad you had to throw away being part of it, Callahan."

The Kid didn't say anything, just rocked along in the saddle as the heat beat down on him. At least Woodson had retrieved his hat and clapped it on his head before they rode away from the railroad tracks. Otherwise the Kid's brains would have been cooked good and proper by now.

Because of the way he was tied, his shoulders ached, his arms were half-numb, and he couldn't feel his hands at all. They were just lumps of senseless flesh. Even if he was freed from his bonds, long minutes would pass before he was able to use his hands effectively again.

Kern allowed them to slow a little once he judged they were north of the border. He called a halt a couple of times to allow the horses to rest. Finally, late in the morning, they came in sight of a dark shape looming on the horizon. Even though the Kid had approached it from a different direction the first time, he knew that was the hacienda where Diego Ramirez intended to establish a second presidential palace.

As the riders came closer, they swung to the east so they could approach the compound from the front. After they had been riding for a few minutes, Bracken sat up straighter in his saddle and said, "What the hell is that? Look there to the left of the gates, Kern."

"I see it," Kern said. "Looks like something happened to damage the wall."

It was true. The wall hadn't collapsed, but the Kid saw that something had gouged out a chunk of it near the base.

The opening went all the way through, but it appeared that the men had erected a makeshift barricade on the other side until the wall could be repaired properly.

"Son of a gun!" Woodson exclaimed. "Somebody blowed a hole in it!"

The Kid thought the same thing. An explosion of some sort had done that damage.

But who would try to blow up Ramirez's stronghold? The Kid couldn't imagine any of the settlers from Saguaro Springs doing such a thing. No one else was around here, though.

Maybe the citizens had decided it was time to fight back at last. If that turned out to be true, it was an interesting development and might have a bearing on what the Kid would be able to do about rescuing Frank and dodging the grisly fate that Ramirez undoubtedly would have in store for him as soon as the general heard what had happened during the train holdup.

The same thought had occurred to Bracken, about who might be responsible for the damage to the wall. The murderous gunman spat some curses, then said, "We're gonna have to ride into Saguaro Springs and teach those sheep a lesson! How about we bring all the gals under twenty years old out here and let them spend a few days with us? After we kill half a dozen of the men, of course."

"How about we let the general decide what needs to be done?" Kern said. "Last time I checked, he was still in command around here."

"Yeah, but he lets them get away with too much."

The Kid thought about the whipping that Florita had received and wondered how anybody could think that

Ramirez let the citizens of Saguaro Springs get away with too much. Bracken's brain didn't work like that of a normal person, though, he reminded himself.

The guards inside the compound had been watching for their return. The gates swung open as they rode up. Kern led the way inside, followed by Bracken, then Woodson and the Kid, then the other men.

Someone had alerted Ramirez. He strode out of the so-called second capitol building, wearing a resplendent green uniform today, as well as a hat with a bright green plume on it. The Kid thought he looked a little ridiculous, but nobody around here was going to say that to the self-proclaimed general.

"Your mission was successful?" Ramirez asked Kern as the *segundo* dismounted.

"We got the gold."

"Excellent!" Ramirez clenched his right hand into a fist and shook it in front of his face in an exultant gesture.

Kern leaned his head toward the Kid and added, "No thanks to Callahan here."

That put a frown on Ramirez's face. He asked, "What happened?"

"He tried to double-cross us." Kern quickly sketched in the violent details of the train robbery, concluding, "I guess the thought of all that gold made him loco. I started to kill him, then decided that you might want to decide what to do with him, General."

Ramirez nodded and said, "I am glad you did, Kern. I need something to brighten my spirits on this unpleasant day, and executing a traitor will do that."

"Unpleasant day?" Kern repeated with a frown. "I don't

understand, General. We got the gold. Together with the ransom we're going to get for Frank Morgan, we'll have enough to field and equip a real army against Díaz."

"There will be no ransom for Frank Morgan," Ramirez said. "He is gone. Escaped."

# Chapter 30

Frank Morgan stood there in the cantina for a long moment after Luciana Hernandez made her bold statement. Then he said, "You and these folks are planning to go to war against Ramirez?"

"See for yourself, señor," she said as once again she gestured toward those assembled in the cantina. "Are those the faces of people willing to continue enduring the abuses Ramirez and his men are heaping on them?"

Frank had to admit that they weren't. The citizens of Saguaro Springs looked both angry and determined. But most of them were more than a little scared, too.

On the other hand, anybody who went into a war without being scared was a damned fool. Even though four decades had passed since Frank had gone off to fight the Yankees as a young man, he still remembered quite well the uneasy feeling in his guts while he waited for his first battle to begin. He'd been scared, all right. Mighty damned scared.

But he had done his duty. These people saw it as their

duty to fight to protect their homes and loved ones, and he couldn't say they were wrong to feel that way.

"All right," he said to Luciana. "Tell me what your plan is."

"Our plan was to get you out of there and then turn to you for leadership, Señor Morgan." She smiled. "You are *our* general."

"Now, hold on! I was in the army a long time ago, but I was just a fella who carried a rifle and marched wherever somebody else told me to march."

"But you are a fighter. More than any of us are. We trust your instincts, and we will follow you into battle."

He cocked an eyebrow at her and said, "You and these other ladies here aren't planning to fight, are you?"

"We are pioneer women, Señor Morgan. We know how to fire a gun, and many of us have suffered mistreatment of one form or another at the hands of those animals at the old rancho. Yes, we will fight if need be."

"We'll do our share," the young blonde said. "Just give us a chance."

"That's right," the older woman who was probably her mother added.

Frank heard the sincerity in their voices and didn't doubt them. But he asked Luciana, "How many men do you have who are willing and able to fight?"

Luciana looked around the room and said, "Not all of them are here right now, but perhaps . . . fifty. We out-number Ramirez and his men."

"Not by much, once the others get back. What do you have in the way of weapons?"

"Shotguns, rifles, a few pistols. And a good supply of ammunition." She smiled. "Enough for one battle, certainly."

Frank understood what she meant by that. If they attacked Ramirez's stronghold, that wouldn't be the first engagement in an ongoing war. It would be an all-or-nothing assault that would see Saguaro Springs liberated . . . or most of the settlement's men slain and an even worse situation for the survivors.

Frank suddenly remembered how Sam Houston had ordered Deaf Smith and some of the other members of his Texican army to burn a strategic bridge as they were advancing toward the enemy in the decisive battle of the Texas Revolution. If you didn't have any way to retreat, your only options were victory or death.

"Are you sure you know what you're letting yourself in for?" he asked.

"We know," the man with the eye patch replied. "We've plumb had all we're gonna take from them varmints."

Nods and mutters of agreement came from nearly all the others in the cantina.

"All right," Frank said, "but remember this: You may outnumber Ramirez, but his men are professional killers, each and every one of them. There might come a time when you'll hesitate before you pull the trigger, but those men won't. They'll kill you before you can blink your eyes, if they get the chance." The settlers pressed closer around him as he went on, "Here's another thing. You can't just saddle up and go charging out there right now. The sun will be up long before you could get there."

"But those men Ramirez sent to hold up the train will be back today," Beatriz protested. "His force is small right now. We must strike while we have the best chance!"

Frank shook his head and said, "Even if he only has ten men, that's enough for them to perch up there on that wall and pick off our men at long range before they ever get there. We might make it to the stronghold, might even get inside and overrun Ramirez's men . . . but at least half of our force will die while we're doing it."

At that blunt assessment, concerned frowns appeared on a number of faces in the crowd.

"Then, what do you suggest?" Luciana asked coolly.

"Somebody was able to sneak up and plant that blasting powder next to the wall last night," Frank said. "I think we need to wait for nightfall again and take advantage of the darkness to get as close to the compound as possible before attacking. If one of your men was able to blow those gates open so we could get inside before Ramirez's men knew what was going on . . ." Frank shrugged. "Taking 'em by surprise like that would go a long way toward giving us a better chance."

The townsman in the storekeeper's apron said, "Do you think Ramirez will wait that long to strike back against us for gettin' you out of there, Mr. Morgan?"

"*Sí*," the Mexican blacksmith said. "The general will be loco with anger that someone dared to defy him!"

"He's not going to try to attack the town with the men he has on hand right now," Frank said. "Anyway, he'll want to wait for those others to get back from below the border to see if they got the gold they went after. We don't know when that will be, so it would probably be a good idea to send a couple of men out there with field glasses to keep an eye on the place from a distance. If Ramirez does make a move toward the settlement once the rest of his bunch gets back, we'll need some warning. In the meantime, we can do some forting up, just in case we do have to defend the town. We need wagons with teams hitched up and ready to go, so we can block the ends of the street with them if we need to. Get some men on top of the tallest building in town to keep watch all around, and have runners ready to spread the alarm if there's an attack. We can only defend a fairly small area effectively, so the women and kids and any men who aren't able-bodied enough to fight should gather in the center of the settlement where they'll be safe."

The young blonde opened her mouth to speak, but Frank held up a hand to forestall the protest she was obviously about to make.

"The women who want to be will be armed and will serve as the last line of defense," he went on. "Everybody else will spread out and try to keep the bandits out of town as long as possible."

"And you claimed you are no general!" Luciana said with an approving smile.

"Everything I said was just common sense," Frank insisted.

"A man with common sense who can think clearly in times of trouble is the best general an army can have, I think." She looked around at the others in the cantina, and a ragged cheer went up.

Frank just shook his head. They were cheering and carried away by emotion now, but sooner or later it would come down to blood and flame and death. It always did.

"I want to talk to the man who planted that blasting powder. I reckon we can get another keg of the stuff?"

"You can have all of it I got in my store, Mr. Morgan," the man in the canvas apron said. "And anything else you need."

Frank rested his hands on the butts of the Colts stuck

behind his belt. He smiled and said, "I could use a box of .45s, I reckon."

The Kid carefully kept his face expressionless as he heard Ramirez say that Frank was gone. He had kept his connection to the prisoner a secret for this long, and he wanted to continue that, if possible.

"He was rescued, I should say," Ramirez went on. "While the peons were blowing a hole in the wall, some of the sluts we brought here to work as servants killed several of our men and helped Morgan get away."

"You know for sure that's what happened?" Kern asked.

"The women were all gone this morning," Ramirez answered, shrugging. "They slipped away during the night. There is no other explanation." His face darkened even more with rage. "But before they left, they cut the throats of some good men!"

There weren't any good men in this bunch, the Kid thought. Whatever had happened to them, they'd had it coming. But if Ramirez was able to carry out his vengeance on Saguaro Springs, it would be fearsome indeed.

"Well, we're back now," Bracken said, "so let's unload this gold and then go burn that damn settlement to the ground! That'll teach those greasers and white trash they can't stand up to hombres like us!"

Ramirez made a slashing gesture and said, "No, not yet! I believe they may be trying to lure us into a trap. Besides, we need the town for supplies. We cannot destroy it, no matter how much I might like to!"

Kern frowned in thought, scratched at his bearded jaw,

and said, "You reckon maybe Morgan is still there? Or do you think he's getting as far away from here as he can, as fast as he can?"

A savage smile creased Ramirez's face. He said, "That is another reason to wait. I believe Señor Morgan may seek revenge for being kidnapped. If we are patient, he may come back with men from the settlement and try to attack *us*, instead of the other way around. And that will put him right back in our hands."

The Kid's spirits sank a little as he listened to the general. The notion that Frank Morgan would run away now that he was free had never crossed his mind. He had known as soon as he heard that Frank had escaped it was only a matter of time until he tried to strike back against Ramirez. Frank had seen Ramirez's evil with his own eyes, and he would be keen to destroy this bandit stronghold.

If he could just manage to stay alive until then, maybe he could get loose and make a difference, the Kid told himself.

That might not be possible, though, because Ramirez turned toward him and said, "In the meantime, we can amuse ourselves by coming up with a painful death for this traitor—"

"No!"

The sudden outburst took the men by surprise, including the Kid. He turned his head to look and saw Antonia striding toward them.

She wore the black leather trousers but today had on a red, long-sleeved silk shirt with them. Her long raven hair was loose around her shoulders and down her back. She stopped and cast an insolent gaze over the Kid, taking in the way his hands were tied behind his back.

"What has he done?"

"Tried to steal all the gold for himself!" Ramirez said as he waved a hand in the air. "He must pay for his madness and his treachery!"

"I agree." Antonia's voice was almost a purr as she went on, "Give him to me."

"What!" The exclamation came from Kern. The Kid watched the way he looked at Antonia, and now that he knew what to watch for, he saw signs that Kern was smitten with her. But at the same time, the suggestion Antonia had just made flabbergasted and upset the gunman.

"I said, give him to me. I will devise a suitable punishment for him."

Ramirez glowered and said, "This is not a matter for women—"

"And I am *not* a typical woman, Papa, you know that. You trusted me to help you capture a notorious gunfighter like Frank Morgan. Why do you not trust me to make an example of a man who would betray us and our noble cause?"

The Kid didn't think for a second that she believed her father's cause was noble. He wasn't sure what drove Antonia Ramirez's actions, but it wasn't any altruistic desire to make things better for Mexico and its people, he was damned sure of that.

For a long moment Ramirez stood there, apparently considering what Antonia had said. Impatience grew on Kern's face, and finally he burst out, "Why not just let me put a bullet through his head, General? I came mighty close to doing that down there in Mexico after he nearly ruined everything."

"If that's what you wanted to do, then you should have done it," Ramirez snapped. "Instead you left the decision in my hands, Kern, and I will make it." His head jerked in an abrupt nod. "And I decide that I will grant my daughter's wish. You can have this dog to do with as you will, Antonia . . . but he must suffer before he dies. That is my only requirement. Otherwise it will not be a suitable demonstration of what happens to those who defy the leader of our glorious revolution!"

Antonia said, "I can promise you, Papa, that Señor Callahan will suffer." She turned and barked an order to some of the men standing nearby. "Take him to the dungeon!"

A couple of them grabbed the Kid's arms and marched him toward the hacienda. They didn't know it, he thought wryly, but their new prisoner was worth just as much money as the one who had escaped. However, he sure wasn't going to tell them that.

His captors hustled him down the stairs and into one of the cells. One of the men cut the ropes around his wrists, then the other gave him a hard shove that sent him sprawling forward heavily on the stone floor. The cell door clanged shut with grim finality, and shadows closed in around him.

As he lay there, he thought about the expression he had seen on Antonia's face after she had watched Florita being whipped. He was still alive, and he had that to be thankful for, but he wasn't sure if he was better off having Antonia in charge of his fate . . . or worse.

# Chapter 31

After the eventful night, and after giving his orders for the settlement's defensive preparations, Frank managed to get a few hours of sleep on a bunk in the cantina's back room. He woke up with Luciana Hernandez perched on the mattress's edge beside him as she lightly rested a hand on his shoulder.

"I have coffee and food for you, Señor Morgan," she told him. "You said you did not wish to sleep past mid-morning."

"Thanks," he said as he sat up. Luciana didn't move, and he was very aware of the soft warmth of her hip pressed against his.

She moved her hand up and down his arm and said, "You are a most impressive hombre, Señor Morgan."

"Call me Frank," he suggested. "You mean I'm impressive for my age?"

"Ha! I can tell by looking at you that you still put many younger men to shame, Frank. A man of your years has much wisdom when it comes to life . . . and women."

"Being wise is something I haven't been accused of too

often," he responded with a grin. "You said something about coffee?"

"Of course." She stood up and indicated a tray she had placed on a small table.

Frank moved from the bunk to a ladder-back chair beside the table and took a swallow of the strong, black coffee, immediately feeling better as he did so. He tucked into the food while Luciana continued sitting on the bunk.

"One of the men we sent out to keep an eye on Ramirez's stronghold rode back into town a few minutes ago with news," she said. "The men he sent below the border have returned. They brought two packhorses with them that appeared to be heavily loaded."

Frank frowned and said, "That means they must have been successful and got that gold from the train. That amount by itself will be enough for Ramirez to recruit more men and buy more guns and ammunition."

"Which means he must be stopped now, before he becomes even stronger."

"That's right," Frank said. "How many men came back?"

"Our watchers counted twenty. Beatriz says that was the number of men who left a couple of days ago."

"I was hoping maybe they lost a few in the holdup. I'll take whittling down the odds any way we can get it."

"Here is something odd, though," Luciana said. "The watchers reported that one of the men appeared to have his hands tied behind his back as he rode, as if he were a prisoner."

"Maybe they did lose somebody in the holdup but brought a man from the train back with them."

"Perhaps. But our men said the one who was a captive

looked like a gunman. They could not make out too many details through the field glasses, but they said he was young and dressed all in black."

That description made Frank's jaw tighten. He asked, "What color hair did this fella have?"

"The watchers could not tell. They were too far away."

Frank sat there, his coffee and breakfast forgotten for the moment. During the brief moment when he had seen his son in the hacienda's dining room, Conrad had been dressed all in black. But some of the other men could be, too, so what Luciana had just told him didn't really mean anything.

And yet, the tightness in his gut was undeniable. It was unlikely Conrad would have let those bandits get away with holding up the train without doing something to try to sabotage their efforts. If he had done that and failed . . . worse, if they had also discovered that he was actually Conrad Browning . . . they might have brought him back to the stronghold for Ramirez to deal with. Frank had absolutely no proof that was what had happened, but he had a father's instinct that told him his son was in trouble.

"I can tell something worries you, Frank," Luciana said. "Do you believe our attack is doomed to fail?"

He shook his head and said, "Not at all." He didn't say anything about Conrad, because he couldn't allow that to influence his decisions. The people of Saguaro Springs had put their faith in him, and he was going to do his best for them. That meant waiting for nightfall to put his plan into action . . . even though a big part of him wanted to gallop out there right now and go in with all guns blazing to find his son.

But if anything *did* happen to Conrad, Frank would see

to it that Ramirez and all his gun-wolves paid for it in blood.

He drank some more of the coffee and said calmly, "I need to talk to that Apache fella and figure out the best way to blow up the gates into that place."


The Kid sat with his back propped against the stone wall of the cell and rolled his shoulders to get the muscles working properly again. He flexed his fingers and felt the sharp stabs of pain as the blood began flowing in his hands. It was uncomfortable but necessary. If he got the chance to make any sort of move against his captors, he wanted to be able to seize the opportunity.

Footsteps in the corridor outside made him lift his head. He suspected he was the only prisoner down here, now that Frank was gone, so whoever it was had to be coming to this cell. Maybe Antonia had decided his fate, and they were coming to drag him to his death.

He hoped they would be careless enough to let him get his hands on a gun. Just a few shots before he died, that was all he asked for. A chance to put a bullet through Diego Ramirez's head and end his reign of terror . . .

"Señor Callahan?"

The voice that came through the barred window in the door was a surprise. It belonged to Antonia. He'd heard only one set of footsteps, he realized. What was she doing, venturing down here alone?

He stood up and moved over to the door, but he didn't put his face up next to the window, just in case Antonia had some sort of vicious trick up her silk sleeve.

"What do you want, señorita?" he asked quietly.

"Just to talk."

"What's the matter? Having trouble coming up with some suitable way to torture me to death, so you thought maybe you'd ask me for suggestions?"

"You should be careful how you speak to me," she snapped. "I hold your life in the palm of my hand."

"If you don't kill me, your father will take care of that for you."

"Not if he is no longer in command."

He frowned. What in blazes did she mean by that? He risked a look out through the bars.

She was alone, all right, at least as far as he could see. Her face was close to the window in the door. The light from a lantern at the end of the corridor burnished one smooth cheek as she peered in at him.

"Listen to me," she said with a note of urgency. "The guard is far enough away that he cannot hear if you keep your voice low."

"All right," the Kid said in little more than a whisper. "What do you want, señorita?"

"I want to save your life, Señor Callahan. Despite what you did south of the border, you are valuable to me. At least . . . you can be."

"The general doesn't agree with you."

She let out a tiny snort and said, "My father and I have often disagreed. We see this revolution of his in different ways."

"You don't want to free Mexico from el Presidente Díaz's grip?"

She waved a hand and said, "Díaz is a brutal dictator and should be removed, but one brutal dictator is much like another, eh? I have no illusions about my father. He is a cruel man, too. And yet he has his virtues. For example, he is not a greedy man."

"He just stole a fortune in gold," the Kid said.

"The means to an end. If he has to, he will spend every penny of it in his quest to gain power."

The Kid was starting to have an inkling of what was going on here. He said, "And you don't really care all that much about power, do you? At least . . . not compared to gold."

"With the wealth that is in this stronghold right now, I could live in comfort for the rest of my days. More than comfort. Luxury. If my father has his way, though, all of it will go to hire more gunmen, buy more guns and bullets."

"I don't see how you can stop him from doing that," the Kid said.

"He cannot waste all that gold," Antonia said, "if he is not alive."

The Kid said nothing. He knew he should have been shocked and horrified by the calm way the girl spoke about her father's potential death, but somehow, he wasn't. This was just one more step in his true understanding of who and what Antonia Ramirez really was.

She expected him to respond, though, so after a moment he said, "It sounds an awful lot like you're saying you'll spare my life if something happens to your father."

"Not *if* something happens, Señor Callahan. When. And your life depends on making certain that it does."

If she wanted blunt talk, he would give it to her. "You want me to kill your father."

"Tonight, you will be taken out to be executed. My father will be there to witness your death. But you will

have a gun, and your hands will be bound in such a way
that you can get free."

He didn't bother asking her how she was going to accomplish that. Probably a dozen men, or more, inside this
compound would do anything she asked them to, and wag
their tails like happy little puppies while they were doing
it, if only she would favor them with a smile. A touch, a
kiss, would purchase their very souls.

She confirmed that by continuing, "When my father
dies, men who are loyal to me will deal with those who
are not. Once there is no one to oppose us, we will load
up the gold again and leave this haunted place."

"Haunted?" the Kid repeated, recalling the story that
Ezra Dawson, the old liveryman in Saguaro Springs, had
told him about how the man who started this ranch had
murdered his partner and gone mad because of it. "Have
you seen some strange things around here?"

"Never mind that," Antonia snapped. "Do you agree,
Señor Callahan?" She took hold of one of the bars in the
window and added tenderly, "Juan?"

"What happens to me after you get what you want?"

She shrugged prettily. "You come to Mexico with me
and help me spend all that gold, no?"

The Kid didn't believe that for a second. She'd probably
put a bullet in his head as soon as possible after he'd done
the dirty work of killing her father for her. Her nature
would demand that. Snakes had to strike, and scorpions
had to sting.

But for now, agreeing with her was his best way out
of this dungeon, his best opportunity to seize a fighting

chance for life. He smiled and said, "No man could resist an offer like that, señorita."

"Antonia."

"Antonia. I'll do what you want."

*"Bueno."* Her face came closer to the bars. "We should seal the bargain . . ."

She didn't have to suggest that twice. The Kid leaned close. Their faces pressed against the bars from opposite sides, and their lips met between the two iron cylinders. If he hadn't known how cold and merciless she really was, the Kid would have enjoyed the kiss. Her lips were warm and sweet and urgent. He didn't let himself forget the truth for an instant, though.

She broke the kiss and whispered, "From the moment I first saw you, Juanito, I knew you were the man to deliver my heart's desire to me."

"Your heart's desire being a pile of gold?"

"And a good man to help me spend it." She laughed softly. "You shall see. Just do your part, and you will have treasures beyond your wildest dreams."

"I don't know. My dreams can be pretty wild."

"I cannot wait to find out."

He had bantered like this with many women in the past. Seldom had it ended well. This probably wouldn't, either. But it was his only chance, so he smiled and kept his true feelings hidden as Antonia eased back from the door and then started toward the far end of the corridor where the stairs were located.

He heard her speak to the guard there and wondered if the man was one of those who had promised to turn on Ramirez and give his loyalty to her. More than likely he was, otherwise he would have run to the general and reported that she had been cozying up to the prisoner instead of coming up with ways to torture him.

Maybe that was what she would claim if her father or anyone else ever confronted her about what had just happened. She could say that she had been offering him false hope in order to make his torment more painful later on. Most men wouldn't believe such a story, but Ramirez might. It seemed like Antonia could do little wrong in his eyes.

And one way or another, that was likely to be the general's downfall, the Kid thought as he sat down again with his back against the wall and waited for the showdown.

# Chapter 32

The mixed-blood Apache's name was Tomás. He was a dour, wiry, dark-faced man who listened in silence as Frank explained the plan. Then he nodded and said, "I can do this."

"It'll be more dangerous than what you did last night," Frank cautioned. "There weren't any guards right above the spot where you planted that keg of blasting powder, but there will be at the gates. They have loopholes to watch through, and they'll be listening mighty hard, too. Ramirez is probably expecting an attack of some sort."

"No one will see or hear me unless I wish it," Tomás said with complete confidence.

Frank nodded and said, "I'll take your word for it, then. We'll make our move as soon as it's good and dark, before the moon comes up."

That information had circulated through the settlement, so the volunteers knew when they had to be ready to go. Ezra Dawson had rounded up enough horses and mules so that all the men could ride. Jonathan Trammell, who owned the general store, had handed out ammunition until his shelves were nearly empty. Harold Griffith, owner of the Cactus Saloon, had provided free drinks . . . but only one per man, according to Frank's strict orders, because he didn't want to have to keep a bunch of drunken fools in line and go into battle with them. One drink might settle the nerves of a man who wasn't used to risking his life, though.

Julio Hernandez and his wife kept the meals coming in their café all day, at no charge to the volunteers. Frank had warned the men not to eat too heavily, either. A fella didn't need too much food weighing him down during a fight.

For some of these men, however, it might well be their last meal . . . although Frank didn't want to point that out. He assumed a lot of them might be making love to their wives today, too, just in case, but that was none of his business.

As for himself, he stayed on the move during the afternoon, checking on the defenses around the settlement, offering words of encouragement to everyone he spoke to, listening to reports from men who had been out spying on the bandit stronghold. They didn't have any news. Ever since the group that had ventured below the border had returned late that morning, the hacienda and the other buildings of the old rancho had just squatted there in the hot sun with no movement visible from outside.

"I have to tell you, though, Señor Morgan," one man said as he mopped his sweaty face with a bandanna, "I do not like it out there on the edge of the desert. Something about it feels . . . wrong. Like there is something foul in the air. And there were times . . ." He hesitated, then went on, "Times that I felt as if someone were watching me, but when I turned around, there was no one. And no place for anyone to hide, either."

Frank recalled the unnerving yips he had heard while he and the others were riding through the wasteland the night before. He had felt a little like he was being watched, too. But nothing was out there. The desert was lifeless except for snakes and lizards and bugs, wasn't it?

"Just knowing that Ramirez and his men are out there is enough to give a man the fantods," he said.

"*Sí, señor*," the man said. "If you say so. These fantods I have, of that there is no doubt."

Late in the day, Florita found Frank as he stood on the porch of the hotel, having talked briefly to Henrietta and Peggy Cole a few minutes earlier. The blond mother and daughter had assured him that when this was over, he would have the best room in the hotel for as long as he wanted it.

When Florita came up to him, she said, "Tía Luciana wishes to see you."

"What about?" Frank asked.

Florita shook her head. "No one questions la Mariposa."

"I'll go and talk to her. But before I do, how are you feeling, Florita?"

She shrugged, but winced a little at the pain the gesture cost her. "My mother knows many healing herbs. She has taken care of my back. There will be scars, but it will heal."

"I'm sorry you had to go through that."

"I would do it again if it meant removing the threat of Ramirez from this town." She paused. "You will kill that man Kern, Señor Morgan?"

"Somebody will," Frank said. "He'll be dead before morning. You can bet a hat on that."

He nodded to Florita and headed to the cantina to see what Luciana Hernandez wanted.

She was waiting for him and led him into the back room where he had gotten some sleep earlier. She had two cups of coffee waiting there and said, "I spoke to Señor Griffith at the saloon. He told me you refused a drink earlier and said that you were not much of a drinking man. So instead of tequila, I thought I would offer you coffee instead. Unless you would rather go with me to my brother's café and have a meal . . . ?"

"Coffee's fine," Frank assured her. "To be honest with you, I don't have much of an appetite right now."

"A nervous stomach before a battle? I would not have expected that of you, Frank."

He shook his head and said, "I'm not nervous for myself." He paused for a second to consider, then went on, "It's possible that my son is in that stronghold and is Ramirez's prisoner."

Her finely arched eyebrows rose higher in surprise. Frank could tell she was curious, so he explained briefly about Conrad, the relationship between them, and the fact that he had seen his son inside the hacienda.

"He's posing as a gunman named Callahan," Frank continued. "According to Beatriz, he was one of the men Ramirez sent to hold up that train. But the men keeping an eye on the place said that when those bandits returned, one of them had his hands tied behind his back. From the description I got, the prisoner could have been Conrad."

"But you do not know this for certain?"

"No, I don't," Frank admitted. "But it's the uncertainty that has me a mite worried. I'd really appreciate it if you didn't say anything to anybody about this, though. My first responsibility is to put a stop to Ramirez's plans and end his spree around here."

"A man's first responsibility is to his children," Luciana argued.

Frank shook his head and said, "Most of the time, sure. But now and then something bigger comes up, something that makes you realize how much is riding on it, and that changes things. What we do tonight could change the future of a whole country. Two countries, maybe, because if Ramirez ever *does* seize power in Mexico, I don't believe he'll be satisfied. From what I've seen of him, sooner or later he'll get ambitious again, and he's liable to turn his sights on the United States."

"You believe he would attack the Americans?"

"It could happen," Frank said. "Unless we stop him now. I promise you, though, if Conrad's in danger, I'll do everything in my power to save him, unless it means letting Ramirez go. Conrad wouldn't want me to do that. Once he would have been selfish enough to feel that way, but the boy's grown up a lot over the past few years."

Luciana smiled and said, "He sounds as if he is no longer a boy."

"Yeah, you're right about that. He's a man, a good man. As fine a man as I've ever known. I ought to remind myself of that a little more often."

She thought about everything he had said, then she slowly began to nod.

"I will say nothing to anyone. This is a private matter."

They had been sipping coffee as they talked. Frank drank the last of his now and stood up.

"Reckon I'd better get back out there," he said.

"It is still several hours until nightfall."

"I've been checking on the defenses—"

She was on her feet, too, and stepped closer to rest both hands on his chest.

"I have been told that everything in town is ready if we must defend Saguaro Springs from attack," she said. "You have done everything that can be done for now, Frank. Why not ease your mind for a time, while you have the chance?"

"I'm not sure how I'd go about doing that."

"Oh," she said, leaning even closer so he felt the soft, rounded warmth of her breasts as she smiled up at him, "I can think of several excellent ideas . . ."


The Kid looked up when he heard several sets of footsteps approaching the cell late in the day. A key rattled in the lock and the door swung open. Diego Ramirez, still wearing his gaudy green uniform and plumed hat, strode into the stone chamber followed by Kern and Bracken, both of them holding drawn guns. They trained the revolvers on the Kid.

Kern looked tense and eager, as if he wanted any excuse to pull the trigger and blast a hole through the prisoner. The Kid expected such an attitude from the sadistic Bracken, but Kern was usually cooler headed than that. Right now, though, fires of rage burned in the *segundo*'s eyes, and the Kid had to wonder why.

He didn't have long to think about it, though, because Ramirez announced, "My daughter has decided how you are to die, traitor. You will be flogged until life has departed from your body." He shrugged. "To be honest, I expected something more creative from her. One of my men who is part Yaqui claims that with a sharp-enough knife, he can remove every bit of a man's skin without that man dying until hours later. I thought perhaps that might be your fate."

"Reckon we'll both have to live with the disappointment," the Kid said dryly.

Ramirez's face hardened with anger.

"You will not be so clever when the whip has fallen for the twentieth, or the fiftieth, time. However many lashes it takes to kill you." Ramirez nodded toward Kern. "Señor Kern will deliver the strokes."

"And I'll enjoy each and every one of them," Kern said with an unexpected vehemence in his voice.

What the hell?

Then a possibility occurred to the Kid. He knew that Kern was sweet on Antonia Ramirez. If he had found out that she'd been down here talking to the Kid alone, he might be jealous, even though she had sentenced the prisoner to death.

Surely Antonia knew how Kern felt about her. Somehow, women were always aware of these things. The Kid wondered why she hadn't approached Kern to get rid of her father instead of him. Maybe she didn't believe he would ever double-cross his leader. Some men were pretty stiff-necked about such things as loyalty and honor, even when faced with the temptation of a beautiful woman.

"If you would like a last meal, now is the time," Ramirez went on. "I hesitate to offer such a courtesy to someone who attempted to betray our cause, but I am not a barbarian, after all."

"I don't think I have much of an appetite," the Kid said.

Ramirez spread his hands and said, "Very well. If such

is your decision, so be it. Tonight, when darkness has fallen and the moon first appears in the sky, your death will begin, Señor Callahan . . . but it may take a long, agonizing time."

He turned and strode out of the cell, leaving the two gunmen to cover the Kid as they backed out and locked up.

Before they left, though, Bracken said, "Hey, Kern, you reckon we ought to make some bets on how long it'll take him to die?"

"I'm not going to gamble on it," Kern said. "I'll take my pleasure in other ways."

# Chapter 33

Frank knelt on the back side of a small, sandy rise about half a mile from Diego Ramirez's stronghold. Tomás was on his right, holding a bundle of six sticks of dynamite obtained from Jonathan Trammell's store. Trammell had been happy to donate them when he found out what Frank intended them for. Dynamite would be easier than using another keg of blasting powder.

The sun had set half an hour earlier, but an arch of fading red and gold remained in the western sky. Behind Frank, to the east, a deep, deep blue that would soon darken to black spread through the heavens. Before too much longer, stars would begin to pop into view. Then darkness would close down over the landscape, relieved only by faint starlight until the rising of the moon half an hour later.

Tomás was confident that he could reach the stronghold and plant the dynamite to destroy the gates before the moon rose.

"We'll be creeping closer behind you, so when the gates are blown, we'll be able to rush in before Ramirez's men know what's happening," Frank said quietly, referring to the forty men with him. A dozen more had been left in Saguaro Springs to join the women and teenage boys in defending the settlement if they needed to. Some of those men were unhappy about not being included in this force, but Frank had picked those with the largest families to stay in town, unwilling to risk their lives unless absolutely necessary.

Frank went on, "Is that fuse long enough to give you time to get away?"

"Too long and they may see it burning," Tomás said. "It must be short enough that they will not have time to open the gates and put it out."

Frank nodded, knowing the man was right. Tomás would be running the biggest risk starting out, but all of them would be in danger of losing their lives before this night was over. That was the price of freeing the settlement from Ramirez's grip and making sure that he didn't go on to do even worse things.

Frank turned to Ezra Dawson, who had also been a soldier during the Civil War, although for the Federals rather than for the Confederacy. After so many decades, Frank didn't care about that anymore. Dawson was serving as his second-in-command.

"Pick ten men and spread them out in front of the compound," Frank told the liveryman. "Pick the best marksmen you can find, because we'll need them to be sharpshooters. When the dynamite goes off, they'll concentrate their shots along the top of the wall so any of Ramirez's men who are up there will have to keep their heads down. It'd be a good idea if all ten men are armed with repeaters, so they can keep up a steady fire."

"Understood," Dawson said with a nod.

"I'll have fifteen men with me," Frank went on. "We'll go in first. Give us a couple of minutes, and then you follow with the other fifteen men. We'll have engaged Ramirez's forces by then, and with any luck we'll be able to catch at least some of them between our two forces."

"If you find Ramirez and kill him, that ought to do it. I'd be willin' to bet that most of his men are in it for the money, not because they really believe in some sort o' revolution."

"You're probably right about that," Frank agreed, "but they're still going to fight, and fight hard, because they'll know they can't expect much mercy from you folks after running roughshod over you for so long."

"They damn sure can't," Dawson said grimly.

Frank checked the sky again. Sunset's aftermath was almost gone, and pinpricks of light had appeared in the eastern sky. The stars were coming out.

"All right," he said to Tomás. "I'll leave it up to you when to start."

"This is a good time," the mixed-blood said. "The shadows are thick."

"I'll pass the word, then," Frank said.

A few minutes later, with Tomás out in front by fifty yards or so, Frank and his group began creeping toward the bandit stronghold, moving slowly and taking advantage of every bit of cover they could find as they closed in on the enemy.


As night approached, the Kid couldn't help but wonder what was going to happen. Antonia had promised that he would be freed and armed, but had she been telling the truth? Maybe that really *was* part of her plan to torment him. He began considering all the possibilities, and not many of them were good.

He had no way to tell what time it was, but it seemed like night ought to have fallen by now. On the other hand, he didn't want to hurry along his potential death. He just sat there and waited, trying to stay calm.

When he heard several people coming along the corridor, he got to his feet. Two gunmen he didn't know came into the cell first and covered him with shotguns. The third man into the cell, somewhat surprisingly, was Sam Woodson. The jovial outlaw didn't have his guitar with him this time, which was good. The Kid was in no mood for a serenade.

"Howdy, Johnny," Woodson said. "I figured you might like to see a friendly face, since this is gonna be a tryin' time for you. You need to turn around."

"What are you going to do?" the Kid asked.

"Orders are that your hands should be tied behind your back. I'll take care o' that."

With the two double-barreled shotguns menacing him, the Kid couldn't do anything except comply. He turned so that his back was to Woodson, who stepped closer behind him.

"Gimme your hands."

The Kid put his hands behind him, and as he did, he felt Woodson shove something into the waistband of his trousers, at the small of his back, and then pull his shirttail out to cover it. The Kid could tell by the object's feel that it was a short-barreled revolver of some sort. He realized that Woodson's body was blocking the view of the other two guards. They couldn't see that Woodson had just given him a gun or tell that Woodson wasn't tying the length of rope he had brought along very tightly around the Kid's wrists.

Woodson grunted as if putting a lot of effort into the binding. The Kid played along with a sharply indrawn breath, then said, "Damn it, you don't have to make that so tight. There's nowhere I could go and nothing I could do, even if I got loose."

"You ain't gettin' loose. It was Señorita Ramirez's orders that I make sure of that."

So he was one of the men loyal to Antonia who was switching sides. That didn't come as a complete surprise to the Kid. Woodson had never struck him as the revolutionary sort. He was more interested in money, and Antonia probably had offered him plenty.

Woodson stepped back and said, "All right, we're ready to go."

The men marched the Kid out of the cell, along the corridor, and up the stairs out of the dungeon. They followed a twisting route to the front part of the hacienda, then out through the big entrance hall. They circled the adobe building that Ramirez planned to use as his second capital someday, after he seized power. The Kid frowned as he saw torchlight spilling over the open area in front of the building. With the exception of a few men posted on the parapet at the top of the wall, what appeared to be Ramirez's entire army had gathered for the execution, and a number of them held blazing brands.

The garish light revealed a wooden post set into the ground so that about eight feet of it stuck up. The Kid realized he wasn't going to be strung up from one of the vigas the way Florita had been. He would be tied to that post with his back to the big, thronelike chairs that had been placed in front of the adobe building. Ramirez and Antonia were seated in those chairs, like royalty.

Kern and Bracken waited to one side of the whipping post. Kern held a coiled whip, either the same one he had used on Florita or a twin to it. Bracken had his thumbs hooked casually in his gun belt and a smirk on his face.

Woodson had a hand on the Kid's back, prodding him toward the post, but Ramirez raised a hand to halt the procession.

"Bring him over here," the general ordered. "I would face the traitor before he dies."

Antonia looked a little uneasy but not actually displeased by this.

"You heard the man," Woodson said quietly to the Kid. "You gonna be able to get loose from that rope?"

"Soon," the Kid breathed.

Woodson marched him over to stand in front of Ramirez. The self-proclaimed general regarded him solemnly for a long moment, then said, "You tried to steal from our cause, Señor Callahan. There can be no greater crime than such a betrayal. Do you have anything to say before you pay for this crime with your life?"

The Kid had been carefully, unobtrusively, twisting his wrists to loosen the bonds even more. Now he pulled harder with his right arm and that hand came free. He reached inside his waistband, under the tail of the black shirt he wore, and smoothly drew the revolver Woodson had slipped him.

He sure wished he'd had a chance to check it and make sure it was loaded.

But he didn't have time for that. Moving almost faster

than the eye could follow, he thrust his arm out and leveled the gun at Ramirez. It was a .32 caliber Smith & Wesson, not a very powerful handgun but deadly enough at short range like this.

Ramirez started to bolt to his feet as shouts of alarm filled the compound at the sight of him being threatened. But the Kid snapped, "Don't move, General! My thumb's the only thing holding this hammer back. Even if your men shoot me, it'll fall and you'll die. So you'd better tell them not to get nervous."

"Hold your fire!" Ramirez called. His voice shook a little from outrage. "Hold your fire!"

"You were wrong about my crime being the biggest," the Kid went on, figuring out his next move on the spur of the moment. "There's a worse one."

He glanced at Antonia, saw the hate-filled daggers shooting from her eyes at him as her hands tightened into claws on the arm of the chair where she sat. That didn't stop him from continuing, "Your daughter wants to replace you as the leader of this bunch."

Ramirez turned his head to stare in astonishment at Antonia. He demanded, "Is this true?"

"Papa, this man lies—" she began.

The Kid interrupted her. "She came to see me by herself, down in the dungeon. She's not interested in your revolution. She wants that gold, and she promised me part of it—along with her—if I'd get rid of you for her."

"You cannot believe him!" she cried. "I would never do such a thing, Papa!"

Ramirez stared coldly at her now as he said, "You told me many times that it would be better if we took the riches we raised for our cause and went someplace where no one would ever find us. But I believed you had come to understand how urgent and noble our cause is—"

"Your cause!" she cried suddenly as she came up out of the chair. "It was always your cause, never mine! I never cared about power, only wealth!"

The Kid said, "You can see now I've done you a favor, General. And to repay that favor, you're coming with me and we're leaving this place. You'll be my safe passage out of here—"

"No!" Antonia screeched. A dagger had appeared in her hand as if by magic, and before the Kid could stop her, she lunged at her father and drove the blade into his chest.

Ramirez started up out of the chair but fell back, his eyes wide with shock and pain. Antonia turned and shouted to the men who had gone over to her side, "Kill them! Kill them all!"

That was when a shot rang out from one of the men posted on the wall, and then the gates into the compound blew up, filling the torchlit air with smoke, flame, and flying splinters.

# Chapter 34

Frank didn't like sneaking around like this. Never had. He preferred facing his enemies straight up, head on. But sometimes stealth was necessary, and tonight was one of those times.

Darkness fell quickly in this part of the country. Seemingly only seconds passed between the time when the stars began to appear and thick ebony shadows completely cloaked the landscape. Frank couldn't see Tomás anymore, but he knew the part-Apache was up there somewhere, ahead of the others.

But then, with eyes adjusted to the dim starlight, Frank saw something flitting across the sandy ground between his position and the bandit stronghold. The vague figure trailed red sparks behind it, and the sudden *yip-yip-yip* of a deranged coyote split the night, followed by a reedy voice that cried, "Steal my rancho, will you, you damned greasers!"

Muzzle flame spurted from the top of the wall as one of the guards fired at the rushing figure. The shape staggered, then fell to its knees, but as the man pitched forward he threw something toward the gates. The sparks coming from the thing told Frank it was the bundle of dynamite. Frank had no idea what had happened to Tomás, but from what the ragged figure had screeched, he guessed it was old Walt Creeger, the man who had built the hacienda and then gone mad.

Then the dynamite exploded just as it landed at the base of the gates. Even though the plan had gotten skewed somehow, the end result was what Frank and the others wanted.

He surged to his feet and bellowed, "Follow me!" as he charged toward the now-destroyed gates with a fully loaded revolver in each hand.

Behind him, shots rang out from the marksmen Dawson had picked. The red glow of torchlight came from within the compound, and by that flickering glare Frank saw chips of adobe fly from the top of the wall. Any guards up there would have to keep their heads down or get them shot off.

Just ahead of him, he spotted a man rising unsteadily to his feet. Frank recognized him as Tomás. From the way he was acting, Creeger must have snuck up on him, walloped him on the head, and taken the dynamite away from him.

"Come on!" Frank barked as he charged past Tomás and continued toward the stronghold. A few more strides and he bounded over the wrecked gates, into the compound, which for some reason was already engulfed in a chaotic battle.

Guns roared back and forth, orange flame slashed the darkness, bullets hummed like giant bees, and men shouted curses and screamed in agony. Frank didn't know what was going on, but since everyone in here was an enemy—

with the exception of Conrad, if he was even inside the stronghold—he didn't hesitate as two men with rifles spun toward him and lifted their weapons.

Both of Frank's revolvers boomed and bucked in his hands. He saw the two men fly backward as his slugs drove into their chests. Then he strode forward, picking out targets and firing left, right, left, right. A bandit went down every time Frank squeezed the trigger.

Then somewhere close by, a man screamed, "Morgan!"

Frank turned and saw Carl Bracken standing there a few yards away. The gun-wolf looked more like a demon than ever with the crimson torchlight playing over his angular features. To Frank's surprise, he grinned, twirled the gun in his hand, and then slapped the iron back in its holster.

With all hell breaking loose around them, he wanted to test the speed of his draw against the notorious Frank Morgan, the Drifter, the Last Gunfighter. Bracken clawed at the gun butt on his hip.

Frank fired both guns. The slug from the one in his left hand punched into Bracken's heart. The bullet from the right-hand gun struck him in the forehead, bored on through his diseased brain, and burst out the back of his head in a grisly spray of blood, brain matter, and bone fragments. He hit the ground hard but was already way too dead to feel it.

Frank swung around, the vicious gunman already forgotten, and looked for his son.

Sam Woodson tackled the Kid and knocked him to the ground just as a hailstorm of lead slashed through the air above them. In the chaos, the Kid didn't know who had fired the shots, but it didn't really matter. The explosion had startled everyone into opening fire. Guns blasted all over the compound.

Woodson came up on his knees and grabbed the Kid's arm, urging, "Come on! We gotta get out of—"

His eyes widened and he gurgled as blood suddenly gushed from a gaping wound in his throat. He let go of the Kid and fell to the side to thrash around as he bled to death. Antonia stood there over the Kid, blood dripping from the dagger she had yanked from her father's chest and used to slash Woodson's throat.

"My God, why did you do that?" the Kid said. "He was on your side!"

"He was in my way," Antonia said calmly, "keeping me from killing you."

She raised the dagger, ready to lunge at the Kid.

Before she could, a man shouted, "You bitch!" and a gun blasted. Antonia rocked back as a red splotch appeared on her shirt. Kern stalked toward her, yelling, "I would have given you everything! *Everything!* But you wanted *him*!"

He continued triggering the gun in his hand as he shouted. The bullets slammed into Antonia, their impact making her stumble backward in a jittering dance as her dark eyes got bigger and bigger. Finally she crumpled into a bloody heap on the ground.

The Kid rolled over onto his belly as Kern fired again, at him this time. The bullet smacked into the ground less than a foot away. The Kid triggered the little Smith & Wesson twice. The first bullet, angling up, hit Kern between the eyes and jerked his head back. The second ripped into his throat and caused blood to fountain high into the air. His knees buckled and he went down, dead by the time his face plowed into the dirt.

The Kid pushed himself up onto his knees and looked around. Diego Ramirez had toppled off his chair and lay on his side, moving feebly but not going anywhere. The stab wound from his daughter hadn't killed him yet. The Kid crawled over to him.

Ramirez stared up at him and gasped, "An . . . Antonia!"

The Kid glanced at the crumpled shape on the ground a few yards away. She was shot to pieces and not moving. He knew she never would again.

Ramirez clawed at his arm and said, "My . . . my daughter! Is she . . . safe . . . ?"

Life was fading from the man's eyes. He had already lost all his dreams of power. The Kid didn't see a reason to take anything else away from him.

"She's fine," he said.

"Ahhhh . . . I forgive her . . . Señor . . . Callahan . . ."

The Kid couldn't resist saying, "My name is Conrad Browning. No, Conrad *Morgan*." He spotted a tall, broad-shouldered figure with a gun in each hand striding toward him through the now-dwindling battle. "And here comes my father now."

Ramirez's final breath rattled out of his throat. The Kid lowered the would-be *presidente*'s head to the ground and then stood up to hug Frank unashamedly. They pounded each other on the back, and Frank said, "How are you, son?"

"Just fine now," Conrad said.

* * *

Far into the night, the celebration continued in Saguaro Springs. Frank and Conrad sat at a table with Luciana Hernandez in one of the cantina's rear corners and drank coffee as they watched the singing and dancing and laughing that filled the rest of the room. Ezra Dawson was doing a jig with Beatriz to a tune played by several men with guitars. Peggy Cole and her mother, Henrietta, were among the spectators clapping along with the music.

Frank and Conrad had spent a while just filling each other in on everything that had happened since Antonia Ramirez, Kern, and Bracken had kidnapped Frank in Tucson. Frank said, "It'll be good to get back up there and pick up Dog and Stormy and Goldy from Pete McRoberts. I sure was relieved when you told me they were all right, Conrad."

"Dog wanted to come with me," Conrad replied with a smile, "but I was afraid it would be too risky. I thought Kern and Bracken might recognize him and wonder why Frank Morgan's dog was traveling with a hardcase named Callahan."

"That was smart thinking. I warn you, though, he holds a grudge, so he may not forgive you for keeping him out of the action."

Luciana said, "You men and your dogs. Whatever trouble is going on, you want to be right in the middle of it."

"You were pretty involved in this ruckus, too," Frank reminded her. "You may not have been in on the shooting part, but you helped put the whole thing together."

"You needed a woman to get it all organized," she responded with a toss of her head.

Conrad grinned and said, "I wouldn't argue with her, Frank."

"Oh, I don't intend to."

Luciana frowned and said, "He does not call you Papa or Father?"

"Maybe I ought to," Conrad said, "but it took me a while to warm up to the old coot, and by then I was used to calling him Frank."

"That's all right . . . boy," Frank said dryly.

He leaned back in his chair, stretched out his long legs, crossed his boots at the ankles, sipped coffee from the cup in his hand, and sighed in a mixture of weariness and satisfaction. Mostly satisfaction, because not one of the men from Saguaro Springs who had gone with him to attack Ramirez's stronghold had been killed in the battle. A few had been wounded, but all of them would recover, including Tomás, who had taken a lick on the head when Walt Creeger jumped him and grabbed the dynamite away from him.

Tomás's pride was hurt worse than anything else, because he had allowed Creeger to sneak up on him and had no idea the crazed old man was anywhere around until it was too late.

"Truly, he must have been a phantom to do such a thing without me knowing he was there," Tomás had said solemnly while explaining to Frank what had happened.

Creeger was flesh and blood, though, and the bullet fired by one of the outlaws on the wall had killed him at last, after years of him wandering the desert alone . . . alone, maybe, except for the ghost of his murdered partner.

Frank wasn't even going to speculate about that. He was just glad Creeger hadn't ruined things for them.

Diego Ramirez was dead, too, of course, along with Antonia, Kern, Bracken, Sam Woodson, and all but a few of the other bandits. The survivors, most of them wounded, had been rounded up and were locked in a smokehouse, since Saguaro Springs didn't have a jail. A rider had already left town on a fast horse, bound for Tucson. The sheriff would have to bring a posse and some wagons down here to transport the prisoners and the recovered gold back to the county seat. That gold would wind up back in the hands of those rich men from Monterrey. What they did with it after that was their business. Frank had already put that part of the affair completely out of his mind.

"You weren't ever going to pay that ransom money, were you?" he asked Conrad now.

"*I* wasn't going to pay it, but Claudius Turnbuckle had instructions to have the company pay it if I didn't come back or if he didn't hear from me in a certain amount of time. I wrote out a telegram for Claudius and sent it with that rider, to send when he gets to Tucson."

"So you would have given a snake like Ramirez a fortune just to save my hide?"

"I just told you, I would have been dead by then."

"He would have killed me anyway, even if he got the money."

"More than likely," Conrad agreed. "But I wouldn't have wanted to give up on you as long as there was a chance. Would *you* have paid if the situation had been reversed?"

Frank snorted and said, "Yeah, I'd have paid him in gunpowder and lead."

"The apple, as they say, does not fall far from the tree," Luciana commented with a smile.

Conrad scraped his chair back and stood up. "I think I'll go ask Miss Cole to dance," he said. "She doesn't like me much, but that's because she thought I was an outlaw. I'd kind of like to see if I can change her mind." He took a step, then paused and turned back. "One more thing, Frank. As Ramirez was dying, I told him my real name."

"You told him you were Conrad Browning?"

"I did. And then I told him my *real* name, the name I plan to go by from now on: Conrad Morgan."

Frank felt a surprising tightness in his chest. He said, "You don't have to do that, son. I know how much you loved your mother."

"I did," Conrad said. "I still do. But I shouldn't deny my true heritage, either. I'm a Morgan . . . just like you."

"And I'm mighty pleased about that," Frank told him.

Conrad smiled and turned away again. Frank watched as the young man approached the pretty blonde from the hotel and spoke to her. Peggy's response looked a little cool at first, but then she smiled and let Conrad take her in his arms and whirl her into the open space where several couples were dancing.

Luciana reached over and rested her hand on Frank's where it lay on the table.

"He is a fine young man," she said. "Like his father."

"I haven't been a young man in a long, long time."

"Perhaps not, but I like a man with some . . . seasoning, shall we say?"

Frank turned his hand and clasped hers, and they sat there listening to the music and watching the dancing and thinking about the celebrating that would come later.

Keep reading for a special excerpt!

# THE
# INTRUDERS
### ❦ A BUCK TRAMMEL WESTERN ❦

by
William W. Johnstone and J.A. Johnstone

Pinkerton. Sheriff. Lawman.
Buck Trammel has spent his life fighting for justice.
Now, he must defend a town against corrupt businessmen
and scurrilous outlaws turning it into
a bloody battleground.

Blackstone, Wyoming, belongs to "King" Charles Hagen.
The rancher bought land, built businesses, and employs
most of the townsfolk. Unfortunately Sheriff Buck
Trammel is not on His Majesty's payroll. The lawdog won't
be tamed or trained to accept King's position as master of
the territory, but neither will he threaten his empire.

Adam Hagen, King's oldest son, is vying to take control of
his father's violent empire in Blackstone.
Sidling up with the notorious criminal Lucien Clay, Adam is
adding professional gunmen to his gang of murderous hired
guns who perform his dirty deeds without question.
But moving against his father means crossing paths with his
former friend Buck—the man who once saved Adam's life.

A civil war is coming to Blackstone.
And when the gunsmoke clears, Buck Trammel is
determined to be the last man standing . . .

Look for **THE INTRUDERS** on sale now!

# Chapter 1

"Clean up Blackstone! Clean up Blackstone!"

So yelled the thirty or so marchers from the Citizens' Committee of Blackstone. Their number was enough to fill the width of Main Street in front of the Pot of Gold Saloon.

Sheriff Steven "Buck" Trammel stood guard in front of the saloon to prevent the crowd from storming the place. He might only have been one man, at several inches over six feet tall and two hundred and thirty solid pounds, he loomed large over the crowd. He looked larger still from the boardwalk.

The piano player from the Pot of Gold mocked the marchers by banging out "The Battle Hymn of the Republic." The patrons joined in, slurring the words loudly.

"Blasphemy!" Mike Albertson exclaimed. Trammel had heard the man with the crooked back was a retired freight driver who had given up the life of a long hauler to do the work of the Lord. He was the leader of the marchers and raised his voice louder than his followers as he said, "How dare they mention the Lord in a den of such call yourself, Trammel. You've got no right to order us to leave."

His followers cheered as Albertson pointed past Trammel toward the Pot of Gold Saloon. "But you do have every right to tell them to leave. To tell them to obey the law. Them and their kind. It's getting so it ain't safe to walk around town, be it morning, noon, or night. Drunken cowhands from the Blackstone Ranch and miners roaming the streets in a laudanum stupor."

Albertson pointed to a shrunken old woman clutching a bag. "Why, Mrs. Higgins here found one of them passed out on her porch the other morning. Gave this poor, God-fearing woman the fright of her life."

"I know all about it." Trammel looked at Mrs. Higgins and said, "I came right over and got him out of there, didn't I, Helen?"

The old lady's scowl turned into something of a smile. "Yes, you did, Sheriff. You came in and dragged him away in no time flat."

Trammel looked back at Albertson. "I kept that drunk in a cell until he sobered up. Then I fined him and threw him out of town. I know you're new around here, Albertson, but this town is used to drunks and knows how to handle them."

The old freighter pointed to the new buildings that had more than doubled the length of Main Street. The locals had taken to calling that section of town New Main Street. "And just how do you expect to handle all of them new places once they're open, Trammel? How many of them are going to be saloons? Your friend Hagen sure ain't telling us."

Trammel said, "Adam Hagen's not my friend, but he

does own those properties. Why don't you ask him what he has planned? Or ask Mayor Welch."

But Albertson and his followers had come to Main Street to shout and argue, not for answers. "Asking either of them is pointless," Albertson said. "Hagen is crafty enough to keep his true plans hidden, and Welch is gullible enough to believe him. And King Charles Hagen is content to look down on us from his ranch house and watch this town crumble without so much as lifting a finger."

The crowd offered a full-throated cheer, and Albertson raised his voice so he could be heard over them. "We will not be deterred by lies and placation. We will not be fooled into thinking Hagen's plans are for the benefit of anyone but himself."

The old freighter's eyes narrowed in defiance as he glared up at Trammel. "And we will not allow a Judas goat with a star on his chest to tell us to be calm and go home."

Trammel snatched Albertson by the collar and pulled him toward himself before he realized what he had done. He easily lifted the man just enough so that Albertson was standing on his toes.

The marchers gasped and now took several steps back.

"You listen to me, Albertson, and listen well," Trammel said. "I'm nobody's Judas goat, got it? I don't belong to either of the Hagens. I don't belong to Montague down at the bank. I don't belong to anyone or anything but the law and the town of Blackstone. If you ever doubt it, come see me at the jail and I'll be more than happy to convince you."

He released Albertson with a shove that sent him stumbling back toward the marchers he led. Several of them rushed to keep him from falling down. He knew he would regret manhandling the rabble-rouser later on, but now was not the time.

He faced the crowd. "You've all made your point. You've had your march. You've spoken your mind and you've been heard. Now it's over. If I see any of you clustered together within the next five minutes, I'll lock you up for disorderly conduct."

Trammel did not have to ask if he had made himself clear. Judging by the looks on their faces, they knew.

And from how they had just seen him take on Albertson, none of them wanted to risk the same treatment.

Trammel stood his ground alone as he watched the marchers reluctantly fold their banners and head back to their homes.

As the crowd thinned out, only one man was left in the middle of Main Street. A thin man in his late twenties, his black hair and spectacles gave him a studious look. This man was not Albertson, but Richard Rhoades of the town's newspaper, the *Blackstone Bugle*.

Trammel shut his eyes and hung his head. He had not seen the reporter during the march. If he had, he would have tried to keep a better handle on his temper. Grabbing Albertson would be the bright bow his story needed for the paper's next edition. And he couldn't blame Rhoades for printing it. He could only blame himself for giving the newsman something to print.

"How long have you been there?" Trammel called out to him over the heads of departing marchers.

"From the beginning." The reporter finished jotting something down in his notebook as he walked toward Trammel. "I was with them when they began gathering at Bainbridge Avenue and followed them the whole way here. They had about thirty marchers by the time you broke it up. An impressive number for a town this size if you ask me."

Throughout his career as a policeman in Manhattan, and then as a Pinkerton, Trammel always had a healthy distrust of newspapermen. They tended to distort the truth to fit whatever message they were trying to convey. But Rhoades was a different sort. Since he had come to town a year before, Trammel found his reporting honest and had even grown to like the man.

"Guess you're happy I grabbed Albertson like I did. That ought to make a nice addition to your story."

"Maybe," Rhoades agreed, "but I'm not going to use it."

Trammel hadn't been expecting that. "Why not? Your readers will love it."

The reporter shook his head. "Albertson said he wouldn't be manipulated by anyone, and neither will I. He goaded you into grabbing him because he knew I was there. When he gathered everyone together, he told me to keep an eye on him because he was going to give me 'one hell of a story' for my article. I won't give him the satisfaction of printing it."

Trammel's mood improved some. "I'll make it a point of keeping a better handle on my temper when he's around. He won't rile me so easily next time."

Rhoades leaned in closer so no one could hear him say, "Personally, I think you should've slugged him for stirring up all this trouble."

Trammel had thought about that a lot since Albertson had first come to town six weeks before. The crippled freighter had started grousing about conditions in the town almost from the start. People were always looking for a

THE INTRUDERS 323

reason to complain, and men like Albertson had a knack for getting the worst out of them. "What do you think his aim is? About starting up all this trouble, I mean. I've known a lot of freighters in my day, and every one of them would prefer whiskey and women over marches and such. It doesn't make any sense to me."

"Me neither," Rhoades agreed. "He claims he was a freighter, but if he was, he's the most eloquent mule skinner I've ever heard."

The small question that had been rattling around in Trammel's mind now loomed large. "That's been bothering me, too. You think he's a phony?"

"He seems sincere in his complaints," Rhoades said. "There's no denying that. Now, as for his motivation, I'm still trying to figure that out." Trammel watched an idea dawn on the reporter's face. "He says he's worked freighter outfits in Texas and Missouri and Kansas. I have colleagues in those areas. I'm going to write them to see if they've heard of him. I doubt we'll learn much, but I'll feel better having tried it."

Trammel watched Albertson walk back toward Bainbridge with two old ladies on his arms. He was gesturing wildly, probably carrying on with the same rhetoric he had used in front of the saloon.

"Think you could wire your friends instead?" Trammel asked. "The town will pay for it."

"In that case, of course." Rhoades looked curious. "But why the urgency?"

"Because I think Albertson is working up to something big," Trammel said. "Today's march proves it. His attempt to barge into the saloon tells me he's looking to escalate things. The sooner we know who and what he is, the quicker we'll know what he's really up to. Might be able to stop him before he does it."

"Let's hope so." Rhoades pushed his hat further back and scratched his forehead. "I've got to tell you, Sheriff, for a small town, Blackstone's sure got a lot of intrigue going on."

Trammel could not argue with him there. "Too much for my taste. When do you think you could get down to Laramie and send out those telegrams?"

He pulled his watch from his waistcoat and frowned. "It'll be well on dark if I leave now and I have tomorrow's edition to get out. I'll do it first thing in the morning. That soon enough for you?"

It wasn't, but it sounded like it would have to be. "I appreciate it, Rich. And I appreciate you leaving my grabbing of Albertson out of your article."

"Don't give it a second thought." Rhoades grinned. "Besides, no one wants to read anything that casts 'the Hero of Stone Gate' in a bad light."

"Knock it off." Trammel had hated that moniker since the day Rhoades had hung it on him after he kept a group of Pinkertons from taking over King Charles Hagen's Blackstone Ranch the previous year. "I told you not to call me that."

"That's the problem with you, Buck. You're too modest. I spelled your name right and gave you a legend. You should be pleased. The people of this territory have put you on a pedestal."

Trammel knew he was right. And he also knew what people did with things on pedestals.

They pulled them down after they were sick of looking at them.

# Chapter 2

Adam Hagen had watched the entire spectacle unfold from the second-floor balcony of the Clifford Hotel. His hotel.

From there, he could watch the whole town. He could see the carpenters working on the structures he had ordered to be built on lots he had purchased along Main Street. He could see the new houses he was building on the new Buffalo Street, too, in anticipation of the people who would flock to Blackstone when his plans took shape. He had even seen the marchers assemble on Bainbridge, then head toward his Pot of Gold on Main Street. He had watched them pick up more followers along the way until they reached his saloon and hurled insults and prayers at the place.

He almost felt sorry for the poor fools. They were so ardent in their righteousness. Strident in their belief that they could change the future of Blackstone.

But Adam Hagen knew there was only one man who could do that, and it was not King Charles Hagen. Soon, it would be King Adam Hagen.

He had ordered the porch to be added to his room to

aid in his convalescence after having been shot in the right arm by renegade Pinkerton men several months before.

He squeezed the small bag of sand in his right hand again for the countless time that day. He ignored the sharp pain that webbed through his body following each squeeze. His convalescence had taken a toll on him, particularly his looks. His fair hair had begun to turn white in places, though he was just past thirty. His smooth skin, which the ladies loved, now had lines brought about by pain that had not been there before.

A doctor down in Laramie had told him the exercise was his best chance of regaining some use of his right arm. The doctor had been cautious enough to tell him that he was unlikely to ever have full use of the arm again, but with diligent exercise, he might be able to hold a fork again. Perhaps even write his name without much difficulty.

But as for gambling and gunfighting, those activities were out. The doctor advised him to learn how to make do with his left hand for now.

But Adam Hagen had no intention of making do with anything. He had made do long enough as the banished son of King Charles Hagen. And now that he knew the man he had called "Father" all those years was actually his uncle, he planned on going far beyond making do.

He intended on making revenge.

Hagen had almost cheered when Trammel snatched Albertson by the neck. The old man had been baiting him and almost got what he deserved. But Buck was a smart man, quick to anger and even quicker to calm down and listen to reason.

It was why the people of Blackstone loved him. It was the quality Hagen had admired most in his former friend.

And it also happened to be the only weakness in his considerable armor. A weakness he intended to exploit when the time came.

He knew Trammel would rebel at first. After all, Hagen hadn't nicknamed him Buck without a reason. But eventually he would see that his old friend was right and had given him an embarrassment of riches. Hagen hoped Trammel would be prudent enough to focus on the message and not the messenger. Hagen still owed him for saving his life by getting him out of Wichita the year before.

If he did not, Hagen just might have to kill him, and that would cast a shadow over all he had dreamed these past months in convalescence.

Hagen watched Trammel finish his conversation with that weasel reporter from the *Bugle*. His first order of business upon taking over the town would be to buy that damned paper and shut it down. But for the moment it served its purpose.

He watched Trammel lumber back toward the jail, which was right next door to the Clifford Hotel. Hagen did not have many regrets in life, but he regretted that he and the big man were no longer friends. Trammel abhorred his selling of laudanum at his saloon and the laudanum he allowed the Chinese to sell in a canvas tent next door.

But he had not regretted it enough to stop selling laudanum. In fact, laudanum played a key role in his plans for revenge.

He saw Trammel cast a quick glance up to his balcony and, upon seeing him, quickly looked away.

Hagen got out of his chair and went to the side railing

as he called out, "Behold the return of the conquering hero! That was a mighty impressive sight to see, Buck. They complain about the new saloons on Main Street, but say nothing of the houses I'm building. They're a fickle bunch indeed. At least you turned them before they got themselves hurt. They wouldn't have received a warm reception in my saloon."

Trammel stopped walking and glowered up at him. Hagen had to admit the sheriff was a frightening sight when he was angry.

"I've told you not to call me that," Trammel said. "We're not friends anymore, Hagen, so quit acting like we are."

"I'm still your friend," Hagen said, "even if you're not mine."

"If you mean that, then quit selling dope," Trammel said. "You've got half the men on your father's ranch using the stuff, and most of the coal miners. Quit rotting their brains and you and me can be friends again."

Adam appeared to think it over, though he had absolutely no intention of stopping the flow of laudanum into Blackstone. If anything, it was just the opposite. He decided to have a little fun with the sheriff. "A wise proposition. Why don't you come up here so we can talk about it instead of shouting at each other like this?"

"And look like I'm up there to kiss your ring?" Trammel shook his head. "No chance."

Hagen laughed. "You always see me in the worst light. Even after all we've been through together. I'm not your enemy, Buck. You saved my life, and I'll never be able to repay you for it."

"Don't thank me," Trammel said. "If I'd known what you'd turn into, I wouldn't have bothered."

"Yes, you would," Hagen told him. "You're a natural hero, Sheriff Trammel, and this world needs heroes. It always has and always will."

Trammel looked like he was going to say something more but didn't. Instead, something in the distance captured his attention.

And when Hagen looked in the same direction, he understood why. Dr. Emily Downs was getting into her wagon.

Hagen imagined some might call her pretty. He had always thought of her as elegant, with an agile mind that made for pleasant company.

She had captured Trammel's heart from the moment they had arrived in Blackstone and, for a time, they had been a very happy couple.

But their relationship had soured after Trammel's troubles with the Pinkertons at Stone Gate. She had been a widow once and had no intention of becoming one again. She'd shut her heart to Trammel, and Hagen knew it had wounded the big man deeply. It had hardened him in a way that had made Hagen angry. She had given up Trammel because he could no sooner change who and what he was than Hagen could grow a new right arm. He had expected more from a woman of science, but as a widow, he could not fault her reasons.

Hagen watched Trammel forget the world around him as Emily released the break and snapped the reins, bringing her horse to a quick trot. He saw Trammel stand a little straighter and something of a smile appear on his face as she steered the wagon toward Main Street. Even the sight of her was enough to make him happy, and Hagen's heart ached for him.

She would pay for hurting him, and soon. But not that day.

She sat ramrod straight and made a point of keeping her eyes forward as she approached the Clifford Hotel. Hagen knew she could hear him as he called out, "And a blessed day to you, our fair Dr. Downs. Our humble town is grateful for you gracing us with your presence."

"Mr. Hagen," she said as she rode by, then added, "Sheriff Trammel."

Buck tipped his hat, entranced as she rode by without the slightest glance his way. "Nice to see you, Emily."

She said nothing more as she continued on her way.

Hagen pitied his former friend. He waited until she had passed out of earshot before saying, "Quite the peacock our Dr. Downs has become since throwing you over. I wonder how she'd fair if she lost her plumage."

Trammel slowly raised his head and looked at Hagen. "If you touch her, I'll kill you."

Hagen had no doubt he would and forced a laugh. "Why would I touch a hair on her head? I happen to like Emily. Besides, she has the virtue of being the only doctor in town. But cheer up, my friend. Fate is a great equalizer and, sooner or later, she'll regret having treated you so poorly."

Hagen watched Trammel's anger fade away before he turned to enter the jail. "Just leave her alone. And quit calling me 'friend.'"

Hagen decided he had given the sheriff a tough enough time already and let him go without another word. He went back to his chair and resumed squeezing the small bag of sand.

He cast an eye up the long hill to where King Charles Hagen's ranch house sat. It was a mighty place that lorded over all beneath it like a behemoth. It looked indestructible from here, but Adam knew nothing built by man would last forever. He looked forward to the day when he watched that house burn to the ground. No, he would not attack the house from the front. He would attack his father's empire at its foundation and watch it fall in on itself.

Yes, King Charles Hagen's end would come soon. But first, Buck Trammel would receive his reward, and sooner than he thought. And Emily Downs would learn what happened to those who displeased him.

He winced as he squeezed the bag of sand tighter as he looked at the Hagen ranch house on the hill and remembered a verse from the Bible. "Your glory, O Israel, lies slain on your heights. How the mighty have fallen!"

# Connect with Us